OCCULT JAPAN

A POSSESSION BY THE GODS UPON ONTAKÉ. Page 6

OCCULT JAPAN

Shinto, Shamanism and The Way of the Gods

PERCIVAL LOWELL

INNER TRADITIONS INTERNATIONAL
Rochester, Vermont

Inner Traditions International, Ltd.
One Park St.
Rochester, Vt. 05767

First edition published in 1894 by Houghton-Mifflin Co.

Library of Congress Cataloging-in-Publication Data

Lowell, Percival, 1855-1916
        Occult Japan / Percival Lowell.
                p.   cm.
        Reprint. Originally published: 1894
        ISBN 0-89281-306-7 : $12.95
        1. Shinto. 2. Cults--Japan. I. Title.
BL2220.L69 1990
299'.561--dc20

Printed and bound in the United States

10 9 8 7 6 5 4 3 2 1

Distributed to the book trade in Canada by Book Center,
Montreal, Quebec

CONTENTS.

OCCULT JAPAN.

ONTAKÉ.

IN the heart of Japan, withdrawn alike by distance and by height from the commonplaces of the every-day world, rises a mountain known as Ontaké or the Honorable Peak. It is a fine volcanic mass, sundered by deep valley-clefts from the great Hida-Shinshiu range, amidst which it stands dignifiedly aloof. Active once, it has been inactive now beyond the memory of man. Yet its form lets one divine what it must have been in its day. For upon its summit are the crumbling walls of eight successive craters, piled in parapet up into the sky.

It is not dead ; it slumbers. For on its western face a single solfatara sends heavenward long, slender filaments of vapor, faint

breath of what now sleeps beneath; a volcano sunk in trance.

Almost unknown to foreigners, it is well
known to the Japanese. For it is perhaps
the most sacred of Japan's many sacred
peaks. Upon it, every summer, faith tells a
rosary of ten thousand pilgrims.

Some years ago I chanced to gaze from
afar upon this holy mount; and, as the
sweep of its sides drew my eye up to where
the peak itself stood hidden in a nimbus of
cloud, had meant some day to climb it.
Partly for this vision, more because of the
probable picturesqueness of the route, I
found myself doing so with a friend in August, 1891. Beyond the general fact of its
sanctity, nothing special was supposed to at-
tach to the peak. That the mountain held
a mystery was undreamed of.

We had reached, after various vicissitudes,
as prosaically as is possible in unprosaic
Japan, a height of about nine thousand feet,
when we suddenly came upon a manifestation as surprising as it was unsuspected.
Regardless of us, the veil was thrown aside,
and we gazed into the beyond. We stood
face to face with the gods.

The fathoming of this unexpected revelation resulted in the discovery of a world of esoteric practices as significant as they were widespread. By way of introduction to them, I cannot do more simply than to give my own. Set as the scene of it was upon the summit of that slumbering volcano sunk in trance itself, a presentation to the gods could hardly have been more dramatic.

We had plodded four fifths way up the pilgrim path. We had already passed the first snow, and had reached the grotto-like hut at the eighth station — the paths up all high sacred mountains in Japan being pleasingly pointed by rest-houses ; we were tarrying there a moment, counting our heart-beats, and wondering how much more of the mountain there might be to come, for thick cloud had cloaked all view on the ascent, when three young men, clad in full pilgrim white, entered the hut from below, and, deaf to the hut-keeper's importunities to stop, passed stolidly out at the upper end : the hut having been astutely contrived to inclose the path, that not even the most ascetic might escape temptation. The devout look of the trio struck our fancy. So, leav-

ing some coppers for our tea and cakes,
amid profuse acknowledgment from the hut-
keeper, we passed out after them. We had
not climbed above a score of rods when we
overtook our young puritans lost in prayer
before a shrine cut into the face of the cliff,
in front of which stood two or three benches
conspicuously out of place in such a spot.
The three young men had already laid aside
their hats, mats, and staffs, and disclosed the
white fillets that bound their shocks of jet-
black hair. We halted on general principles
of curiosity, for we had no inkling of what
was about to happen. They were simply
the most pious young men we had yet met,
and they interested us.

The prayer, which seemed an ordinary one,
soon came to an end; upon which we expected
to see the trio pack up and be off again.
But instead of this one of them, drawing
from his sleeve a *gohei*-wand, and certain
other implements of religion, seated himself
upon one of the benches facing the shrine.
At the same time another sat down on a
second bench facing the first, clasped his
hands before his breast, and closed his eyes.
The third reverently took post near by.

No sooner was the first seated than he launched into the most extraordinary performance I have ever beheld. With a spasmodic jerk, pointed by a violent guttural grunt, he suddenly tied his ten fingers into a knot, throwing his whole body and soul into the act. At the same time he began a monotonic chant. Gazing raptly at his digital knot, he prayed over it thus a moment ; then, with a second grunt, he resolved it into a second one, and this into a third and a fourth and a fifth, stringing his contortions upon his chant with all the vehemence of a string of oaths. Startlingly uncouth as the action was, the compelling intentness and suppressed power with which the paroxysmal pantomime was done, was more so.

His strange action was matched only by the strange inaction of his vis-à-vis. The man did not move a muscle; if anything, he grew momentarily more statuesque. And still the other's monotoned chant rolled on, startlingly emphasized by the contortion knots.

At last the exorcist paused in his performance, and taking the *gohei*-wand from beside him on the bench, placed it between the other's hands, clenched one above the other. Then he resumed his incantation, the motionless one as motionless as ever. So it continued for some time, when all at once the hands holding the wand began to twitch convulsively; the twitching rapidly increased to a spasmodic throe which momentarily grew more violent till suddenly it broke forth into the full fury of a seemingly superhuman paroxysm. It was as if the wand shook the man, not the man it. It lashed the air maniacally here and there above his head, and then slowly settled to a semi-rigid half-arm holding before his brow; stiff, yet quivering, and sending its quivers through his whole frame. The look of the man was unmistakable. He had gone completely out of himself. Unwittingly we had come to stand witnesses to a trance.

At the first sign of possession, the exorcist had ceased incanting and sat bowed awaiting the coming presence. When the paroxysmal throes had settled into a steady quiver — much as a top does when it goes off to sleep — he leaned forward, put a hand on either side the possessed's knees, and still bowed, asked in words archaically reverent the name of the god who had thus deigned to descend.

At first there was no reply. Then in a voice strangely unnatural, without being exactly artificial, the entranced spake : " I am Hakkai."

The petitioner bent yet lower; then raising his look a little, preferred respectfully what requests he had to make ; whether the peak would be clear and the pilgrimage prove propitious, and whether the loved ones left at home would all be guarded by the god? And the god made answer : " Till the morrow's afternoon will the peak be clear, and the pilgrimage shall be blessed."

The man stayed bowed while the god spake, and when the god had finished speaking, offered up an adoration prayer. Then leaning forward, he first touched the possessed on the breast, and then struck him on the back several times with increasing insistency. Under this ungodly treatment the possessed opened his eyes like one awaking from profound sleep. The others then set to and kneaded his arms, body, and legs, cramped in catalepsy, back to a normal state.

No sooner was the ex-god himself again

than the trio changed places ; the petitioner moved into the seat of the entranced, the looker-on took the place of the petitioner, and the entranced retired to the post of looker-on. Then with this change of persons the ceremony was gone through with again to a similar possession, a similar interview, and a similar awakening.

At the close of the second trance the three once more revolved cyclically and went through the performance for the third time. This rotation in possession so religiously observed was not the least strange detail of this strange drama.

When the cycle had been completed, the three friends offered up a concluding prayer, and then, donning their outside accoutrements, started upward.

Revolving in our minds what we had thus so strangely been suffered to see, we too proceeded, and, being faster walkers, had soon distanced our god-acquaintances. We had not been long upon the summit, however, when they appeared again, and no sooner had they arrived, than they sat down upon some other benches similarly standing in the little open space before the tip-top

shrine, and went through their cyclical possessions as before. We had not thought to
see the thing a second time, and were almost
as much astounded as at first.

Our fear of parting with our young god-
friends proved quite groundless. For on returning to the summit-hut after a climb
round the crater rim, the first thing to catch
our eyes amid its dim religious gloom was the
sight of the pious trio once more in the full
throes of possession. There were plenty of
other pilgrims seated round the caldron
fire, as well as some native meteorologists
in an annex, who had been exiled there for
a month by a paternal government to study
the atmospheric conditions of this island in
the clouds. Up to the time we met them the
weather had been dishearteningly same, consisting, they informed us somewhat pathetically, of uninterrupted fog. The exorcists,
however, took no notice of them, nor of any
of the other pilgrims, nor did the rest of the
company pay the slightest heed to the exorcists; all of which spoke volumes for the
commonplaceness of the occurrence.

We again thought we had seen our last of
the gods, and again were we pleasurably

disappointed. At five the next morning we had hardly finished a shivery preprandial peep at the sunrise, — all below us a surging sea of cloud, — and turned once more into the hut, when there were the three indefatigables up and communing again by way of breakfast, for they took none other, and an hour later we came upon them before the tip-top shrine, hard at it for the fifth time. And all this between four o'clock one afternoon and six the next morning. The cycle was not always completed, one of the three being much better at possession than the other two, and one much worse, but there were safely ten trances in the few hours that fringed their sleep's oblivion.

And nobody, apparently, took any cognizance of what was going on, except us and the meteorologists, who came out to fraternize with us, and volunteered comments in a superior manner on the senselessness of the proceeding, — an imported attitude of mind not destitute of caricature.

Truly the gods were gracious thus to descend so many times; and truly devout their devotees to crave so much communion. Doubtless an inordinate desire for their

society is gratifying to the gods, but the
frequency of the talks fairly took our breath
away, though it had no perceptible effect on
the young men's nor on the god's, even at
that altitude. The god possessed his devotees with comparative ease ; which was edify-
ing but exhausting ; for to let another inhabit one's house always proves hard on the
furniture. And all this took place on top of
a climb of ten thousand feet toward heaven.
In spite of it, however, these estimable
young men were equal to a tramp all over
the place during the rest of the morning.
They ascended religiously to all the crater-
peaks, and descended as piously to all the
crater - pools — and then started on their
climb down and their journey home of three
hundred and fifty miles, much of it to be
done afoot. That night saw them not
only off the mountain, but well on their way
beyond. How far their holy momentum
carried them without stopping I know not,
for the last we saw of them was a wave of
farewell as they passed the inn where we
had put up for the night. But the most
surprising part of the endurance lay in the
fact that from the moment they began the

ascent of the mountain on the early morning of the one day, till they were off it on the late afternoon of the next, they ate nothing and drank only water.

Such was my introduction to the society of the gods ; and this first glimpse of it only piqued curiosity to more. No sooner back in town, therefore, than I made inquiry into the acquaintanceship I had so strangely formed upon the mountain, to receive the most convincing assurance of its divinity. The fact of possession was confirmed readily enough, but my desire for a private repetition of the act itself was received at first with some mystery and more hesitation. However, with one man after another, offishness thawed, until, getting upon terms of cordiality with deity, it was not long before I was holding divine receptions in my own drawing-room. Exalted and exclusive as this best of all society unquestionably was, it proved intellectually, like more mundane society we agree to call the best, undeniably dull. I mention this not because I did not find it well worth knowing, but simply to show that it was every whit the company it purported to be.

II.

The revelation thus strangely vouchsafed me turned out to be as far-reaching as it was sincere. There proved to exist a regular system of divine possession, an esoteric cult imbedded in the very heart and core of the Japanese character and instinct, with all the strangeness of that to us enigmatical race.

That other foreigners should not previously have been admitted to this company of heaven may at first seem the strangest fact of all. Certainly my introduction cannot be due to any special sanctity of my own, if I may judge by what my friends tell me on that subject. Nor can I credit it to any desire on my part to rise in the world, whether to peaks or preferments — an equally base ambition in either case — for Ontaké, though not of every-day ascent, has been climbed by foreigners several times before. Rein, that indefatigable collector of facts and statistics, managed some years ago to get to the top of it and then to the bottom again without seeing anything. The old guide-book, in the person of an enthusiastic pedestrian, contrived to do the like. Other visitors of good locomotive powers also accomplished this feat without penetrating the secret of the mountain. And yet the trances were certainly going on all the time, and the guides who piloted these several gentlemen must have been well aware of the fact.

The explanation is to be sought elsewhere. The fact is that Japan is still very much of an undiscovered country to us. It is not simply that the language proves so difficult that but few foreigners pass this threshold of acquaintance ; but that the farther the foreigner goes, the more he perceives the ideas in the two hemispheres to be fundamentally diverse. What he expects to find does not exist, and what exists he would never dream of looking for.

Japan is scientifically an undiscovered country even to the Japanese, as a study of these possessions will disclose. For their importance is twofold : archæologic no less than psychic. They are other-world manifestations in two senses, and the one sense helps accentuate the other. For they are as essentially Japanese as they are essentially genuine. That is, they are neither shams nor importations from China or India, but aboriginal originalities of the Japanese people. They are the hitherto unsuspected esoteric side of Shintō, the old native faith. That Japanese Buddhists also practice them is but appreciative Buddhist indorsement of their importance, as I shall show later. We must begin, therefore, with a short account of Shintō in general.

SHINTŌ.

I.

SHINTŌ, or the Way of the Gods, is the name of the oldest religious belief of the Japanese people. The belief itself indefinitely antedates its name, for it has come down to us from a time when sole possession of the field precluded denomination. It knew no christening till Buddhism was adopted from China in the sixth century of our era, and was then first called Shintō, or the Way of the Gods, to distinguish it from Butsudō, or the Way of Buddha.

If it thus acquired a name, it largely lost local habitation. For Buddhism proceeded to appropriate its possessions, temporal and spiritual. It had been both church and state. Buddhism became the state, and assumed the greater part of the churches; paying Shintō the compliment of incorporating, without acknowledgment, such as it fancied of the Shintō rites, and of kindly recognizing the more popular Shintō gods for lower avatars of its own. Under this generous adoption on the one hand, and relegation to an inferior place in the national pantheon on the other, very little, ostensibly, was left of Shintō, — just enough to swear by. Lost in the splendor of Buddhist show, Shintō lay obscured thus for a millenium; lingering chiefly as a twilight of popular superstition. At last, however, a new era dawned. A long peace, following the firm establishing of the Shogunate, turned men's thoughts to criticism, and begot the commentators, a line of literati, who, beginning with Mabuchi, in the early part of the eighteenth century, devoted themselves to a study of the past, and continued to comment, for a century and a half, upon the old Japanese traditions buried in the archaic language of the Kojiki and the Nihongi, the history-bibles of the race. As science, the commentators' elucidations are chiefly comic, but their practical outcome was immense. Criticism of the past begot criticism of the present, and started a chauvinistic movement, which overthrew the Shogunate and restored the

Mikado — with all the irony of fate, since these littérateurs owed their existence to the patronage of those they overthrew. This was the restoration of 1868. Shintō came back as part and parcel of the old. The temples Buddhism had usurped were purified; that is, they were stripped of Buddhist ornament, and handed over again to the Shintō priests. The faith of the nation's springtime entered upon the Indian summer of its life.

This happy state of things was not to last. Buddhism, and especially the great wave of western ideas, proved submerging. From filling one half the government, spiritual affairs were degraded, first to a department, then to a bureau, and then to a sub-bureau. The Japanese upper classes had found a new faith; and Herbert Spencer was its prophet.

But in the nation's heart the Shintō sentiment throbbed on as strong as ever. A Japanese cabinet minister found this out to his cost. In 1887, Mori Arinori, one of the most advanced Japanese new-lights, then minister of state for education, went on a certain occasion to the Shrines of Ise, and studiously treated them with disrespect. It was alleged, and apparently on good authority, that he trod with his boots on the mat outside the portal of the palisade, and then poked the curtain apart with his walking-stick. He was assassinated in consequence; the assassin was cut down by the guards, and then Japan rose in a body to do honor, not to the murdered man, but to his murderer. Even the muzzled press managed to hint on which side it was, by some as curious editorials as were ever penned. As for the people, there were no two ways about it; you had thought the murderer some great patriot dying for his country. Folk by thousands flocked with flowers to his grave, and pilgrimages were made to it, as to some shrine. It is still kept green; still to-day the singing-girls bring it their branches of plum blossoms, with a prayer to the gods that a little of the spirit of him who lies buried there may become theirs: that spirit which they call so proudly the Yamato Kokoro, the heart of old Japan.

For in truth Shintō is so Japanese it will not down. It is the faith of these people's birthright, not of their adoption. Its folk-lore is what they learned at the knee of the

race-mother, not what they were taught from
abroad.   Buddhist they are by virtue of belief ; Shintō by virtue of being.

Shintō is the Japanese conception of the
cosmos.   It is a combination of the worship
of nature and of their own ancestors.   But
the character of the combination is ethnologically instructive.   For a lack of psychic
development has enabled these seemingly
diverse elements to fuse into a homogeneous
whole.   Both, of course, are aboriginal in-
stincts.   Next to the fear of natural phenomena, in point of primitiveness, comes the
fear of one's father, as children and savages
show.   But races, like individuals, tend to
differentiate the two as they develop.   Now,
the suggestive thing about the Japanese is,
that they did not do so.   Filial respect lasted,
and by virtue of not becoming less, became
more, till it filled not only the whole sphere
of morals, but expanded into the sphere of
cosmogony.   To the Japanese eye, the universe itself took on the paternal look.   Awe
of their parents, which these people could
comprehend, lent explanation to dread of
nature, which they could not.   Quite co-
gently, to their minds, the thunder and the

typhoon, the sunshine and the earthquake, were the work not only of anthropomorphic beings, but of beings ancestrally related to themselves. In short, Shintō, their explanation of things in general, is simply the patriarchal principle projected without perspective into the past, dilating with distance into deity. That their dead should thus definitely live on to them is nothing strange. It is paralleled by the way in which the dead live on in the thought of the young generally. Actual personal immortality is the instant inevitable inference of the child-mind. The dead do thus survive in the memories of the living, and it is the natural deduction to clothe this subjective idea with objective existence.

Shintō is thus an adoration of family wraiths, or of imputed family wraiths ; imaginaries of the first and the second order in the analysis of the universe. Buddhism with its ultimate Nirvana is in a sense the antithesis of this. For while simple Shintō regards the dead as spiritually living, philosophic Buddhism regards the living as spiritually dead ; two aspects of the same shield.

The Japanese thus conceive themselves the direct descendants of their own gods. Their Mikado they look upon as the lineal descendant of Niniginomikoto, the first God Emperor of Japan. And the gods live in heaven much as men, their descendants, do on earth. The concrete quality of the Japanese mind has barred abstractions on the subject. The gods have never so much as laid down a moral code. "Obey the Mikado," and otherwise "follow your own heart" is the sum of their commands; as parental injunctions as could well be framed. So is the attitude of the Japanese toward their gods filially familiar, an attitude which shocks more teleologic faiths, but in which they themselves see nothing irreverent. In the same way their conception of a future life is that of a definite immaterial extension of the present one.

To foreign students in consequence, Shintō has seemed little better than the ghost of a belief, far too insubstantial a body of faith to hold a heart. To ticket its gods and pigeon-hole its folk-lore has appeared to be the end of a study of its cult.

Nor is its outward appearance less uninvitingly skeleton-like. With a deal barn of a building for temple, a scant set of deal paraphernalia, and so to speak a deal of nothing else, its appearance certainly leaves something to be desired. For in all save good Puritan souls, the religious idea craves sensuous setting. Feeling is the fuel of faith which sights, sounds, and perfumes fan into flame. Sense may not be of the essence of religion, but incense is.

II.

In but one thing is Shintō patently rich — in gods. It has as much to worship as it has little to worship with. It has more gods than its devotees know what to do with. From the Goddess of the Sun to the gods of rice and agriculture, few things in heaven or earth stand unrepresented in its catholic pantheon. Biblical biography puts the number roundly at eighty myriads, but in Japanese speech "eighty" and "myriad" are neither of them mathematical terms, the one being a mystic number and the other a conventional confession of arithmetical incompetency; both expressions being rigorously rendered in English by the phrase "no end."

Nobody ever pretended to count the gods. Indeed, to do so would be pious labor lost ; for the roll is being constantly increased by promotions from the ranks. Any one at death may become a god, and it is of the entailed responsibilities of greatness that the very exalted must do so.

Of course no merely finite man can possibly worship so infinite a number of deities, though time be to him of oriental limitlessness. So each makes his choice of intimates, and clubs the rest in a general petition, from time to time, to prevent accidents.

His first choice is made for him by his parents. A week after birth the babe is presented at the temple (*miya mairi*) and put under the protection of some special deity. The god's preference is not consulted in the affair ; he becomes tutelary god on notification, as a matter of course.

Next in importance to the tutelary god is the patron god. For every branch of human industry is specially superintended by some god. Men may deem it beneath them to be in business, but the gods do not. Each has his trade, and spends much time looking after his apprentices. But it is work without worry, befitting the easy-going East; the god of honest labor being portrayed as a jolly, fat fisherman, very comfortably seated, chuckling at having just caught a carp.

Pleasures, too, have their special gods with whom perforce their notaries are on peculiarly intimate terms, inasmuch as such gods are very boon-companion patrons of the sport. Furthermore, every one chooses his gods for a general compatibility of temper with himself. He thus lives under congenial guardianship all his life.

Simple as such conceptions are, there is something fine in their sweet simplicity. The very barrenness of the faith's buildings has a beauty of its own, touched as it is by Japanese taste. Through those gracefully plain portals a simple life here passes to a yet simpler one beyond; and the solemn cryptomerea lend it all the natural grandeur that so fittingly canopies the old.

So are the few Shintō rites perfect in effect. Finished fashionings from a far past, they are so beautifully complete, that one forgets the frailty of the conception in the rounded perfection of the form.

One sees at once how aboriginal all this

is. Childish conceptions embalmed in an exquisite etiquette; so Shintō might have been ticketed.

III.

But the mythologic mummy showed no evidence of soul. By the soul of a faith, as opposed to its mere body of belief, I mean that informing spirit vouchsafed by direct communion between god and man which all faiths proclaim of themselves, and pooh-pooh of all the others. It was this soul that so unexpectedly revealed itself to me upon Ontaké.

We must now see what the Japanese conceive this soul to be. Now Shintō philosophy is not the faith's strong point. The Japanese are artists, not scientists. And in their revelations their gods show the same simple and attractive character. If, therefore, the Shintō scheme of things seem at times incompatible with itself, the gods themselves are responsible, not I, errors and omissions on my part excepted. For I have it all from one whose authority is nothing short of the god's own words, vouchsafed to him in trance, my friend the high priest of the

Shinshiu sect. So that my knowledge of the subject is but second-hand divine, much nearer the source of inspiration than I can ever hope in reason to come again.

To begin with, then, all things in heaven and earth are composed of three elements, (*gotai* or *karada*) body, (*shinki*) mind or spirit, and (*tamashii*) soul. Stocks and stones, plants, animals, and some men have no soul, being made up entirely of body and mind. The behavior of some men seems to lend support to this theory. Gods, on the other hand, are bodiless and consist of spirit and soul, except the supreme god, Ame-no-minaka-nashi-no-mikoto, who is all soul.

Shinki, lit. god-spirit, is related to *tamashii*, soul, much as a substance with its attributes is related to the same substance without them. If you can manage the conception of the first of these philosophic vacuities, you will find no difficulty with the second. Furthermore, spirit and soul may coexist separately in one body. As the spirit clarifies, that is, becomes more and more blank, it approaches soul and finally becomes it.

The one thing common, therefore, to all

things, both of this world and the next, is
spirit. Everything, from gods to granite,
has its god-spirit. Each spirit is as separate
and particular as the body it inhabits ; yet
it is capable of indefinite expansion or contraction, of permeating matter and of going
and coming according to laws of its own.
It may, perhaps, be looked upon provision-
ally as a gas.

Spirit never dies, it only circulates.
When a man or animal or plant dies its
body duly decays, but its spirit either lives
on alone or returns to those two great res-
ervoirs of spirit, the gods Takami-musubi-
no-kami and Kami-musubi-no-kami. From
them a continual circulation of spirit is kept
up through the universe. Whether a spirit's
personality persists or not is a matter decided by the supreme god, and depends upon
the greatness or the goodness of the defunct. For example, Kan Shojo, the god of
calligraphy, has persisted thus posthumously
for almost a thousand years. It is to be
hoped for the sake of Japan's beautiful
brushmanship, that he will continue to survive and be worshiped for some time yet.

Spirit is by no means necessarily good.

It is manifest that, viewed from the human standpoint, some things are harmful, some harmless, both among plants, animals, and men. The harmful ones are therefore bad ; the harmless ones may or may not be good. Why certain inoffensive animals, for example, have got a bad name, or even a good one, is as inscrutable as the cause of the gender of Latin nouns. They are given a bad name, and that is cause enough. It will be observed that in this system of ethics man has no monopoly of original sin.

Similarly the gods themselves are divided into the sheep and the goats, but by a merciful dispensation of something or other the good gods are mightier than the bad. Indeed, a certain evolutionary process is going on throughout the universe, by which the bad spirits grow good and the good better. It is described as a continued clarification, terminating in total blankness.

Spirit not only circulates after death ; it may do so during life. Usually it does not wander in this way, simply because it is at home where it is and inertia keeps it there. But in some cases it is not so wedded to the body with which it is associated, and the purer it becomes the more is it given to occasional volatilizing.

Now esoteric Shintō consists in compelling this spirit to circulate for particular ends. This is not a difficult matter, if it is properly undertaken. It is accomplished through self-purification. For the degree of purity determines the degree of possession. Possession is simply the entrance into one body of another body's spirit, and the simultaneous expulsion or subjugation of the spirit originally there.

This shift of spirit may take place between any two bodies in nature. Nor does such interchange differ in kind, no matter what the bodies be. But for the sake of psychology rather than religion, we may profitably consider it under the two aspects of god-possession of things and god-possession of people. The one gives rise to the miracles; the other to the incarnations. Both kinds of possession occurred spontaneously, that is, at the will of the gods, in olden times, and presumably so occur at the present day; but the gods have also graciously granted pure men the power to pray for them acceptedly.

In the case of people the act of possession is nowadays known as *kami-oroshi, kami-utsushi,* or *kami-utsuri,* that is, "the causing of the god to come down," "the causing the god to transform" or "god transformation." The first two names thus view the thing from the human standpoint, the last from the divine. But this is matter of the temporary point of view, all three expressions, with others such as *nori-utsuri,* "to change vehicles," being used indifferently according to the speaker's preference.

Possession may be partial, complete, or intermediary, that is, the alien spirit may share the head of the person with the native spirit, or it may drive it out, or it may drive it down into the belly. But such degrees of tenancy are grades rather of the proficiency attained during novitiate into the cult. In actual possessions the chief distinction consists in the character of the god who comes.

Possession of things are in like manner possible through purity in the person who would bring them about. They are called *kamiwasa* or god-arts, because originally only the gods, and now only the gods and the godly, can perform them.

IV.

Before entering upon the miracles, it is necessary to explain the present position of Shintō with regard to these esoteric practices generally. For, though as we shall see when we look later into their history, it is probable that originally they were the common property of all Shintōists, they are not so to-day.

Of the present ten sects that compose the Shintō church, only two practice the possession-cult, the Shinshiu and the Mitaké sects. That they do so while the others do not is not matter of creed, but of tradition. Though called sects, the Shintō sects are not properly so much sects as sections. For they differ not by differently worshiping an identical god, but by identically worshiping different gods. Each of them likewise worships, though with less assiduity, all the others' gods. Each looks specially to the great shrine dedicated to its special gods; and all but two, one of which is a sort of general bureau of church organism, make pilgrimages to their shrine once or twice a year.

These sects date only from since the time

of the revival of pure Shintō twenty years ago. But under another name the professors of the cult hold it in unbroken practice from the far past. Whether during the time of Shintō's long eclipse the possession cult was kept up by the few remaining pure Shintōists, if indeed there can be said to have been any pure Shintōists then at all, is doubtful, although the priests to-day assert that it was always practiced by the pious in secret. Certain it is, however, that during the lapse of Shintō from national regard practice of the cult passed to all intents and purposes to a hybrid of Shintō and Buddhism known as Ryōbu or Both, because it was indeed manufactured of both creeds.

The great Kōbō Daishi is the reputed father of Ryōbu. This worthy soul — who by the way was never called Kōbō Daishi while he was called anything ; he was known as Kūkai so long as he was known at all — was the founder of the Shingon sect of Buddhism in Japan. He seems to have been singularly energetic. The peaks he climbed, the pictures he painted, and the divers deeds of one sort and another which he accomplished, would have kept Methuselah on the jump for the whole of his millennial life. Nevertheless, he found time amid it all to invent Ryōbu. His invention consisted in a judicious hodge-podge of Shintō and Buddhist popularities. His diligence met its reward. The newly invented faith instantly became very popular, because it let everybody in. It was essentially an open air faith, much given to mountaineering, a trait it might be supposed to have inherited from its father, were it not instinctive in a Japanese to climb.

Ryōbu has more than one sect, but it was only the Ontaké sect of the belief that practiced god-possession. It kept the cult alive for a thousand years, and then, when pure Shintō was revived at the time of the Restoration, and hybrids were abolished by imperial edict, the Ontaké Ryōbuists came back again into the Shintō fold.

Besides Ryōbu, some of the Buddhist sects early saw the advantage of being intimate with deity, and Kōbō Daishi, after being taught the means to it by the Shintō Emperor Sanga, so it is said, not satisfied with inventing Ryōbu and incorporating it in that, boldly took it for his own Shingon sect of

Buddhism. And the Shingon sect still practices the cult to-day. Denkyō Daishi, the founder of the Tendai sect, was likewise captivated by it and incorporated it into his belief. Lastly, the Nichiren sect learned the art and indulges in it now more than either of the other two.

We thus find at the present time among the professors of the cult some Shintōists, some Ryōbuists, and some Buddhists, each claiming it stoutly for its own.

MIRACLES.

I.

DULLARDS will always deem delicacy incompatible with strength. To touch a subject lightly is for them not to touch it at all. Yet the phrase "dead in earnest" might perhaps hint to them that there is more virtue in liveliness than they suspect. It is quite possible to see the comic side of things without losing sight of their serious aspect. In fact, not to see both sides is to get but a superficial view of life, missing its substance. So much for the people. As for the priests, it is only necessary to say that few are more essentially sincere and lovable than the Shintō ones ; and few religions in a sense more true. With this preface for life-preserver I plunge boldly into the miracles.

Kamiwaza or god-arts are of many sorts, but to Japanese piety are all of a kind, though some are spectacular, some merely useful. Causing the descent of the Thunder-God ; calling down fire from Heaven ; rooting burglars to the spot, and so forth, to say nothing of killing snakes and bringing them to life again, together with innumerable like performances, are all included in the category, and are all simple enough affairs to the truly good. Nichiren, for example, broke in two the blade of his would-be executioner by exorcism taught him of the Shintō priests. The fact without the explanation may be read of in histories of Japan.

In Shintō the miracles are not so important matters as the incarnations ; for good reason, since the god but shows his power in the one case, his self in the other. Yet the church takes pleasure in displaying them for pious purposes. Any fête-day of the possessing sects is more likely than not to have a miracle for central show, and for his great semi-annual festivals my friend the head priest of the Shinshiu sect has announcement of a couple of them printed regularly as special attractions on his invitation cards.

So far as piety classifies them at all, it

does so according to their scenic effect or for the difficulty of doing them. From a psychologic point of view, however, they fall very conveniently under two heads: subjective miracles and objective ones. An account of the former may properly precede, since it includes those which, on the whole, are considered the greater.

Chief among the subjective miracles are what are called collectively the *Sankei* or the three great rites. The bond connecting the trio is apparently purely extrinsic, consisting solely in agreement in greatness. In consequence, on very important festivals lasting two or three days, they are performed in turn successively.

II.

The first and simplest of these Three Great Rites is the *Kugadachi* or Ordeal by Boiling Water.

The word *kugadachi* is archaic Japanese. In Hepburn's dictionary a dagger stabs it obsolete. Furthermore, the departed is given no character, being epitaphed solely in the Japanese sidescript. Such absence of ideograph implies for the expression an

age antedating the time when the Japanese
learned to write; an inference fully borne
out by folk-lore. For the ordeal is mentioned more than once in the Kojiki, and
seems to have been quite popular in prehistoric times. In those direct days it was
applied as touchstone to actual guilt; in
these more teleologic times merely as test
of theoretic guilelessness.

The arrangements for the rite are prim-
itively picturesque. A huge iron pot, as it
might be some witches' caldron, is ceremoniously set in the midst of the garden or
court. About it is then built a magic
square. Four cut bamboo, tufted at their
tops, are stuck into the ground some eight
feet apart. From frond to frond are hung
hempen ropes. This makes an airy sort of
palisade, designed to keep out the undesirable devils. Just outside of the space thus
inclosed is placed a deal table, on which one
or more deal boxes, open on the side, make
consecrated pedestals for the *gohei*. The
gohei are very important affairs, of which I
shall have much to say later. For the moment it will suffice to state that they are zigzag strips of paper festooning a wand, and

are the outward and visible symbols of the
gods. In front of them upon the table
stands a saucer of salt; while behind them
bamboo fronds stuck into stands rise into a
background of plumes.[1]

Spring water is then brought in and
poured into the caldron. On my first occasion of witnessing the miracle I was at
this point graciously permitted to dab my
little finger into the water. I quite fail now
to see why I desired to do so, but I am very
glad I did. My request turned out a most
discreet indiscretion, productive of much
spiritual significance later on.

A fire was then kindled beneath, and we,
professionals and amateurs, stood round
about the square, watching for the water to
boil. When at last the steam started to
rise, the officiating acolyte emerged from
the holy bathhouse near by, where he had
been purifying himself, clad in a single
white robe. That is, the robe was white

---

[1] The wood I have here and elsewhere translated "deal,"
on account of its appearance, which is simple to a degree,
is the *hinoki*, lit. "sun-wood," the *Thuya obtusa*, or *Arbor
vitæ*. Its name sun-wood is said by some priestly exposi-
tors to be due to its having furnished the prehistoric two
sticks from whose rubbing first came fire.

theoretically; practically it was a post-diluvian gray, a hue which the rite soon sufficiently explained.

On entering the mystic square he clapped his hands; the invariable Japanese method this, of summoning anybody from gods to servants. It is worth noting here, as instancing the familiar terms on which the Japanese stand with their gods, that they should thus indifferently summon deities and domestics.

The young priest then started to circumambulate the kettle through a whole series of rites, each made up of an endlessly similar basis of speech and action. Now it is all very well to preach against vain repetitions, but with anthropomorphic gods, as with ordinary mortals, it simply has to be done if one would succeed in one's request. The Shintō priests realize this fact, and thoroughly act upon it, too thoroughly to suit one who looks impatiently past the repetitions to their result. Like all good works, its practical effect is on the worker.

Pantomime and prayer wove the double strand on which his more particular beads of rosary were told; uncouth finger-twists and monotonic formulæ pointed by expressive guttural grunts. Upon this undercurrent of wellnigh automatic action the man was insensibly carried along through successive cycles of rite. Beginning at the north end of the square, he first made incantation facing the caldron ; then walking absorbedly round to the south, digitating as he did so, he faced the kettle and repeated his spell. Continuing as before, he went through the same performance at the west side ; then at the east, the northwest, the northeast, and the southwest, making thus at least a half circuit between each point. All this was most particular ; though as a matter of fact the orientation of the points was hypothetical.

This constituted the simple motif, as it were. No sooner was it completed, than he started on it again with variations. First it was salt. From the saucer on the stand he helped himself to a handful of this, and making circuits of the kettle as before, deposited a pinch of it at each of the compass points in turn, digitating with the free hand as he did so, after the manner of one enjoining implicit compliance with his act. After this he tossed more salt into the air toward each of the four quarters of the heavens.

In the same way he made the rounds with a flint and steel, scattering sparks at the proper places. Then he took the *gohei-*wand, and exorcised the water in like fashion, by cuts in the air of imprecatory violence. Lastly, he made the circuit with two bamboo fronds, one in each hand, which he dipped into the seething liquid, and then, lifting them loaded with boiling water, lashed the air above his head, the spray falling in a scalding shower-bath all over him. This he did north, south, east, west, and then over again from the beginning, on and on, in one continuous round.

To this boiling shower-bath there seemed no end. Round and round the man went, religiously compassing his points, repeating the scalding douche at each with ever-growing self-abandonment. Up to this final phase of the affair he had seemed to be carrying on the rite ; now, the rite seemed to be carrying him on. Still, circuit after circuit he made, his exaltation rising with each fresh dip ; till he was as one possessed, lashing maniacally first the water and then the air with the fronds, scattering the scalding douche not only over himself, but over all

the innocent bystanders as well, giving them
thus, by the way, the most convincing proof
of the genuineness of the feat. Higher and
higher rose the pitch of his possession till,
at last, nature could no farther go, and from
the acme of his paroxysm he all at once collapsed into a lump of limp rag upon the
ground. The others rushed in and bore him
away, the wilted semblance of a man.

While he was gone to prepare himself once
more for this world, the high priest explained
to me the spirit of the rite.

The moon, it seems, is the cause of it all;
a first step in elucidation, to follow which
requires less stretch of the western imagination than the next succeeding one. For that
lunacy-inducing body is, it appears, the origin
of water; on the *lucus a non* principle, we
must suppose, inasmuch as it has none to
speak of. But, whatever the cause, the spirit
of water resides in the moon; the spirit of
cold water, be it understood, cold water and
hot water being, in Japanese eyes, quite different substances with different names. The
spirit of hot water is the spirit of fire. This
rose to the water in the caldron from the
fire below at the moment the water boiled.

" Now," as the priest quaintly put it, " just
as there are veins in man's body, and fissures
in the earth, so are there arteries in the air ;
and to each spirit its own arteries. When,
therefore, the spirit of water is properly besought, it descends from its abode, the moon,
by its appropriate paths, and dispossesses
the spirit of fire, which sinks back again to
the charcoal whence it came." And of course
the hot water is no longer hot.

This happy result is worked to easier perfection amid the purity of the peaks. It is,
of course, an irrelevant detail that water at
those altitudes should boil at a lower temperature. The thin air of the peaks is, for
purely pious reasons, conducive to all manner
of etherealization.

In addition to the lunar action on the
boiling water, the performer himself is, so
the priest said, temporarily possessed by the
lunar spirit, and so is rendered insensible
to the heat, which, as we just saw, does not
exist, so that the second action might seem
to savor of the superfluous. A double nega-
tive of the sort appears, however, to make
assurance doubly sure.

When the man returned, clothed and in

his right mind once more, he was asked whether he felt the heat of the water during the ordeal. He replied that sometimes he did and sometimes he did not; in this instance he said he had felt nothing. He was a frail-looking youth, of ecstatic eye, evidently a good "subject," though still in the early stages of his novitiate. The head priest, a much stronger man, and an adept, said he always felt the water, but not the heat of it; an interesting distinction.

Here came in the importance of my dabble in the basin. Though it had been but to the extent of a little finger, — and that by religious permission, — it had, it appeared, partially spoiled the miracle on that side of the caldron, preventing the water there from becoming as cold as elsewhere. For the acolyte averred that he had perceived a difference between the two. But he had just said that he had not felt the heat of any part of it. He had therefore detected a distinction without a difference, a degree of divinity quite transcending the simply not feeling at all. Yet he was unconscious at the time, and conscientious afterward. By partially spoiling the miracle, then, it would seem that I had considerably improved it.

III.

The second miracle of the Three Great Rites is the Hiwatari or the Walking Barefoot over a Bed of Live Coals.

To the faithful this is one of the regular stock miracles, and when you become well known to the profession for a collector of such curios, you shall have offers of performance in your own back-yard. If also you be friend to the high-priest of the Shinshiu sect, you may have a chance to witness it in spring and autumn in special glory in the grounds of the sect's head temple in town. There, beside the miracle itself, shall you see its scarcely less curious setting, an intent multitude framing the walkers round about, worked up at last to part participation itself. For in its working the miracle is eminently democratic. Even professionally it is not a star performance, but an exhibition by the whole company. Fellowship, they say, adds to the purity of the rite. It certainly conduces to exaltation. In the second place, performance is not confined to the professionals. They indeed have the *pas*, but after they have thus broken the ice the populace is permitted to indulge itself in the same way to satiety. For while the bed is possessed by the god any sufficiently pure person may tread it with impunity to his cuticle and great gain to his good luck. The two go together. The difficulty comes in, in accurately estimating the degree of one's own purity. If one be pure enough he will cross unscathed ; if not, his more material understanding will speedily acquaint him of his deficiency. It proves a sad trial to doubting Thomases. In their case, to previous anguish of spirit is added after agony of sole.

The bed to be traversed is usually from twelve to eighteen feet long and from three to six feet wide. The width of the bed is not so vital to the miracle as the length of it ; the length it is that has to be walked over and grows tedious. And the purity needed to do this increases *pari passu* with the length — only in geometrical progression. Here it is not the first step that costs, but the last one.

In Ryōbu the bed of state is an eight-poster. Eight bamboo, still fronded, are stuck into the ground, making slender posts to a palisade about the pyre. Between them runs a hempen rope from frond to frond about five feet above the ground. From this hang forty-four *gohei*. These details are important in ordinary cases, as the bamboo are dedicated to the eight heavenly dragons, rainmakers and drawers of water generally. But if the ground be holy, such outer guarding becomes unnecessary; and indeed it is a fundamental principle in esoterics that the purer the performer the less paraphernalia he needs. Pure Shintō is more simple in its rites than Ryōbu.

Ordinarily the bed is made as follows: A mattress of straw mats is laid upon the ground, and on this a sheet of seashore sand. This is done in order that everything may be as pure as possible. On top of this sheet are laid first twigs and then sticks criss-cross, after the usual approved principle of laying a fire. In the very centre of the pyre a *gohei* is stood up on its wand.

In theory the bed is laid four-square to the compass points. In practice one side is conveniently assumed to be north, which is just as good in the eyes of the gods, who are sublimely superior to such mere matters of fact.

For fuel, pine wood is the proper article. Sticks free from knots are preferred, for resin lurks in the knots and has a spirit hard to quell. So long as a man is truly good he does not care. But the least admixture of sin in his soul causes him to mind these knotty spots acutely.

Pine is still used in the country and in town when the authorities are not aware of the fact. Legally, however, charcoal is enjoined instead, owing to the danger of conflagration from flying wood-ashes ; and at the high-priest's functions the law is dutifully observed.

To give life to the drama, I will set the scene of it where I first saw it, in the grounds of the head temple of the Shinshiu sect, in Kanda, the heart of Tōkyō. The crowd had already collected by the time we arrived ; the bed had been laid and fired, and the whole temple company, with the exception of the high-priest himself, were at the moment busied about the pyre, some fanning the flames assiduously with open fans strapped to the end of long poles, while others pounded the coals flat again with staves. All were robed in white and were barefooted. The thing made a fine pageant, framed by the eager faces of the multitude, and set in the cool, clear light of a September afternoon.

When they judged the bed to have been sufficiently made, they began upon the invitation to the god to descend into it. A good old soul full of devoutness and dignity led off. Proceeding solemnly to the northern end of the glowing charcoal, he faced the bed, clapped his hands, bowed his head in prayer, and then with energetic finger-twistings cabalistically sealed the same. Then he started slowly to circumambulate the pyre, stopping at the middle of each side to repeat his act.

When he was well under way, another followed in repetition ; then a third and a fourth, and so on down to the youngest, a youth of ecstatic eye, who threw himself body and soul into the rite. Seven of them in all were thus strung out in line walking round about the pyre and sealing it digitally in purification. As it was not incumbent on the exorcists, once started, to travel at the same rate, the march soon took on the look of a holy go-as-you-please race.

The bed was circuited interminably, beyond the possibility of count, so riveting to
one's attention was the pantomime. At the
conclusion of the dedicatory prayer the salt
made its appearance. For, damaging as the
statement may sound, every Shintō miracle
has to be taken with a great many grains of
it. In this instance the salt was used unstintedly. A large bowl filled with it stood
handily on one corner of the temple veranda,
and each priest, as he came up, helped himself to a fistful, and then proceeded to sow it
upon the coals, finger-twisting with the free
hand as he did so. The sowing was done
with some vehemence, each throw being
pointed by a violent grunt that so suited the
fury of the action it sounded ominously like
an imprecation. But it was only an emphatic command to the evil spirits to avaunt.

After considerable salt had thus been sown
from the cardinal points, the head of the
company struck sparks from a flint and steel
in the same oriented way over the bed, the
others still throwing on salt promiscuously
for general efficacy. In addition to what
was thus scattered over the coals, a mat at
either end of the bed was spread with salt.

During all this time the high-priest, who took no active part in the rite himself, being busied with his duties as host, was nevertheless engaged upon a private furtherance of the affair, quite obliviously, he told me afterward. It consisted in breathing modulately in and out of his pursed-up lips. This action is a great purifier ; as we shall see later. It is only to the godless that it suggests an inexpert whistler vainly attempting a favorite tune.

A pause in the rite now informed everybody that the god had come, and everybody watched intently for what was to follow ; with mixed emotion, I fancy, for the entertainment partook of the characters of a mass, a martyrdom, and a melodrama all in one.

The original old gentleman once more led off. Taking post at the bed's northern end, he piously clapped his hands, muttered a few consecrated words, and then salting his soles by a rub on the mat, stepped boldly on to the burning bed and strode with dignified unconcern the whole length of it. He did this without the least symptom of discomfort or even of notice of his own act.

In their order the others followed, each crossing with as much indifference as if the bed were mother-earth. When all had gone over, all went over again.

It was now the turn of the laymen. The passing of the priests had been a pageant, dignified and slow; the procession of the common folk was its burlesque. The priests had seemed superior to the situation; their lay brethren often fell ludicrously below it.

Any one who would was invited to try his foot at it; not, I may add, in the spirit of somewhat similar secular invitation at the circus. No deception whatever lay hidden behind the permit. For the pure are sure to cross in safety, and to him who crosses with impunity, substantial benefits accrue.

Many bystanders availed themselves of the privilege. Indeed, not a few had come there for the purpose. Some did so on the pious understanding that the fire could not longer burn; others apparently upon a more skeptical footing. One firm believer incurred no little odium for the extreme character of his convictions. So persuaded was he of the now harmless state of the charcoal that he sauntered solemnly across, rapt in revery, quite oblivious to a string of less devout folk whom his want of feeling kept in mid-bed on tenterhooks behind him. In the extremity of their woe they began hopping undignifiedly up and down, and finally in their desperation pushed him off at the last, to his very near capsizing. For in spirit he was somewhere else, utterly unsuspicious of a sudden irreligious shove from behind.

Another individual found it hotter than he had hoped, and, after taking one step stolidly enough, lost all sense of self-respect at the second, and began skipping from foot to foot in vain attempts at amelioration, to the derision of the lookers-on, especially of such as did not dare venture themselves. Apparently, he thought better of it a little later, or perhaps he found himself more scared than scarred. For soon after I noticed that he had adventured himself again, and this time, to his credit, with becoming majesty of march.

Indeed, the procession was as humorous as humanity. All sorts and conditions of men, women, and children went over first and last. All were gain to religion, for nothing showed more conspicuous than the buoyant power of faith. It was not the sole, but the self that trod there, stripped of social covering. In the heat of the moment the walkers forgot their fellow-men and walked alone with their god. Characters came out vividly in the process, like hidden writing before the fire. Each contrasted oddly with its neighbors, often treading close on its opposite's heels, jostling emotion itself by the juxtaposition. Now a sturdy jinrikisha man, persuaded that the crossing would bring him fares, went over as a matter of business, and in his wake a small boy, unable to resist so divine a variety of tittle-ties on thin ice, followed for doubtless a very different reason. Then a family in due order of etiquette ventured successfully along in a line. Now a dear old grandam, bent by years to a question mark of life, hobbled bravely across notwithstanding; and now a fair little girl, straight and slim as an admiration point, performed the feat vicariously, but I doubt not as effectively, in the arms of one of the priests. A touch of the fine in all this that tended to film the eyes, and lend the scene a glamour which, if not strictly religious, was its very close of kin.

Many of the lay-folk, not content with one crossing, returned for more; the church kindly permitting any number of repetitions. Indeed, the performance was exceedingly popular.

When the last enthusiast had had enough, the embers were prodded by the poles into pi. This airing of his bed causes the god not unnaturally to depart. After he has gone no one may cross unscathed; and no one attempted to do so. Under coals are certainly more fiery than surface ones, especially if the latter have been well sprinkled with salt.

A final prayer pointed with finger-pantomime closed the function.

The use of the salt deserves further mention. In this instance it was a salient feature of the rite, and had been enjoined by no less a personage, it appeared, than the god himself. But as the deity had commanded it under the somewhat poetic title of " Flower of the Waves," the high-priest had been at first at a loss, so he said, to comprehend the divine meaning. Later the god had condescended to an explanation. Nevertheless, this flowery title, so I am given to understand, is in common secular use.

To the undevout mind the salting of the bed would seem to conduce to the success of the feat. For salt is a very glutton of heat, and will do pretty much anything to get it, however menial, from melting snow on horse-car tracks to freezing ice-cream. Cooling coals is therefore quite in character for it. This, its unappeasable appetite for caloric is not unknown to the profession. The priests nobly admitted that the salt mitigated the full rigor of the miracle.

The miracle does not, however, depend for performance upon its use; only one has to be holier to work the miracle without it. At times fire-walking is done quite fresh; preferably amid the purity of the hills, with whose freshness its own is then in keeping. But it is occasionally so performed in town.

The origin of the rite mounts back to extreme antiquity. It dates from before there were men to walk, having been instituted of the gods in the days when they alone lived in the land. Walking, indeed, is not of its essence; peripatetic proof being but a special mode of showing one's immunity to fire. The possibility of such immunity was first demonstrated by a lady, the goddess who rejoices in the simple but somewhat protracted name of Ko-no-hana-saka-ya-hime-no-mikoto. It sounds better when translated : the Goddess who makes the Flower-buds to open. She is perhaps better known as the Goddess of Fuji. She invented the miracle in order to persuade her doubting spouse, the god Ninigi-no-mikoto, of the falsehood of certain suspicions which he had been ungallant enough to entertain about her. She built herself a house against her confinement, and then, after the babe was born, burnt it to the ground over her head, without so much as scorching herself or the baby. This of course reassured Ninigi-no-mikoto, and is chiefly noteworthy as an instance of a miracle converting a god himself. Those who care to read all the evidence in the case will find it in the Nihonshoki, an invaluable work in fifteen volumes of archaic Japanese.

Walking over the coals with impunity is attributable only in part to virtue in the performer. Immunity from harm is chiefly due to the fact that the fire has lost its power to burn. It has parted with its spirit. Materially considered, the fire is still there, but spiritually speaking it is extinct. This is why, when it has been once exorcised, the veriest tyro may cross it without a blister. The spirit of water has descended to it from the moon and driven the spirit of fire out of the coals. Any skeptic might soon prove this to his own satisfaction by just walking over the coals himself, were true piety compatible with doubt.

"The object of the rite," so the high-priest expounded it to me, "is that the populace may see that the god when duly besought can take away the burning spirit of fire while permitting the body of it to remain. For so can he do with the hearts of men; the bad spirit may be driven out and the good put in its place while still the man continues to exist."

To the coldly critical eye of science two things conduce to the performance of this feat. One is the toughness of the far eastern sole. The far Oriental inherits a much less sensitive nervous organization than is the birthright of a European, and his cuticle is further calloused to something not unlike leather by constant exposed use. This leaves the distance to be traversed between the natural sensitiveness and the induced insensitiveness considerably less than it would be with us. The intervening step is the result of exaltation. By first firmly believing that no pain will be felt and then inducing a state of ecstasy whose preoccupation the afferent sensation fails to pierce, no pain is perceived.

More than this, the burn is probably not followed by the same after-effects. For there is a more or less complete absence of blisters. The part burnt is burnt like cloth, and that is the end of it. No inconvenience whatever follows the act among the truly good. In less devout folk small blisters are raised, but without noticeable annoyance. The fact is that in burns generally it is the cure that constitutes the complaint. It is the body's feverish anxiety to repair the damage that causes all the trouble. Even in the severest burns very little of us is ever burnt up, but our own alarm that it may be induces our consequent inflammation. Delbœuf showed this conclusively upon one of his hypnotized patients.

Faith, therefore, does in very truth work the miracle. We know this now that miracles have ceased to be miraculous; which is perhaps a little late for purely pious purposes.

IV.

We now come to the third miracle of the three; the *Tsurugi-watari*, or the Climbing the Ladder of Sword-blades.

Among the incredible feats that we are asked to believe of Indian jugglers, not the least astounding is their reputed power of treading and even of lying with impunity upon sword-blades; an ability which some of us are inclined to credit to the verb in its other sense. Nevertheless, the same startling if unnecessary bit of acrobatism may be seen every spring in Tōkyō quite secularly done among the peep-shows about Asakusa. To such, however, as still remain skeptical on the subject, it may prove convincing to learn that the thing is a miracle, one of the great miracles of the Shintō church.

It dates from a dateless antiquity. In the Nihonshoki mention is made of it older than Jimmu Tennō himself, the first human

Emperor of Japan. Its first instance seems to have been a case of necessity. When the two gods, Futsu-nushi-no-kami and Také-mika-tsuchi-no-kami were sent from heaven to request O-ana-muchi-no-kami to resign the Japanese throne, we are told that on coming into his presence they imposingly planted their swords hilt downwards in the ground, and then, arms akimbo, seated themselves stolidly upon the points. Unlike the bashful individual who sat down upon the spur of the moment only to rise hastily again, their seats seemed to have proved quite comfortable, for they delivered a long and somewhat tedious harangue in that not ineffective attitude.

This style of camp-stool had, however, gone out of fashion when I made the acquaintance of the miracle last September; the modern mode of doing the thing being to set the blades edge up and then walk over them. The walking was about to be performed, so rumor said, at Hachioji, which it appeared was one of the habitats of the miracle. For shrines have their pet miracles as they have their patron gods. Upon investigation rumor turned out to be correct in all but date, the walking having unfortunately taken place the previous April, at the annual festival of the shrine of which it was the specialty, and would not be repeated until the April following. Seven months seeming long to wait even for a miracle, I ventured to suggest to the priests a private performance. They instantly expressed themselves as very willing to give it, stipulating merely for a week's prior mortification of the flesh. Such indulgence being a necessity to any Shintō miracle, the date fixed on for the spectacle was set duly ahead, and some ten days later, on a veritable May morning in early October, we left Tōkyō for Hachioji by the morning train to witness it.

There were five of us, including two globe-trotting friends of mine, who, having seen one miracle, had developed a strong amateur interest in religion, and Asa, my "boy."

From Hachioji we were bowled in jinrikisha some four miles out of the town to a small temple known as Hachiman Jinja, situate on the outskirts of the hamlet of Moto-Hachioji. The temple buildings, well parasoled by ancient trees, stood upon a spur overlooking the little valley where the

grass-grown roofs of the village peeped
domestically from amid the crops. An army
of mulberry bushes in very orderly files
flanked them round about, silk-worm rearing
being the village occupation ; so much so
that it had given its name to the local pil-
grim-club under whose auspices the function
was to be performed.

Two gods shared the temple very cordially ; O-ana-muchi-no-kami, the right-hand
god of the Ontaké trio, and Hachiman Daijin,
the god of war. O-ana-muchi-no-kami was
the patron god of the feat we had come to
see. He himself was wont not only to walk
upon the blades, but at times went so far as
actually to go to sleep upon them, a seemingly useless bit of bravado only paralleled
by the pains some people are at to tell you
how they doze in their dentist's chair.

From the head priest's house we made our
way up a hill to the temple. As we turned
the corner of the outer buildings we caught
sight, at the farther end of the grounds,
of so startling a scaffold that we all instinctively came to a point — of admiration —
before it. Evidently this was the material
means to the miracle, for against it a ladder,

with notches suggestively vacant of rungs,
led up to a frail plank platform raised aston-
ishingly high into the air. We had somehow
assumed that the sword-walking took place
on the flat, and not, as it appeared it was to
be done, skyward.

When we had sufficiently recovered from
our first surprise to examine this startling
structure, we found it to consist of four stout
poles, planted securely in the earth, and
braced by cross-ties, holding two thirds way
up the above-mentioned platform, upon which
stood a shrine. The height of this upper
story above the ground proved to be thirteen
feet. Upon a secular ladder at the side some
priests were giving a few finishing touches
to the work.

Inclosing the scaffold stood four fronded
bamboo, one at each corner of a square, connected eight feet up by a straw rope, with
sixteen *gohei*, four on a side, pendent from
it. This poetic palisade kept out the evil
spirits; a bamboo railing below kept out
small boys.

Upon the shrine above, which was simply
a deal table, stood, dignifiedly straight, and
commandingly lined in a row, three *gohei*

upon their wands. In front of them, upon a lower table, stood five others, colored respectively, yellow, red, black, white, and blue, the five far eastern elemental colors. The upper row represented the gods of construction, placed here to keep an eye on the scaffolding; the lower, the gods of the earth. Flanking the *gohei* stood two branches of *sakaki*, the sacred tree of Shintō, draped with lace-like filaments of *gohei*. At the corners of the platform four tufted bamboo, joined by a straw-rope hung with *gohei*, made a second palisade, miniature of the one below; while from a pole at the back floated a banner inscribed: Heavenly Gods, Earthly Gods.

Half way up the scaffold two paper placards, one on either side the ladder, challenged the eye. The right-hand one gave the functions and functionaries of the festival: the Principal Purifier, the Vice-Purifier, the Chief of Offerings, the Purifying Door, and the God-Arts; the offices preceded, the names of the persons followed. The other specified the various functions of the God-Arts themselves, and the names of those who bore them, a certain Mr. Konichi being down as Drawing the Bow. This, it seemed, was to

be taken in a purely ceremonial sense, the
real archer being Mr. Kobayashi.

For his benefit, four short posts about four
teet high had been planted directly under the
platform, ready to receive two swords, on
the blades of which he was to stand while
engaged in his act. We could not help wondering how he was to get upon them. Indeed, the elevating nature of the whole performance was not the least impressive part
of it. The reason for this lay, we were told,
in the intrinsic purity of high places, because
above the ordinary level of mankind. Certainly, with a ladder of sword-blades for sole
means of approach, the platform above did
not seem likely to prove overcrowded.

On the left stood the *Kagura-dō* or dancing-stage, filled with musicians, who were at
the moment engaged in tuning up — not a
highly melodious performance at best. They
kindly desisted to let us lunch upon the
stage, which we did while the other preparations went on, to the open-mouthed enjoy-
ment of many small villagers, who had already
begun to collect for the occasion. As soon
as lunch was over the swords were brought
out. They had not been lashed in place

before, in order that we might first inspect
them. This we now did to our satisfaction.
They were, one and all, old samurai blades,
as sharp as one would care to handle — from
the hilt — and much sharper than he would
care to handle in any less legitimate manner.
They certainly did not seem adapted to treading on, even tentatively. There were twelve
of them, all loans from the neighborhood,
and heirlooms, every one, from knightly
times — not so great an antiquity as it
sounds, since the middle ages were but
twenty years ago. But I should never have
imagined so many retired knights or their
heirs in so very retired a hamlet. The blades
themselves bore evidence, however, of having been possessed and probably used for
quite an indefinite time by their owners ; and
this touch of local domesticity imparted a
certain sincerity to the act artistically convincing in itself.

The swords were then lashed in place.
But as the divine archery was to precede
the divine climb, and there were twelve sets
of notches in the ladder and but twelve
blades in all, those destined for its two lower
rungs were lashed first upon the shooting-

stand. The ladder measured fifteen feet in length, the rungs being about a Japanese foot, fifteen inches of our feet, apart; doubtless such distance being found in practice the most comfortable. After securely tying on the swords, blades up, the priests departed to dress for the function.

Meanwhile a capital pantomime was in progress upon the dancing-stage. A dance-hall is an invariable feature of every well-appointed Shintō temple, and is put in play on every possible occasion. The performers are sometimes girls, sometimes men, the former doing the serious dancing and the latter the jocose mimes. Both are always capital, and on this occasion I think the show outdid itself. Certainly it proved comic enough to keep the religious in roars. Three buffoons in fine pudding-faced masks engaged in turn in an altercation with an impressive gray-beard. The altercation was of an intermittent character owing to the necessity felt by the pudding-faced citizen of taking the audience into his confidence by elaborate asides of side-splitting simplicity, digressions which in no wise prevented the row's proper emotional increase, till at

last it culminated in a fight which the gray-
beard, who did nothing but stalk round with
a fine woodeny walk, invariably won. This
was due quite simply to his god-like greatness, and not to the fact that his adversary
went through the fight with his scabbard in
lieu of his sword, having with elaborate in-
advertence drawn the one for the other, a
mistake at which he was subsequently proportionately surprised. All this, of course,
detracted not a whit from the sanctity of
the performance, which, like that of orato-
rios, came in with the historical characters
the performers were supposed to represent.

In the mean time the countryside had
been silently gathering. The ubiquitous
little girl with the pick-a-back baby appeared
first. Her familiars followed ; the waifs
growing in stature as they grew in numbers.
I did not see them come ; I only saw them
there. And they made as modest a setting
to the miracle as do the mountings to a
Japanese painting. There was about them,
indeed, a little of the ecstatic stupor of the
cow, but the usual bovine stare of modern
Japanese curiosity was here tempered by
instinctive old-fashioned politeness.

A Japanese street-crowd pleasingly lacks that brutality which distinguishes a western one ; on the other hand, it has a stare of its own, an unobstrusively obstrusive stare, which knows no outlawing limit of age, and has a vacancy in it that almost bars offense. Apparently it is never outgrown. It alone would convict the race of a lack of self-consciousness and very nearly of a lack of any consciousness whatsoever. I love the Japanese urchin for all that, whether staring or not, but to me advanced age in the starer stales the infinite unvariety of his act. Orderly, however, and good-natured, a Japanese crowd is past praise, and one would think past policemen, which is not, I suppose, why the latter always turn up at such seasons. Here, however, I was much pleased to note their conspicuous absence. And still the concourse grew. When I first counted the folk they numbered one hundred and fifty. Shortly after, as near as I could estimate, there were two hundred and fifty people on the spot, of all ages, sizes, and conditions. The whole countryside had turned out, with or without the baby, according as it existed or not. Nobody's occupation seemed to in-

terfere with his presence there in the least,
from the village ragamuffin to the village
belle. Charming girls I noticed in the act
of commenting upon us, I trust favorably;
for, as one of my friends puts it about his
books, I would rather please the young girls
than the old men.

But though we had not reckoned without our host, we had reckoned, it soon turned
out, without our uninvited guest — the inevitable policeman. Just as we had taken
chairs on the oratory platform, and had forgotten his existence, he turned up. He did
so inopportunely for himself, for the first
prayer had begun, and he had perforce to
wait till it was over to put his official questions. The prayer was the first of the purification rites, and was offered before an im-
provised altar on the oratory. The altar was
set out as the customary divine dinner-table
and displayed the usual choice collection of
indigestibles; fortunately always to be taken
in a strictly immaterial manner. For every
Shintō service is nothing but a divine din-
ner-party, with the god for sole guest. In
this case the aboriginal banquet was offered
to the *gohei* of O-ana-muchi-no-mikoto, the
patron god of the occasion.

The adjournment made the policeman's opportunity. Stiffly lifting his hat, as if the action were itself part of bureaucratic automatism, he challenged a lay brother on the oratory steps and proceeded to interview him on the cause of the crowd. Apparently the lay brother worsted him, for at the end of the colloquy he was so far humbled as simply to send me his card, with the modest request to know if I were a noble, as in that case he wished to salute me properly; to which I returned mine with the reply that I was not a noble, but an American, and therefore only the sixty-millionth part of a sovereign, and left him to figure out the respect due in so complicated a case.

The occasion, however, soon had a humanizing effect even upon his officialdom, so that he shortly grew quite tame and accepted at the hands of the lay brother a seat upon the platform beside us.

Meanwhile the priests were busy with prayers and finger-charms on the mats at the foot of the ladder, and when enough of them had been restored there took place a solemn walk-round by the whole company about the staging.

Mr. Konichi, the Sacred Bow, and Mr. Kobayashi, the Chief of God-Arts, then armed themselves with two beautiful bows beribboned at the end with a tangle of colored *gohei* of the five elemental colors, and proceeded, the one to mount by the secular ladder, which had not yet been removed, to the altar above, where he went through much pantomimic archery; the other to do like effigy-shooting below. The Chief of the God-Arts was specially effective. Stretching his bow at each corner of the square in turn, he made semblance to shoot at the demons, and accentuated his performance by quite unearthly grimaces. He knotted first his fingers and then his face in a truly startling manner. Nature had endowed him with a remarkably expressive physiognomy, which even in repose bordered perilously upon caricature. When this came to be further heightened by art, as enthusiastic performance of the rite demanded, the effect was extreme, quite capable of driving off devils, which was its object, and very nearly of driving off the bystanders, which was not. The pious saw in it the most realistic piety. What the children saw I will not pretend to guess, but I can conceive the nightmares they may have had in consequence.

When he had thus successfully frightened off the evil spirits without, he entered within the staging, and before the arrow-stand further scared the imps. As the exorcism drew to an end and we began once more to wonder how he was going to mount his hobby-horse, the big drum was brought by somebody and set up beside the stand. This solved the enigma and enabled the Chief of God-Arts, with the help of a pole, to rise carefully to the ends of the posts and to place first one foot and then the other lengthwise upon the blades, the forward edges coming out between his great and second toes. He then discarded the pole, as I have seen more secular performers do, to the catch of an assistant, and stood poised upon the knife-edges. Not content with standing upon them, he must needs tilt himself up and down as one does in testing the breaking power of a plank. This, of course, merely showed how much at home he felt upon the blades. Then with due deliberation he fitted an arrow into its notch, raised the bow, and drew it to his shoulder. In this effective pose he remained a long time, uttering what sounded uncommonly like an oath, but was in fact a song, sister to this : —

"The God of the Bow bends down from on high,
And at twang of the string, lo ! the demons fly."

The string, however, did not twang. For the exorcism continued, and the bow stayed bent. Indeed, the one was as long drawn out as the other, and the suspense was becoming positively painful, when at last he released the arrow into the air. The demons had evidently taken the hint, for the arrow buried itself harmlessly in the bushes.

With the assistance of the pole he then changed his pose a quarter way round, planting first one foot and then the other carefully across both blades. Then discarding the pole, he again went through the same pantomime as before, ending in a second release. His pose at this point was quite magnificent, and his intentness such that as with his eye he followed the arrow's flight, his whole audience instinctively did the same. We failed to see the shaft strike, and, turning back, behold ! there it was still in his hand.

Whether economy or the remains of original sin prompted this pious fraud, I know not, but he thus deceived us more than once, as he turned round quarter-wise upon his holy pedestal. Once he hit a tree, quite by accident, and the crowd applauded. After he had thus revolved several times, he called again for the pole and carefully descended from his pinnacle. I examined his soles and found them not only uncut, but barely lined; an unhurt condition which he shortly proceeded to demonstrate practically upon the ladder.

The divine shooting was no sooner over than the purification rites for the climbing of the ladder began; the usual thread of prayer knotted with finger-twists being gone through with upon the mats in front. Then, that there might be no mistake in the minds of the populace as to the genuineness of the miracle, the Chief of God-Arts ascended the secular ladder, which still leaned against the platform, and producing sheets of paper from his sleeve, cut them elaborately into little bits upon each blade in succession, and let the pieces flutter to the ground. When he had finished the secular ladder was removed.

Nothing now led up to the goal of this acrobatic pilgrimage but the consecrated ladder of sword-blades. *Ad astra per aspera* with a vengeance. Nevertheless the Chief of God-Arts, calling once more upon the gods, prepared to mount. Girding up his loins that his feet might not catch in his tunic, and grasping parts of the upper blades with his hands, he planted one foot lengthwise along the lowest sword-edge, and then, drawing himself up to its level, placed the other similarly on the blade above. Then he rose in like manner to the third rung, and the fourth, and so on heavenward. He did this carefully but deliberately. Evidently it was merely a question of foot-placing with him.

The higher he got the less he seemed to think of his footing and the more of effect, till in mid-ascent he was minded to try a religious *pas seul.* Posing on one foot, he turned deftly to face the crowd, and with the appropriate swing kicked out with the other high into the air, flaunting his foot before the rapt concourse of people in the most approved *prima assoluta* manner. At this unexpected terpsichorean touch the

populace burst into applause ; and the Chief
of God-Arts, turning triumphantly to his
climb, continued boldly up till amid a general gasp of relief from the crowd below he
topped the last rung and stepped out unscathed upon the platform.

Instantly he sank in prayer before the
shrine. While he was at his devotions the
second or secular ladder was brought round
to another side of the scaffolding and tilted
up against it, for what purpose did not at first
appear. For, his prayer finished, the Chief
of God-Arts turned again to the ladder of
swords and exorcised it afresh. Then just
as he was about to set foot on it for the
descent, as we thought, he turned back and
to our astonishment came quietly down the
secular ladder instead. I was unavoidably
reminded of the devout but inconsequent
lady who told a friend that " She thought
she should go to New York on Wednesday,
D. V.," but, reflecting a moment, "that she
should come back on Saturday anyway."

That his taking to the back-stairs for the
descent was not due, however, to any in-
ability on his part to come down by the
front ones was shortly evident by his mak-

ing soon after the ascent of the sword-blades
nonchalantly a second time. The truth was,
the miracle was supposed to end at the top,
and the secular ladder to be as invisible a
return to the original position as back-stairs
generally.

As the Chief of God-Arts came down thus
incognito by the back way, a second priest
made ready to go up by the front one. His
performance was largely a repetition of the
first's ; except that before starting the others
weighted him with some boxes full of charms,
which they strapped upon his back, to be
consecrated by the ascent for subsequent dis-
tribution. What he carried made apparently
no difference to him. He stepped up boldly
and, after due suspense on the part of the
populace, stepped out safely at the top.

The next to ascend was the head priest
himself. This was a special compliment to
us, since the head priest no longer habitu-
ally climbs, being well on in years. He
got up, however, with impunity, save for a
slight cut upon one palm. The third blade
from the top did the business. We had noticed that the others had shied at it as if it
were very thin ice, and when it came to

the older skin of the head priest, he simply went through. This mishap conclusively showed, the priests stated, that for some cause the blade was impure. They were afterwards able to prove their prognostication quite right, for on subsequent investigation the blade was found to have recently killed a dog and not to have been properly purified since.

After the head priest all the others went up in turn, including the lay-brother; some of them several times. Planting the feet lengthwise was the favorite mode of procedure, but when more convenient the foot was put across the blade instead. To one man in particular it seemed to make small difference how he trod. He jumped jauntily up as if the blades were an every-day set of rungs and he in a hurry.

Inasmuch as imitation is the sincerest flattery, the priests should have been greatly pleased when at this point Asa, my houseboy, fired to emulation, suddenly pulled off his European boots and socks, rolled up his European trousers, and presented himself as candidate for the climb. To my eye the outlandishness of his dress, amid the archaic

costume of the priests, gave him at once
that unsuitable appearance to the deed so
consecrated to the supposed countryman
who volunteers at the circus. I should certainly have had my doubts about the genuineness of his inexperience had I not known
him for my own "boy." The priests, however, received him most kindly, and after
sprinkling him with a shower of sparks and
properly finger-twisting over him, to purify
him as much as possible, — and I doubt not
he needed it, — showed him how to plant his
feet on the rungs and started him up the
ladder. To my surprise, and I think his
own, he went as well as the best of them.
We watched him with some vanity and more
concern, and were suddenly electrified when,
half way to the top, he turned, and, with a
triumphant smile, made, he too, the approved
coryphée kick high into the air. It brought
down the house but not the boy, who continued on successfully till at last he stepped
out triumphantly at the top. He was obliged
to abbreviate the prayer, from not knowing
it, and then he too came down the regulation
back-stairs.

Exactly what happened after this is a mys-

tery. Whether in his exaltation and hurry
to get back to his place he forgot the projecting tips of the sword-blades, or whether
in coming round the corner he collided with
one of the priests, was not clear, for the first
thing we knew, the boy was on the ground
bleeding pretty freely from a gash in the top
of his foot, while the priests did their best to
stanch the blood. The point of one of the
swords had ripped him as he passed. Nevertheless, he shortly after hobbled to the oratory veranda and then, while a proper bandage
was being fetched, promptly fainted. When
duly swathed he was dispatched to the head
priest's house, where he underwent considerable exorcism, which, as he informed me later,
did him a world of good. Evidently he possessed more latent piety than I had given
him credit for.

How many more enthusiasts might have
gone up the divine ladder had it not been for
this regrettable diversion will never be
known. For by tacit consent the episode
closed the performance.

It by no means, however, ended the fes-
tivity. Several pleasing adjuncts to this had
miraculously appeared, unperceived, during

the performance of the miracle itself. A long line of booth - mats had suddenly sprouted mushroom-like out of the ground beyond the oratory and was now attempting to beguile the crowd by every species of toy and gimcrack, visibly connected or unconnected with the occasion. There were paper masks and clay foxes and baby bows and arrows and papier-maché swords. The last caught our fancy, as being suited for presentation to some of the urchins who were standing interestedly about, and who instantly put them to proper use by making us the objects of pantomimic attack as soon as ever our backs were turned.

Through this running fire we made our way safely to the head priest's house, from which, loaded with charms consecrated by the miracle, we were bundled into our jinrikisha and trundled regretfully toward home.

And now to explain the miracle : —

Doubtless credulity is the mother of miracles, but doubtless, also, with the far eastern family of them a pachydermatous sole stepfathers the process. For most of them are questions of cuticle. Of the three great Shintō rites: the Ordeal by Boiling Water ;

the Walking across Live Coals; and the Climbing upon Sword-blades, all depend upon it for easy performance. That the average Japanese sole is equal to the feat without preliminary purification is evident from the success of my boy, who simply picked up his skirts and walked.

But a certain other physical fact enters this last miracle not commonly appreciated, to the innocent manipulation of which by the priests the miracle is due; to wit, the immense difference in cutting power between a stationary and a moving blade. Everybody is aware that there is a difference, but few people realize how very great it is. If you press your finger upon the sharp edge of your knife, you will be surprised to find what a pressure you can put upon it with impunity; but if, ever so gently, you draw the knife-blade across the skin, it instantly sinks in.

The principle involved is the principle of the wedge. By drawing the blade along in the direction of its edge at the same time that you press down, you thin its angle to any desired tenuity. You have but to graduate the horizontal motion to the vertical force. As the angle of the wedge thus sharpens, the force necessary to make it enter is lessened indefinitely. We unwittingly apply this principle whenever we cut anything. And as this is our normal state, we forget that the blade is, statically used, not as cutting as we think.

Furthermore, it will be remembered that, as a rule, the priests took heed in placing their feet. Most of them were careful to minimize the impact.

These are some of the points that make miracle-working possible; but a good audience is equally necessary. A sympathetic populace renders Japan a very paradise of miracles. There is thus a twofold reason for a miracle's success; a thicker skin in the priests, and a thicker skull in the people. This double lack of penetration makes it easier both to do, and to be done by, a miracle than it would be elsewhere.

Pondering in this wise upon the great advantages for successful miracle-working possessed by priests of an artistic, pachydermatous people over those of a thin-skinned, scientific one, and half lamenting the lost grandeur of that pious past whose childish

imaginings loomed so large and life-like, and
vanish so sadly before our bull's - eyes of
search, we were rolled through the broad
quiet twilight of tillage toward the growing
twinkle of the town.

V.

To give a full account of Shintō miracles,
we have now to consider quite a different
class of them ; the objective ones, pure and
simple. The nomenclature is not mere
matter of distinction. For the first kind
are brought about by the unintentional but
efficient subjective action of the miracle-
performer himself ; the latter take place
independently of him. It is a distinction
unimportant as regards the things, but of
vital consequence as regards the people.
For though it be open to the looker-on to
doubt whether the water or the fire in the
two ordeals above be rendered any the less
hot by having parted with its spirit, it is
not open to him to doubt the difference of
perception of that heat in the man's normal
and abnormal states of consciousness. This
question is quaintly begged by believers, by
stating that the god withdraws the spirit of

the fire or permits it to return momentarily, according to the character of the tester. Skeptics settle the whole matter off-hand by denying the fact. But it is unscientific to call upon a noumenon unnecessarily, even of an annihilating character. Universal negation of a sense distinction implies universal charlatanry; and men are both too simple and too astute for that to be possible. Charlatans ape but they do not originate. A counterfeit implies a genuine, and a shammer something to sham.

To the objective miracles there is no psychic or divine side; they are due to undivined psychical principles merely. The *Odojigokushiki,* or "The Descent of the Thunder-God," is one of these. He descends into so plebeian a thing as a kettle of steaming rice, the rice being afterward offered in banquet to the temple deities. For to have rice taste like thunder is said to be peculiarly pleasing to the gods. The manner of working this miracle is as follows : —

Upon a small urn was placed a kettle and upon the kettle a rice steamer, the lid so set on as to leave a slit on one side. A young acolyte then appeared in the usual pilgrimage robe, his hair dank from the bath and his whole person shivering with cold, and, striking a spark from some flint and steel, proceeded to light the fire and then to encourage its combustion by the usual finger-twisting, scattering of salt, prayer, striking of sparks, and brandishing of the *gohei*-wand.

After the exorcism was well under way, the head priest came forward and sat down before the kettle in order to perfect the rite, the acolyte falling back to the part of mute. In keeping with the good man's extreme purity, his finishing touches were very simple. They consisted of a soundless whistle which he kept up through his pursed lips and of certain archaic finger-charms symbolic of pulling some very heavy substance toward him. Then, still mutely whistling, he sat perfectly still and watched.

He had not long to wait. Suddenly a roar rose out of the body of the kettle, and at almost the same instant the priest's own body began to sway back and forth. Steam followed the roar; then, after a couple of seconds, the roar ceased. We did not have to be told that it was the voice of the Thunder-

God ; and when it ceased we knew the god had gone.

Press of business the priest gave as excuse for the shortness of the divine visit. But indeed we were very fortunate, it seemed, in getting him to come at all, for often the deity does not deign to descend, even for a moment, being otherwise occupied. Besides, if every accessory be not perfectly pure he refuses to come on conscientious grounds.

The priest averred that at the moment of possession he always felt a violent punch in his stomach. He also said that the swaying of his body was to induce by symbolic traction the presence of the god, though it had seemed a trifle late for the purpose. Doubtless the god can be so constrained, but doubtless, also, the kettle is for something in the subsequent conversation. The slit in its lid has been suggested as capable of explaining the miracle, could it only talk as well as it can roar.

VI.

We now come to a miracle which might possibly be turned to practical account. It is perhaps the most wonderful of the objective ones. It consists in bringing down fire from heaven by simple incantation. The spark thus obtained may be used to light anything, the prehistoric two sticks preferably for purposes of warmth. At the time I was shown this miracle, I was not in need of caloric, — it was seventy-five degrees Fahrenheit in the shade, — so I was permitted to witness its working upon the comparatively vile body of my own freshly filled, unlighted pipe.

This is a very difficult miracle. Indeed, even when it succeeds it is scarcely an economical method of firing one's tobacco daydreams, so much time and trouble does it cost. But to epicureans who hunt new sensations and to whom the one meaning of the word "dear" is synonymous with the other, it may safely be recommended. For it is not likely as yet, if I may argue from my own experience, to be generally taken up.

To insure success in the city, the day should be sunshiny. Among the mountains even a cloudy day will do, so I am informed. I cannot speak confidently on this latter point, because my own investigations were confined to the ridge-pole of my house in town, and to the turf immediately below it.

The priest who performed the miracle began by douching himself in the bathroom,
from which, between the plumps of water,
issued uncouth sounds, sputterings of formulæ and grunts as he finger-twisted. He
emerged with nothing on but a blue pocket-
handkerchief for loin-cloth, the small blue
and white rag with which the Japanese dab
themselves in lieu of towel. In this attire
he sallied forth into the garden, and select-
ing the side of a hill as a propitious spot,
squatted in the ordinary Japanese posture on
its slope.

Cradling the pipe between his hands, he
prayed over it exhaustively. Then he put
it, tilted toward the sun, in front of him, and
exorcised it very energetically by finger-
charms, one of which strikingly resembled
an imaginary burning-glass. There was, however, nothing between his fingers but air.
He had spent fifteen minutes thus in digital
contortions, when he suddenly stopped, distressed, and, complaining that the ants tickled
him by promenading over his bare skin, said
he thought he would go upon the roof. So
a ladder was brought and tilted against the
eaves, and up it he mounted to the tiles, and

thence by easy slopes to the ridge-pole. In this conspicuous yet solitary position he continued the incantation. Part of the time I sat beside him on the roof; part of the time below upon the ground, looking intently up into heaven for the advent of the god.

Three quarters of an hour passed thus in momentary expectation of his descent, but nothing happened. At last, much chagrined, the priest informed us from the ridge-pole that it was of no use that day, and came down; but he signified his intention of repeating the rite till he succeeded, and, with this pious resolve, left.

True to his word, he was there again two days later, and remembering poignantly the disturbing ants, he decided to ascend at once to the ridge-pole. Before he did so, I examined him to a certain extent, although he had on only one of my own very smallest towels. Then two of us took post in the garden commanding the ridge-pole, and watched him for the better part of an hour from our vantage points. In another part of the garden had been set the lunch table, also commanding the ridge-pole, for the expected divine visit was sublimely ill-timed, and we hoped thus, if necessary, to be able to combine god and mammon. We put the evil hour off as long as possible, till at last nature could wait no longer, and we decided to sit down to our delayed repast, firmly purposing to keep one eye constantly on the exorcist. We did so religiously till we forgot him a moment for the *vol-au-vent*. Suddenly the man on the roof uttered a cry, went into incipient convulsions, and threw the pipe off into the garden, lighted. We instantly repented our forgetfulness of the god, and cursed our love of mammon. But too late, as the miracle had been wrought.

Exactly how the miracle was managed, I am unable to guess. The man certainly had scant means of concealment about his bare person. Naturally, however, we were not satisfied, and he professed himself willing to repeat the act. He tried the trick after this time and time again, but never succeeded more. So there this miracle remains, very much in the air. But I should say that it is said to be very commonly done; a more common thing, indeed, in Japan, than I can conceive burning-glasses to be.

To make the catalogue complete, I ought

to mention what, spiritually viewed, are ornamental miracles — such as killing snakes and bringing them to life again, rooting burglars to the spot, arresting the attempts of assassins in the act, and defending one's self against discourteous dogs. But all such acts need not be dwelt upon at length, as they are very simple affairs to the truly good, and, like some scientific inventions, too expensive for general use.

INCARNATIONS.

I.

AFTER the miracles, or possessions of things, follow, in order of esoteric ascension, the incarnations, or possessions of people.

The miracles, as I have hinted, are performed largely with an eye, at least one eye, to the public. To drench one's self with scalding water or to saunter unconcernedly across several yards of scorching coals are not in themselves feats that lead particularly to heaven, difficult as they may be to do. Esoterically regarded, they are rather tests of the proficiency already attained in the Way of the Gods than portions of that way needing actually to be traversed. The real burning question is whether the believer be pure enough to perform them pleasurably. To establish such capability to one's own satisfaction in the first place, and to the wonder of an open-mouthed multitude in the second, are the objects the pious promoters have in view.

Not so the incarnations. They too, indeed, serve a double purpose. But whereas they are, like the miracles, measures of the value of the purity of the man, they are also practical mediums of exchange between the human spirit and the divine. Foregone for directly profitable ends, loss of self is the necessary price of an instant part in the kingdom of heaven.

Perhaps the most startling thing about these Japanese divine possessions is their number; unless it be that being so numerous they should have remained so long unknown. But it is to be remembered that what no one is interested to reveal may stay a long while hid. For, with quite Anglican etiquette, the Japanese never thought to introduce their divine guests and their foreign ones to each other. Once introduced, the two must have met at every turn. Indeed, the visitants from the spirit-world remind one of those ghost-like forms of clever cartoonists, latent in the outlines of more familiar shapes, till, by some chance divined, they start to view, to remain ever after the most conspicuous things in the picture.

Thoroughly religious, the possessions are not in the least hierarchic. In theory esoteric enough, in practice they are, in the older sense of that word, profane. For god-possession is no perquisite of the priests. It is open to all the sufficiently pure. The reason for this lack of exclusiveness is to be sought in the essentially every-day family character of Shintō. Everybody is a descendant of the gods, and therefore intrinsically no less holy than his neighbor. Indeed, if ease of intercourse be any proof of kinship, the Japanese people certainly make good their claim to divine descent. For they pass in and out of the world beyond as if it were part of this world below.

Purity is the one prerequisite to divine possession, and though to acquire sufficient purity be an art, it is an art patent rather in the older unindividualized sense of the word. Any one who is pure may give lodgment to a god, just as any plutocrat may entertain modern royalty. The gods, like latter day princes, are no respecters of persons. They condescend to come wherever due preparation is made for them. It is the host's house, not the host that they visit; the presence of the host himself being graciously dispensed with. The man's mind must have been vacated of all meaner lodgers, including himself, before the god will deign to habit it, but who the man is, is immaterial. Such humble folk as barbers and fishmongers are among the most favored entertainers of divinity.

But though the social standing of the man be immaterial, the social standing of the god, on the other hand, is a most material point in the matter. For mere association with the supernatural is not in Japan necessarily a question of piety or even of impiety. Often it is pure accident. To become possessed by a devil, of which bewitchment by a fox is the commonest form, may be so purely an act of the devil that no blame beyond carelessness attaches to the unfortunate victim. Religion claims no monopoly of intercourse with the unseen. What religion does claim is the ability to admit one to the very best heavenly society. For, to say nothing of mere animal spirits, there are all grades in

gods, good gods and bad gods, great gods
and little ones. Access to the most desir-
able divinities is the privilege to which the
church holds the keys.

Capability to commune is thus in a general
way endemic, much as salvation is held to be
in some places, or infant damnation in others.
And to Japanese thought the gods are very
close at hand. Unsuspected as such presence be by foreigners, in the people's eyes
the gods are constantly visiting their temples
and other favorite spots, in a most ubiquitous manner. Indeed, after introduction to
their Augustnesses, one is tempted to include them in the census and to consider
the population of Japan as composed of
natives, globe-trotters, and gods.

The gods resemble the globe-trotters in
this, that both are a source of profit to the
people. For finding themselves in communi-
cation with the superhuman, the Japanese
early turned the intimacy to practical account. They importuned these their relatives for that of which men stand most in
need, the curing of disease. Out of this
arose a national school of divinopathy.

Civilized cousins of the medicine-men of

North America, of the shamans of savage
tribes the world over, and of Christian scientists generally, the Japanese practitioners
differ from most members of the profession
in the widespread popular character of their
craft.   For though all the practitioners are
religious men, they are by no means all
priests.   Except for a difference in degree,
the distinction between the priests who
practice and the practicing lay brethren lies
in the professional or avocational character
of their performance.   The priests, of course,
have no other business than to be pious,
and to be temporarily a god is an easy extension to being perpetually godlike.   The lay
brethren, on the other hand, practice such
possession only as an outside calling, each
having his more mundane trade to boot.   The
above-mentioned barber, for example, besides
industriously shaving man, woman, and child,
— this detail of the toilet being universally
indulged in, in Japan, — was able to carry on
a very lucrative business as a popular other-
world physician.   But he made no analogue
of the European barber - surgeon of times
gone by.   No particular pursuit has privilege of the divine practice, barbers being no

better than other folk in the eyes of the god. A divinopathist's earthly trade may be anything under heaven. Plastering and clerking in a wine-shop are among the latest specimen occupations I have met with of men thus engaged in business both with this world and the next.

These doctors of divinity receive regular diplomas, without which they are not allowed to practice. Nominally they are not allowed to practice with them, for in the certificates no mention is made of the special object for which the certificates are issued, permission being granted merely to perform prayer, which comprehensive phrase covers a multitude of saintly acts.

The reason the certificates read so beautifully vague is not that religion conceives her esoteric cults to be profoundly secret, but that the government imagines them to be barbarous because not in keeping with foreign manners and customs. At the same time, the paternal powers-that-be dare not proscribe them. The fact is, they are both too Japanese to be countenanced and too Japanese to be suppressed ; so the authorities wink at their practice. The Japanese government is, in more matters than this one, in much the same awkward state of mind as the Irish legislator, who declared himself to be "for the bill and agin its enforcement."

Divinopathy has one great advantage over other schools of medicine : by the very preparation for healing others the physician heals himself. For mere qualification to be a practitioner is itself a preventive to earthly ills ; much as vaccination precludes small-pox. The only question might be whether the cure be not worse than the complaint. After an account of the rigid self-discipline to be undergone before a diploma be possible, and then largely kept up for it to continue in force, I think it will seem uncommonly open to the doubt. Yet there are plenty of men who lead this life of daily hardship and renunciation for the explicit purpose of enjoying the life they renounce ; just as many an invalid will give up all that makes life worth living for the sake of living the undesirable residue longer.

But if the self-martyrdom be duly performed, the god practically always descends on application, and vouchsafes his opinion as to the cure of the complaint. Of course his prescriptions are religiously followed, and if report speak truth, with an unusually large percentage of success. Any and all diseases are thus cured on presentation, subject only to the willingness of the god. This proviso satisfactorily explains the few unfortunate failures.

Divine possession is not limited in its applications to the curing of disease. Naturally the divine opinion is quite as valuable on other subjects as on medicine, and is consequently quite as much in demand. From the nature of the gods themselves to the weather of the coming month, anything a man may want to know is thus inquired about of deity. Due care only must be exercised to grade the importance of the question to the importance of the gods. For gods of high rank stand as much on their dignity as men both in the matter of coming and in the matter of talking after they have come. I remember once a most superior person, as gods go, who grew very angry because I asked him a question he deemed it beneath him to answer, although he had descended on purpose to impart information, and told me, quite up and down, to go to the

god of agriculture (Inari-sama) for trivialities
of the kind.

The character of the company sought is
what renders excessive self-mortification necessary. It is only to the very best heavenly
society that introductions are so hard to get.
Inferior gods permit intimacy on much easier
terms. Ordinary *ichiko,* or trance-diviners,
for instance, whose deities rank much lower,
go through a preparation which is mild in
comparison.

II.

The one thing needful to insure divine
possession is purity. If you are pure, that
is, blank enough, you can easily give habitation to a god. Now some men are born
blanker than others, but none are by nature
quite blank enough for religious purposes,
though secularly they often seem so. Addi-
tional vacuity must somehow be acquired,
the amount varying not only with the man,
but with the rank of the god by whom he
desires to be possessed. To reach this state
of inanity is the object of the austerities
(*gyō*).

In the days of Ryōbu there were two

classes of men who indulged in mortification of the flesh to the attainment of thus losing themselves, — *gyōja* and *shinja*. With pure Shintō, that is, the present resurrection of the past pure faith, these names are naturally not popular, inasmuch as they savor of the millennial lapse from orthodoxy. But the course in practical piety pursued by the would-be pure, having itself always been *de rigueur*, remains still substantially the same.

Gyōja, translated, means "a man of austerities;" and heaven is witness that he is. Short of actual martyrdom, I can imagine few thornier paths to perfection. He would seem to need a cast-iron constitution to stand the strain he cheerfully puts upon it. Even to be a *shinja* necessitates a regimen that strikes the unregenerate with awe. Though *shinja* means simply "a believer," the amount of works this simple believer must perform before his faith is enough to be accepted would appall most people.

The curriculum has this in common with more secular ones, that whoso goes in at the one end usually comes out at the other, unless protracted austerity fall upon him; in which case he quits in the middle. The fact

that so many graduate shows that no extraordinary capacity is required to do so ; indeed, it is the capacity for incapacity that is
necessary. Plodding perseverance is what
wins the day. For the course is terrifically
arduous and terribly long.

To the purification of the spirit, the road
lies through the cleansing of the body. To
this end the two chief exercises are washing
(*suigyō*) and fasting (*danjiki*). Unlimited
bathing, with most limited meals ; such is
the backbone of the regimen. The external
treatment, being the more important of the
two, claims notice first.

Washing is the most obvious kind of purification the world over. Cleanliness, we say,
is next to godliness ; though at times in individual specimens the two would seem not to
have made each other's acquaintance. But
in Japan cleanliness very nearly is godliness.
This charming compatibility is due possibly
to the godliness being less, but certainly
chiefly to the cleanliness being more.

Even secularly the Japanese are supernaturally cleanly. Every day of their lives
forty millions of folk parboil like one. Nor
do they hurry themselves in the act. The

nation spends an inordinate amount of time in the national tub ; as becomes pecuniarily apparent when you hire a man by the day, or, stranger yet, by the job. You are tempted at times to suppose your toiler continuously either tubbing or teaing. Doubtless such totality is due to emotional exaggeration on your part, but it is beyond prejudice that he soaks in his tub a good working minority of his time.

When it comes to religious matters, it would seem as if this estimable quality were carried to its inevitable defect. For, from a pardonable pastime, bathing here becomes an all-engrossing pursuit. The would-be devotee spends his waking life at little else, and he sleeps less than most men at that. Not only is it his bounden duty to bathe six appointed times in every twenty-four hours, but he should also bathe as often as he may between. The more he bathes the better he becomes.

Now, if he simply soaked in a hot water tub as his profane friends do, this might be merely the ecstatic height of dissipation. But he does nothing of the kind. No gentle parboiling is his portion ; perpetual gooseflesh is his lot. For in his case no such amelioration of nature is allowed. Whatever the season of the year, his ablutions must be made in water of untempered temperature, fresh from the spring; in the depth of winter a thing of cold comfort indeed. It then goes by the expressive name of *kangyō*, or the cold austerity. What is more, he takes this uncongenial application in the mode to produce the most poignant effect — with the shock of a shower-bath.

Esoterically there are grades in the cleansing capabilities of shower-baths. For him who would reach the height of holiness the correct thing is to walk under a waterfall and be soused. This luxury is, of course, only to be had in the hills. In default of a waterfall, a douche from a dipper will do. But on religious grounds it is not to be recommended.

Man-made methods are imperative in town owing to the lack of natural ones, which is one reason why the hills are the proper habitat for novitiates into the higher life. In the good old days such habitat was a necessity, not that men were less pure then, but, on the contrary, that they strove to become

yet purer, so *gyōja* aver ; pure Shintō says it
was because they had then lapsed from orthodoxy. However that be, when *gyōja* were
gyōja they were anchorites pure and simple.
They dwelt as hermits among the hills, seeing
no man by the space of three years, and re-
ducing themselves as nearly as might be to a
state of nature ; of the inoffensive kind, for,
as their diet will show, they belonged rather
to the herbivorous than to the carnivorous
order of wild animal. After they had become quite detached from all that distinguishes humanity, they returned to the world
to live hermitically in the midst of it, repair-
ing again at suitable seasons to mountaineering meditation. Such were the men who
opened, as the consecrated phrase is, On-
take, that is, who first succeeded in reaching
its sacred summit. There are still a few of
these estimable creatures at large in the hills.
I have myself met some of them, there and
elsewhere, after their return to society, and
have gazed with interest at caves pointed out
to me which they had once inhabited.

But *gyōja* generally have deteriorated with
the world at large. They are far from being
what they were, so far that a conscientious

man hardly feels that he has the right to call himself a *gyōja* at all, as one of the class humbly informed me. He blushed, he said, when he thought of the austerities of the olden time. A modern *gyōja* was little more austere than a *shinja* who made his summer pilgrimages when he could. This was perhaps a gloomy view to take of the situation, for one usually finds the past not so superior to the present as report represents. But even at its worst, the deterioration would seem a case only for professional sympathy. For whatever the regimen may have been, there is at all events enough severity left it to satisfy any decent desire for self-martyrdom.

That mountains should be deemed peculiarly good points for entering another world is not unnatural. With inclines incapable of cultivation, they do not conduce to sociability, but enable the dweller there the more effectively to meditate himself into inanity. Unjogged by suggestion, the average mind lapses into a comatose condition, till the man comes eventually to exist upon the borderland of trance. But as it is not convenient for everybody to retire to the hills for three

years at a time, even for this sublime purpose, it has been found possible to combine
purity enough for vacuity with a tolerably
secular existence. The *gyō* in the two cases
differ only as a state of nature differs from
a condition of civilization.

This brings us back again to the bath,
for we are not half through with it yet. If
the neophyte be not taking the waterfall in
all simplicity on his head, he is outdoing
Diogenes by living not simply in his tub, but
tubbing. A cold water douche begins the
day, another marks its meridian, and a third
brings it to a close. But the day does not
bring the douche to a close. Just before
turning in the neophyte must take another
dip, after which it might indeed be thought
that he should sleep in peace. But such
would savor of pandering to the flesh. The
most vital ablution of all, therefore, the *crux
purificationis*, occurs at two A. M. (*yatsugyō*).
At this unearthly hour the poor creature
must wake himself up, stagger half asleep
to the waterfall or bathroom, souse himself
with a dipper or be soused by the fall, while
his teeth chatter a prayer and his fingers
twist themselves into cabalistic knots, he

himself shivering the while from top to toe ; then, brought up standing in this manner, try if he may to sleep again. Even should he succeed, his doze may not be for long, for with the dawn he must douche again, the sunrise austerity (*hi-no-de-gyō*).

Unearthly the midnight hour may advisedly be called, for it is for precisely such attribute that the time is chosen. At that dead of night, when every sound is hushed, and even the plants, they say, lie locked in sleep, the gods can the better hear. And this, oddly enough, in spite of their being very much engaged with their own spatterings and sputterings, for the gods themselves are then taking their baths, — the gods of the mountains under their waterfalls, and the gods of the plain in the rivers thereof. In Japan, even the gods wash and are clean, and, like their human poor relations, apparently make of the bath a time of social reunion and merriment. They hear, nevertheless, and reward the bather accordingly.

With a *shinja* this nocturnal exercise is optional. It all depends upon how pure he intends to become. Of course it is a great deal better to be thorough, and not for the sake of the flesh to shirk what shall etherealize the soul. A little more bathing can do no harm — unless it kill, which is beside the point.

Extras, that is baths at odd hours, are to be taken *ad libitum* by all. The rule is: When in doubt, douche.

This extreme lavatory exercise lasts indefinitely — as long as the devotee can stand it. And in diminishing doses it is kept up through life. To those who perform it in all its rigor under the waterfalls in the hills, the gods graciously show signs of accepted favor. For round the head of the holy, as he stands beneath the fall, the sunlight glancing through the spray rims a halo which all men may see and the reverent recognize as proof of sanctity. The skeptic may possibly ascribe it to a different cause, having perchance seen the like around the shadow of his own head cast, as he sat in the saddle, upon the clipped grass of a polo field. He will certainly do so when he perceives similar halos about the heads of his godless friends. Yet that abandoned character, Benvenuto Cellini, on suddenly remarking one

day an aureole radiating from the reflection
of his head in the water, as he leaned over
the side of a boat, took it at once for sign
certain that his salvation was assured.

So much for the fresh-water cure. To sum
it up in a maxim, — adapting to its gentler
warfare with the spirits of evil Danton's
celebrated one about war in general, — we
may say that the three essentials to success
in it are : "De l'eau douce ! de l'eau douce !
et encore de l'eau douce ! "

III.

Fasting (*danjiki*) is the next mortification
to the flesh. The poor brute of a body un-
equally yoked to so indomitable a spirit fares
ill. For it is deprived at once both of superficial gratification and of solid nourishment.
The would-be pure must abstain from meat,
from fish, from things cooked, and, compre-
hensively, from whatever has taste or smell.
In short, he should lead gastronomically an
utterly insipid existence. He may not even
indulge in the national tea, a beverage taste-
less and bodiless enough in all conscience
to escape proscription. Salt is specially to
be shunned (*shiwodachi*). It is worth noting

that on the way to a higher life the apparently harmless chloride of sodium should work as banefully within a man as it works beneficially without him.

Greater deprivation than all these, even tobacco falls under the ban. In that earthly paradise of smokers, the Japanese Islands, where the use of the weed rises superior even to sex, it seems indeed hard that only those dedicate to deity should be debarred it. But the road to immaterial peace of mind knows no material narcotic by the way. After he has attained to a holy calm without it, the lay brother returns to moderate indulgence in this least gross form of gluttony. The professed ascetic continues to abjure it his life long.

Nuts and berries form the staple of the *gyōja's* diet, if he be living a hermit among the hills ; buckwheat flour if, though not of the world, he be still in it. He may also eat vegetables and dried persimmons and grapes in their season; but he must eat most sparingly of whatever it be. One bowl of buckwheat and a dish of greens at noon is sustenance enough for the day. Breakfast and supper are forbidden panderings to the flesh. To wash this next to nothing down cold water is allowed him, if his external applications have not already given him enough of it.

Not unnaturally a diet of such subtraction speedily reduces him to his lowest mental terms, a state which he still further simplifies by purely mental means.

To start with, the general character of his existence conduces to that end. Whether he be living an actual anchorite among the mountains or only a would-be one in town, solitude complete or partial tends by well-known laws to convert him into either a maniac or a simpleton. To a species of the latter it is his ambition to attain.

To this end untold repetitions of elementary prayers admirably conduce. It would be hard indeed to overestimate the efficacy of such process for producing utter blankness of mind. The subdued chanting by rote over and over again of words to which any thought has long since bade good-by tends in a twofold manner to mental vacuity. There is just enough mental action going on to keep the mind from thinking of anything else, and yet it is so ineffably uninteresting that attention, do what it will, inevitably nods. It is a mistake to suppose that the soothing effects of church are wholly due to sound sleep during the sermon. Any auditory routine is competent to compel it. Rhythmic monotone is as potent a lullaby as more consecrated cradle-song. The eventual end of both would be sleep; as we see with the latter in the case of an infant in his crib or of middle-aged gentlemen in their pews, and in our own case with the former when we conquer our insomnia by methodically counting to a hundred an indefinite number of times. The chanter does not attain to this supreme nirvana because it is he himself that is preaching the sermon; but the soporific power of these rites in helping to a virtuous vacancy of mind is quite specific, and partly accounts incidentally for the long-windedness of preachers.

To this same intent, the more searching brother practices upon himself further ingenious devices. One of the most effective of these is the concentrating his whole attention upon his own breathing. Mentally, he scrutinizes each expiration — the in-

spirations appear to be somewhat better
able to look after themselves — with molecular minuteness. Each breath as it passes
out is thus subjected to the spirit's picket
challenge. By giving his whole mind in this
manner to the mere method of existence, he
effectually prevents any ideas from stealing
into that mind unawares. After prolonged
duty of the sort, consciousness, like all really
good sentinels, nods at her post ; in which,
unlike the good sentinels, lies the virtue of
the deed, though unsuspected of the doer.
For divine possession in Japan, like other
Japanese things, is not a science but an art.
The reason given by religion for this inspection of one's breathing is that by prayerful
concentration upon the source of spirit one's
evil spirit may be expelled and a good
afflatus drawn in. One of the truly pious
when quantitively questioned told me that
he had thus kept watch on himself for three
weeks at a time, only pausing in the pursuit
unavoidably to eat and sleep. It is sadden-
ing to think to what farther tenuities he
might not have attained had he not been
thus grossly shackled to the flesh.

Ablutions and abstinence are thus the two

great *gyō*, which endless prayers, mechanical finger-charms, and careful breathing help accentuate.

But besides the regular stock austerities, there are several supererogatory ones. There is, for example, the *gyō* called *tsumadachi*, which consists in walking on the tips of one's toes wherever one has occasion to go. A species of pious ballet-dancing this.

Then there is the austerity of never looking upon a woman's face. This martyrdom the ascetic who had practiced it spoke of as a very severe self-infliction indeed. But in view of the vast subjective disturbance wrought even unconsciously by the sex, I should judge it to be one of the most essential austerities of all. For no man who is a man can take that absorbing interest in nothing at all which the rules require while a pair of piquant eyes and a petticoat lead his imagination their irresistible dance. To be insensible to such charm were to have attained to complete insensibility already.

Compared with this renunciation, the next *gyō* must be a positive pleasure. It consists in letting unlimited mosquitoes bite one to satiety for seven consecutive nights.

The aptitude of all these artifices to the end desired is more or less apparent: some tending to slow down the whole machine; or by weakening the body, or by tiring the mind, some to dull the sense perceptions by persistent attention to what is essentially incapable of holding it, — all to reduce the brain to an inactive state. The road is unnecessarily long because originally discovered by chance, and then blindly followed by succeeding ages without rational improvement. An immense amount of labor is thus in point of fact thrown away. How much quicker a like result can be obtained by the application of a little science, modern hypnotism shows.

Now there will have been noticed in the list of austerities a steady departure from primitive simplicity. This decrease in simplicity is strictly paralleled by the decrease in their respective use. Everybody washed, though comparatively few poised on their toes. The several vogue of the austerities is further paralleled by the position occupied by those who practiced them, in that long chain of mixed belief which, dependent from pure Shintō at the one end, is supported by

Buddhism from the other. The mosquito ordeal, for example, is quite Buddhist, while abnormal ablutions are not. The significance of these two parallelisms will appear later on.

What the Japanese sensations are during the process may be gathered from the personally narrated experience of a certain believer, who sufficiently expresses the type. The given individual was first minded to become a practitioner in consequence of the surprising cure, through god-possession, of his master's sick son. He was at the time apprenticed to a dyer, and was away on a journey when the cure was wrought. Much impressed by what he heard on his return, he determined to seek out the holy man who had effected the miraculous result, and, by following in his footsteps, to attain to proficiency himself. The *gyōja* received him cordially, and kindly indulged him in his desire by putting him to the washing (*suigyō*) and the fasting (*danjiki*) austerities in all their rigor for three weeks. At the end of that time he was so used up that he could hardly stand. One bowl of rice and a dish of greens a day are little enough to help one through such a course of ablutionary training. Nevertheless, for fifty days more he kept on with but little addition to his meagre diet, washing lavishly the while. At the close of this second period he relaxed somewhat and ate, as he expressed it, in moderation, that is, immoderately little; which ameliorated treatment of himself he kept up for the next three years. He was twenty when he went through his novitiate, and sixty-three when he told me of it; for the intervening forty-three years he had dieted and douched daily.

No very definite sensation, follows, he says, the exercise of the austerities. He simply feels an increase in virtue, whatever that may mean. Fortunately it would seem to show itself in a practical form. For as he continues in the regimen he gets to know, he says, good and evil spontaneously. When a bit of good luck is coming to him or his family, or a misfortune about to befall them, he feels it beforehand by a certain mental light-heartedness, or a corresponding oppression of spirit. Finally he arrives at being able to predict everything. Whether he can always avert what he is able to foretell may be open to doubt. For consequent upon this exposure of his capabilities the poor man contracted a very bad cold, and was confined for a couple of weeks to his house.

He was, as the mention of his family showed, a married man. In this he made no exception to the rule. All lay brethren marry as a matter of course. Indeed, in Shintō proper, the priests wed like anybody else. Nor do such as follow the austerities commit themselves in the least to celibacy. For matrimony and self-consecration to the gods do not, it appears, conflict. In spite of the great advantage that accrues to piety from never looking upon a woman's face, mentioned above, mere matrimony would seem innocuous. Either femininity in repeated doses loses its intoxicating effect, or acquired sanctity renders the believer superior to it. Perhaps, as one of my married friends suggested to me, marriage is sufficient austerity itself.

However that may be, certain it is that nowadays even *gyōja* wed without detriment to their souls. I am by no means sure that they did not in the olden time, for so commonplace a detail of a far oriental's life as matrimony might well have escaped chronicling. Still there is no doubt that times have changed for the worse with *gyōja*, as my *gyōja* averred. Even pecuniarily so much is evident.   In the good old days they supported themselves in peace and plenty from the offerings of grateful patients ; now alas, as he said pathetically, these gratuities do not suffice, and many a worthy soul is forced to eke out a slender subsistence by secular work in secret. Making toothpicks was the industry he affectingly instanced, when pressed to be more explicit. To be driven to such extremity must seem indeed pitiable, even to the undevout.

Thus, then, do the pious get themselves into a general potentiality of possession. Before possession becomes a fact, however, a short renewal of extreme austerities must be undergone ; like the slight shake that crystallizes the solution. On notice of a case to be cured the practitioner enters again the rigors of the washing and the fast, and keeps them up for a week if he be very thorough, two or three days if that will suffice. The amount of abstinence depends upon the gravity of the case. There is something highly satisfactory in this dieting of the physician in place of the patient. From the patient's point of view it instantly raises divinopathy above all other pathies on earth. Besides, it is more thoroughly logical. For why, indeed, should not the physician, if well paid for it, be expected to furnish all the elements of his cure!

IV.

We have now reached the function itself. That this is imposing in the first sense of that word, that is, impressive, the hold it has had on man sufficiently testifies ; that it is imposing in the second sense, that is, a sham, is a supposition which the first view of one of these trances would suffice to dispel.

We will first take up the Ryōbu form which is the commonest one. The ceremony with which Ryōbu has surrounded the act is finely in keeping with the impressiveness of the act itself. So sense-compelling a service you shall find it hard to match in the masses of any other church. But more constraining still are the energy and the sincerity with which the whole is done. It is small wonder that the already susceptible subject feels its charm when even bystanders are stirred.

As with the *gyō*, purification is of its essence. For not only must a general purification antecede the act, but a special purification must immediately precede it. And first the spot must be holy. Now only one spot is holy by nature: the sacred mountain Ontaké or its affiliated peaks. All others must be purified. These may be of two kinds : temples, public or private, — for most houses have what is called a gods'-shelf, (*kamidana*), which does them for family shrine, — and ordinary rooms. The first are kept perpetually purified ; the second are specially purified for the occasion.

If there be no permanent shrine, a temporary one is constructed. Its central motif is a *gohei* upon a wand, stood upright on a pedestal. By the side of the *gohei* are lighted candles, and flanking these, sprigs of *sakaki*, the sacred tree of Shintō. In front of the *gohei* is set out a feast for the god. The feast varies in elaborateness according to the occasion, its principal dishes being a bowl of rice, a saucer of salt, and a cup of *saké*, the national wine. In addition to these indispensables, any form of uncooked human food may be offered to the god, according to the sumptuousness of the repast it is desired to give him.

The shrine is set up in the *tokonoma,* or recess of honor, of the room. At the back is placed a hanging-scroll of the gods of Ontaké. Some five feet in front of the *tokonoma,* in the centre of the sacred space, a porous earthenware bowl is placed upon a stand, and in the bowl is built a pyre of incense sticks, usually beginning as a log-hut and terminating as a wigwam.

Then the place is purified. This is done by inclosing the room, or the part of it in front of the shrine, by strings from which depend at intervals small *gohei.* These are usually arranged after the so-called seven-five-three (*shichi-go-san*) pattern ; seven of them being nearest the shrine, five on each side, and three at the farther end. From the space so inclosed all evil spirits are driven out by prayer, by finger-charms, by sprinkling of salt, by striking of sparks from a flint and steel, and by brandishing of a *gohei-*wand used as an exorcising air-broom.

After the purification of the place, the next duty of the officiators is the purification of their persons. For this purpose they

all go out to the well or to the bathroom to
bathe, and return clad in the Ontaké pilgrim dress, a single white garment stamped
with the names of the Ontaké gods, with the
name of the mountain itself, and with the
signs of their *kō* or pilgrim club. For, as
we shall see more particularly later, all
Ryōbu adepts, whether priests or laymen,
are enrolled in some Ontaké pilgrim club.
This solitary garment is bound about the
waist by a white girdle.

In its full complement the company consists of eight persons. There is, first, the
man whom the god is to possess. He
is called the *nakaza,* or seat-in-the-midst.
Equal to him in consideration is the man
who presides over the function and who is
to talk with deity, the exorcist, so to speak,
called the *maeza,* or seat-in-front. Next in
religious rank is the *wakiza,* or side - seat.
He is one of the *shiten,* or four heavens, specialized as the *tōhō,* or eastern side, the *hoppō,*
or northern side, the *nambō,* or southern side,
and the *saihō,* or western side. Their duty
is to ward off evil influences from the four
quarters. The two front ones also have the
charge of the paraphernalia, and the *nambō*

the care of the patient. In addition to these six there is a deputy *maeza* and a sort of clerk of court. The impersonality of these names is worth noting. It is the post, not the person, that is designated.

Severally clapping their hands, the performers now enter upon the ceremony proper. This consists of two parts : a general purification service, separated by a pause and a rearrangement from the communion service itself. The one is an essential preface to the other.

When the last man is fairly launched upon the general incantation, the *maeza* starts one of the purification prayers (*harai*), into which the others instantly fall. The prayer chosen to begin with is usually the *misogi no harai.* It is a chant chiefly in monotone, only occasionally lapsing for a note into the octave or the fifth. Every now and then a chanter sinks into a guttural grunt as if mentally fatigued, very suggestive of a mechanical dulling of the mind.

The *harai* over, or rather bridged by some of the company, the *maeza* starts another, the rest take it in swing, and the eight are off again together. In this manner prayer

after prayer is intoned, and *uta* or songs
chanted in like cadence between.   Shakings
of the *shakujō*, a small crosier with metal
rings, emphasize the rhythm, and the pilgrim
bells rung at intervals point the swift processional chorus of the whole.

The pyre is then lighted, and as the flames
leap into the air, prayers ascend with them
to Fudō-sama.   Meanwhile, pieces of paper
with characters inscribed on them are rapidly passed to and fro through the flame by
the *maeza* an unlimited number of times ; yet
do they not burn, an immunity due to possession by the gods.   Then he holds each
for a moment stationary in the flame, upon
which it catches fire and is caught upward
by the air current, to float away, the shriveled shape of its former self.   The paper is
in effigy of the disease, and, according as it
ascends or fails to do so, will the disease
itself depart or stay.   Some exorcists, with
more wisdom, perhaps, say that the manner
of its ascension only is significant.   But
mark how pitying are the gods.   For since
the flame makes its own draft, that must
indeed be an unlucky wraith of tissue ash
that fails of being well caught up with it to
heaven.

More chanting brings the purification service to a close.

The bowl that held the pyre is then removed, and sheets of paper are laid in the centre of the sacred space in the new places the performers are to occupy. Then the *gohei*-wand is brought down from the shrine and stood up in the midst.

The men take their seats for the descent of the god. Up to this time they squat on their heels in the usual Japanese fashion; from now on they sit with folded legs, which some say is the exalted seat of old Japan, and others ascribe to Buddhist influence. The *maeza* seats himself first, opposite and facing the shrine, folds his legs in front of him, and, drawing his dress over them, ties it together from the sides and then brings the farther end up and ties it to his girdle. This is the usual Japanese mode of tying up a bundle. The others do the same, the *shiten* seating themselves at the four corners, and the deputy *maeza* and clerk by the side of the *maeza*. The *nakaza* is as yet unseated, officially speaking.

All face the *gohei* and go through a further short incantation. Then the *wakiza*

reverently removes the *gohei*-wand and holds
it while the *nakaza* seats himself where it
was, facing from the shrine, tucks himself in
as the others did, and closes his eyes. After
some private finger-twistings and prayer on
the part of the *nakaza* and the *maeza*, the
nakaza brings his hands together in front
of him and the *maeza*, taking the *gohei*-wand
from the *wakiza*, places it between them.
Then all the others join in chant, and watch
for the advent of the god.

For a few minutes, the time varying with
the particular *nakaza*, the man remains perfectly motionless.   Then suddenly the wand
begins to quiver ; the quiver gains till all at
once the man is seized with a convulsive
throe — the throe, as we say in truth, of one
possessed.   In some trances the eyes then
open, the eyeballs being rolled up half out
of sight ; in others the eyes remain shut.
Then the throe subsides again to a permanent quiver, the eyes, if open, fixed in the
trance look.   The man has now become the
god.

The *maeza*, bowed down, then reverently
asks the name of the god, and the god an·
swers ; after which the *maeza* prefers his

petitions, to which the god makes reply.
When he has finished asking what he will
and the god has finished replying, the *nakaza*
falls forward on his face.

The *maeza* concludes with a prayer ; then
striking the *nakaza* on the back, with or
without the ceremony of previously writing
a cabalistic character (a Sanskrit one) there,
the *maeza* wakes him up. One of the others
gives the man water from a cup, and when
he has been able to swallow it, the rest set
to and rub his arms and body out of their
cataleptic contraction. For at first it is practically impossible to take the wand from his
unnatural grasp.

Although eight men are considered the
proper number by Ryōbu canons for a full
presentation of the function, so many are
not really vital to its performance. Two are
all that are absolutely essential; one to be
possessed, and one to hear what the god
may deign to say. I have seen trances with
officiators in number anywhere from two to
eight. One man alone would be sufficient,
were it not a part of the rite that some one
should hear the god's words; for one man
can take the parts of both *maeza* and *nakaza*

in turn, doing the *maeza's* part for the preliminary purification, and the *nakaza's* for
the possession itself. In this case the second
man acts as *wakiza.* Ordinarily, however,
when two men take part, one is the *maeza*
and the other the *nakaza* from the beginning to the end. With three men, the third
is *wakiza.* Of this kind was the possession upon Ontaké, in the case of the three
devotees.

From the moment he claps his hands each
begins upon a chain of finger-charms, of the
effective uncouthness of which it is difficult
to convey any idea in words. Their uncanny
character is distinctly the most impressive
thing in the function. They are called *in-
musubi* or seal-bindings, which describes
their intent, and incidentally their appearance. In form it is playing holy cat's-cradle
with one's hands, but in feeling it is the most
intense action imaginable. The fingers are
tied into impossible knots with a vehemence
which is almost maniacal; and the tying is
timed to consecrated formulæ that, in consequence of the performer's exaltation, take
on much of the emotion of a curse.

The several twists typify all manner of

acts. The position of the fingers in one symbolizes a well, raising which above the head and then upsetting it souses one with holy water. Another represents a very realistic pull, which constrains a good spirit to enter the performer. A third compels evil spirits to avaunt; and so forth and so on. There is quite an esoteric library on the subject, and so thoroughly defined is the system that the several finger-joints bear special names.

The seal-bindings are themselves sealed by a yet simpler digital device wrought with one hand, and called cutting the *kūji* or the nine characters. It consists in drawing in the air an imaginary five-barred gate, made of five horizontal bars and four vertical posts. This gate is to keep out the evil spirits. The reason there are nine strokes and not ten, which is the far-eastern dozen, is due to the far-eastern practice of always providing an enemy with a possible way of escape. If the Japanese devils could not thus run away it is said they would become dangerous. For, as a far-eastern proverb hath it, --

" The cornered rat
Will bite the cat."

At first I was inclined to believe these finger-charms Buddhist. But although the Ryōbuists say that they are, I have never seen a Buddhist practice them. On the other hand, they are professedly not Shintō, and are shunned by pure Shintōists accordingly. Their most devoted admirers are the Ryōbuists themselves.

The finger-charms are knotted upon one or other of the great purification prayers (*harai*). Of these there are three chief ones : the *misogi no harai*, the *nakatomi no harai*, and the *rokkon shōjō no harai*. The *misogi no harai* I believe to be pure Shintō. The *nakatomi no harai* undoubtedly is a native production, and is said to have been composed by an ancestor of the present high-priest of the Shinshiu sect. The *rokkon shōjō no harai* is of Ryōbu origin. It is the great Ontaké processional, chanted by the pilgrims as they toil slowly up the mountain's slopes.

V.

Having thus sketched the possession cult, I will now present some specimen trances of the various Ryōbu varieties of it. These

shall be followed by the Buddhist possessions, and these in turn by the pure Shintō
ones. When we shall thus have looked at
the possession objectively in the manner, we
will consider it subjectively in the man.

Heading the list comes the first possession
that I succeeded in obtaining, — a parlor-pos-
session in my own house. After very proper
coquetting with mystery, a priest of the
Shinshiu sect consented to visit me for the
purpose with a friend as side-seat (*wakiza*).
His performance was a case of playing con-
secutively two parts in the function: first
that of exorcist, and then of entranced.
Although he was a pure Shintō priest, the
ceremony was according to Ryōbu rite; for
he was a reformed Ryōbuist, and his refor-
mation did not extend to the rite.

His introductory scene-setting enabled me
to gaze for the first time upon the faces of
the Ontaké gods. For he began by hanging
up in the room's recess of honor a scroll
depicting those deities; whom as yet I knew
only as voices — *voces et præterea nil.* But
inasmuch as talking is their chief characteristic, I accepted unhesitatingly their portraits
for speaking likenesses. There were nine

of their Augustnesses in all, standing pedestaled respectively on precipitous points
of the conventional tri-peaked mount in con-
ventionally inapt attitudes. They all wore
the comfortable cast of countenance and generally immaculate get-up quite incompatible
with ever getting up a mountain. This, of
course, proved their divinity. The great god
of Ontaké towered commandingly on the
highest peak, flanked by two lesser Shintō
divinities perched on somewhat lower pin-
nacles. Below these stood Fudō-sama — a
conglomerate god from nobody knows exactly where, popularly worshiped as the god
of fire, which it is certain he was not, but
possessing, however, for some inscrutable
cause a certain lien on the land. He, too,
was flanked by two companions on suitable
inferior vantage points. These peopled the
mid-heaven of ascent. Still lower down came
three canonized saints of Ryōbu, the men
who had opened the mountain by first succeeding in getting to the top; for which feat
they were now rewarded by being placed
humbly at the bottom. The relative posi-
tions of the three classes of gods is worth
notice, for such is their invariable ranking

in Ryōbu pictures; a grading in greatness which says something about the Shintō ancestry of the act.

After the priest had duly hung up this happy family portrait and arranged the altar and incense pyre, he went and bathed, returning clothed in his Ontaké pilgrim robe, the very one in which he had himself several times made the ascent of the mountain, and which was therefore correspondingly pure. It showed this unmistakably. I think it was perhaps the dirtiest garment I have ever seen; at all events it was the most self-evidently so. It convinced at once of holiness in spite of the fact that it fortunately lacked all odor of sanctity. For it was internally as clean as externally it was dirty; it being, as we have seen, as imperative upon a palmer to wash himself as it is not to wash his robe.

Through the garment's present grimy gray glimmered traces of red characters; the stamped certificates, these, of his ascents. Their glory, enhanced by being hidden in an ideographic tongue, shone all the more resplendent for being thus mellowed by travel-stain. It was a pious thought that induced the wearer later to let his mantle fall, in gift, upon me; for it now rests from its wanderings among my most valued possessions.

The pale gray of his ascension robe took on a further tinge of glory from the glow of the burning incense pyre. The seemingly conscious flame lapped the pyre eagerly about, and then leaped searchingly up into the void, to send its soul in aromatic surges of smoke in curling rise toward heaven, into every highest nook and cranny of the wood-paneled ceiling of the room. From without, the glow of dying day stole through the sliding screens, tinging the gloom within; while pervading it all like a perfume rose the chant of the pilgrim-clad petitioner, rolling up in surges of its own, smothering sense to some delicious dream. Behind, silent and immovable, sat the assistant, a statue bowed in prayer.

Through the flame the priest passed, one after the other, written sheets emblematic of disease; passed each deliberately to and fro an amazing number of times, yet without so much as scorching it. After which he held it there motionless for a moment and it swiftly took fire. As it did so his chant swelled.

The shriveled shape wavered, poised, and then rose with the chant toward the rafters of the room. Its prayer had been heard and granted.

When the last embers of the pyre had burned themselves out, and the orange was slowly fading to ash, the priest brought his chant to a close, and, rising, removed the bowl. Then, spreading pieces of paper in a sort of Greek cross upon the mats where the bowl had been, he seated himself upon them in the *nakaza's* place, facing out from the shrine and prefacing his act by a short prayer, took the *gohei*-wand in both hands and shut his eyes. After some minutes of hushed suspense the wand suddenly twitched; the twitching grew to convulsions, the wand striking the man first on the forehead with quite irresponsible violence, and then with like frenzy on the floor. Finally it came back still quivering to its former position before his face. I say "it," for in truth it seemed rather the wand than the man that caused the shaking. Trembling there a few moments, it went off again into another throe; and so the action continued intermittently rising and falling, till at last the man himself fell face forward upon the floor.

The assistant advanced, raised the possessed to a sitting posture, and fell to thumping him on the back and chest to wake him. This energetic treatment brought him sufficiently to himself to be able to articulate for water. But when the glass was put to his lips he bit it to pieces in his frenzied efforts to drink. By good luck he neither cut himself nor swallowed any of the pieces.

After his senses had fully returned and his arms had been well kneaded, we carried him out upon the veranda, his legs still rigid in catalepsy. There they had to be violently rubbed and jerked into a natural state again. His pulse had been eighty-four at the time when he began upon his incantation; it was one hundred and twenty as he came to himself again.

When sufficiently recovered he went and bathed, and on returning, his first question was whether he had spoken in the trance. On being told that he had not uttered a syllable, he was much chagrined. He had hoped, he said, to have astounded us by speaking English when possessed, a tongue

of which, in his normal state, he knew nothing. That he might be permitted to do so
had been his petition as exorcist. Such supernatural powers, he assured us, were often
vouchsafed by the gods; and he mentioned
an Englishman (the only trace I have come
across of a previous foreigner in this other-
world) who had been thus possessed twenty
years before in Kōbe, and who, though
knowing no Japanese in his natural state,
spoke it fluently in the trance. A parallel
to this is to be found in the illiterate ser-
ving-girl of the German professor, who, in the
hypnotic trance, astounded the bystanders
by repeating whole pages of Greek, which,
it turned out, she must unconsciously have
learned from simply hearing her master read
Greek plays aloud, while she casually came
in and out to tend his fire.

I will next present a function with the full
force of the *dramatis personæ*. It also was
performed in my own house, by the Mi-
Kagura-kō, or August Dancing Pilgrim Club.
There were eight performers, the parts of
maeza, *nakaza*, the four *shiten*, the deputy
maeza, and the clerk of court, being taken
respectively by a plasterer, a lumber dealer,

a rice shopman, a carpenter, a pawnbroker, a pattern designer, a fishmonger, and a maker of *mizuhiki,* those red and white paper strings with which the Japanese tie bow-knots about their gifts. Quite a representative board of trade, in fact. The plasterer was the president of the club, and the pawnbroker its treasurer. This last combination was a mere coincidence, the man's earthly calling not being, so I was informed, any special recommendation to his heavenly office.

On the day appointed they turned up, *more Japanico,* pre-punctually. A polite, but at first aggravating national custom, this appearance of a guest considerably before the time for which he was invited. They came in detachments, the baggage leading, with the president and clerk. It was at once set up in scene, together with several other properties provided by me beforehand at the request of the club. The list of the latter articles was the better part of a foot long, and footed up to exactly thirty-one cents and a third.

A picture of Kuni-to-ko-dachi-no-mikoto, the great god of Ontaké, suitably pedestaled upon the mountain and flanked by his followers, was suspended in the recess, in front of which stood a *gohei*, bosomed in sprigs of Shintō's sacred tree, the dark green gloss of the leaves bringing out vividly the white paper flounces of the symbol of the god. On either side of it stood a candle speared upon its candlestick. A modest repast of salt and raw rice lay below, and flanking it a *saké* bottle not innocent of real *saké*. In front of the feast, in a pair of saucers, two tiny wicks floating in rape-seed oil made holy twinkles of light.

In the middle of the sacred space, duly inclosed by a frieze of pendent *gohei*, was built the symbolic primeval house of incense sticks. The place was then purified by prayer, by striking of sparks from a flint and steel, and by air-dusting with the *gohei* at each of the four corners, after which the eight officiators severally left for the bathroom to bathe, and returned one after the other clad in the pilgrim dress. The bathing, though in this case privately done, is often publicly performed. On the occasion of a fire-crossing (*hi-watari*), I have seen the holy performers strip and bathe quite naturally at a convenient well, in the face of the waiting populace of men, women, and children.

When the last man was back again before the altar, the eight launched in a body swingingly upon one of the purification prayers, the *maeza* as usual leading off. Exceedingly impressive these purification prayers are, if one will but devoutly refrain from understanding them. I had some of them translated, and am a wiser and sadder man in consequence.

As the chant swelled it sounded like, and yet unlike, some fine processional of the church of Rome. And as it rolled along it touched a chord that waked again the vision of the mountain, and once more before me rose Ontaké, and I saw the long file of pilgrims tramping steadily up the slope.

Intoned in monotone, it was pointed with pantomime, those strange digital contortions, the finger-twists. I suppose to one looking on for the first time nothing about the function would seem so far out of all his world as these same finger-charms. The semi-suppressed vehemence with which the knots are tied, the uncanny look of the knots themselves, and the strange self-abandonment of

the performer to the act, produce an effect
that is weird in the extreme. Symbolic of
bodily action, the force of the originals is felt
in these their effigies. A whole drama takes
place in them, done by a true magician, as
he bids the devils avaunt and calls the good
spirits to his aid; and so realistic are the
signs, the beings to whom they are addressed grow real, too. Like a talk at a
telephone, the half that is heard conjures
up of itself the half that is inaudible. And
their uncanniness clothes these conjurings
with the character of the supernatural. You
almost think to see both the devils and the
gods.

About them there is a compelling fasci-
nation in spite of their repellent uncouthness. If one seek to unravel his sensation
from the mesh in which it lies caught, he
will find the charm of the thing to consist,
I think, in energetic rhythm. For it has
something of the cadence of a dance; yet,
unlike a dance, it is not pleasing in itself.
It is indeed the height of inartistic art; its
very uncouthness has a certain grace, the
grace of the ungraceful masterfully done.

If such be the force of the charm acting

quite simply upon the dispassionate, how great its hold upon the believer, set as it is by the mordant of faith! And then, as chant and charm roll on in their swift processional, suddenly the brass-ringed crosiers (*shakujō*) ring together in double time, joining with it their jingle as of passing bells.

Prayer after prayer followed thus in purification. Each in turn rose, swelled, and sank only to rise again, in long billows of sound, buoying one's senses to sensations as of the sea, indefinitely vast. Crest after crest swept thus over thought, drowning all reflection in a fathomless feeling of its own. One felt quite contentedly full of nothing at all; in that semi-ecstatic state when discrimination has lapsed into a supreme sense of satisfaction; when the charms seemed as enchanting as the chant, and the chant as charming as the charms. The portal this to the seventh heaven of vacuous content.

A lull like a loud noise broke in upon our half-dream when the *maeza* stopped to light the pyre. As the flame leaped ceilingward the chant rose with it, the one carrying the other up with it. Tongues of flame three feet high darted ceilingward to transform themselves suddenly into clouds of opal smoke, that, surging, floated off, and then slowly settled down. Through the flame the *maeza* passed the written sheets emblematic of disease; passed them as usual to and fro unharmed; till, letting each stay still a moment there, it caught and was carried up into the crannies of the room. Many ills of life thus vanished into thin air.

Other things were likewise passed through the flame to gain like virtue; each man thus purified his rosary, with which he afterward rubbed what part of his body he wished to be pure and strong; and finally the *gohei* itself, for quintessence of purification, was taken from the altar, purified by the fire, and put back in place.

This finished the first service. The incense altar was then removed, sheets of paper were spread on the mats in its stead, and the *gohei*-wand was taken from the shrine and set upright in the midst. Plain paper! plain pine-wood! plain pilgrim dresses! Truly the neutral tints of self-effacement as near nothing as symbols can well show; the very apotheosis of vacancy.

All the performers except the *nakaza*

now took post for the possession, seating themselves in the prescribed places, facing the *gohei;* the *maeza* directly in front of it, the "four heavens" (*shiten*) at the cardinal points on the side, and the clerk and the deputy *maeza* flanking the *maeza* to the left and right.

After a short incantation the *maeza* removed the wand and gave it to the *tōhō,* the "eastern heaven," who held it ready in his hand. The *nakaza* came forward and solemnly seated himself where the *gohei* had been, facing from the altar. Folding his legs under him, he drew his robe carefully round them, and tied the ends of it together as one would a bundle-handkerchief. The result gave him the look of certain rubber toys of one's extreme childhood, that began as a man and ended in a bulb. After he had thus arranged himself the others did the same.

For such is the conventional Ryōbu-Shintō attitude during possession. Whether this by no means easy pose is modeled after that of the contemplative Buddha, or is merely the exalted seat of old Japan, is doubtful. The two differ in certain technical details of the knot that one ties in one's legs, and the knot is sometimes of the one kind and sometimes of the other. The tying is done to tether the possessed that he may not prove too violent in the trance. For, as may be imagined, the pose is one from which it is next to impossible to rise. Nevertheless, I have seen a god hop round on this his pedestal with astounding agility.

After a little private finger-twisting and prayer, the *nakaza* folded his hands before him and closed his eyes, the others of course incanting. The *maeza* took the wand from the *tōhō* and put it between the *nakaza's* hands. The man at once fell slowly forward on it, resting one end on the mat and the other against his forehead, near the hollow at the base of the nose.

The others took up in chorus the stirring processional chant known as the *rokkon shōjō no harai*. As the measured cadence rolled on, suddenly the wand began to quiver; and the chant increased in energy. Moment by moment the wand gathered motion by fits and lulls, as when a storm gathers out of a clear sky. Slowly, as it shook, it rose till it reached his forehead. The paroxysm came on and then the wand settled with a jerk to a rigid half-arm holding before his brow, a suppressed quiver alone still thrilling it through. The god had come.

The *maeza* leaned forward, bent low before the outstretched *gohei*, and reverently asked the god's name. The eyes of the possessed had already opened to the glassy stare typical of trances, the eyeballs so rolled back that the pupils were nearly out of sight. In an unnatural, yet not exactly artificial voice, the god replied, "Matsuwo," at which the *maeza* bowed low again, and then asked what questions he had previously inquired of me my preference to have put. They were about the health of those beyond the sea, and prognostications for my approaching voyage. All of which were answered with Delphic oracularity; after which the god spoke on of his own accord. He spoke to the *maeza*, but at me; he wished to thank me, he said, for making the ascent of the mountain (Ontaké) two years before. At which divine encomium, considering that the pious are convinced that no foreigner may scale the sacred peak and return alive, I was proportionately pleased.

After delivering himself of this politeness he settled forward heavily into a lethargic swoon. From it he was roused by further incantation to fresh fury. Slowly raising the wand, he suddenly beat the air above his head, and proceeded to hop excitedly round on his folded legs, stopping at each of the four compass points to repeat his performance. Then he came back to his previous commanding pose, and, in reply to the *maeza*, spoke again.

Once more he relapsed into his lethargy, and once more he was roused, and answered.

When he had fallen into his comatose condition for the third time, the *maeza*, after a sort of *benedicite*, made the sign of a Sanskrit character on his back, and slapped him energetically on top of it. One of the four "sides" stood by ready with a cup of water, and, the moment he had come to enough, put it to his lips and helped him to drink. Under this treatment he gradually revived, but it took some kneading before the wand could be loosed from his cataleptic grip.

Three gods, it appeared, had come in turn, which accounted for the rise and fall in the character of the possession : Matsuwō Sama, or O-yama-zumi-no-mikoto, Fukan Gyōja, and Hakkai San.

The last example of the Ryōbu form shall be one typical of the average unpretentious trance, the participants being all simple-minded farmers of the suburbs of Tōkyō. There were five of them, all members of the Five Cardinal Virtues Pilgrim Club. The shrine was the simplest possible, and so was the banquet offered the god. No picture was hung in the recess, and the pyre was not elaborate.

The *maeza* and *nakaza* had both been up Ontaké more than once; the other three were as yet ascensionless, but hopeful the lot to go might soon fall upon them, their finances having up to date only permitted them to travel so far in fancy.

Purification prayers and purification songs —the *misogi no harai*, the *rokkon shōjō no harai*, and the *nakatomi no harai*—were duly intoned, the *nakaza* in this case being specially active, because otherwise the leading spirit of the company. All five were clad in their Ontaké ascension robes, although the greater number were simply, as has been said, piously anticipating that event.

The possession itself took place with open eyes, and was interesting only for the rise and fall of its crises. The wand shook frenziedly, settled before the man's face, the god spoke, and then with an *agaru*, " I ascend," the man fell forward collapsed. The incantation began again, and a second god came down. Five several times this cycle was gone through before the possession was brought to a close and the man waked up. Five separate gods had come in turn.

VI.

The Buddhist trances introduce a new feature in the shape of femininity. For in the Buddhist variety of these divine possessions the god shows a preference for feminine lips.

The first one I was shown was a possession by the Nichiren sect. This is a sect of purely Japanese origin, having been founded by Nichiren, who had learned much of the Shintō priests six hundred years ago, — a sect with no prototype or affiliations elsewhere. It is the Buddhist sect that now chiefly affects possession. In this instance the mouthpiece of the god was the mouth of a maiden, and the man who parleyed with

her a mouse-like priest of a certain not un-
popular temple.

It too was a parlor possession in my own
house, and I have since learned that in consequence of the temple company having
been thus invited out to perform, the fame
of the temple has gone abroad and its holy
trade has amazingly increased.

There were three persons in the company.
For with the priest and the maiden, who was
about eighteen, came a female friend of
maturer years, not indeed to chaperone the
fair one so soon to be more than metaphor-
ically divine, but merely to assist at the divine audience. The three all belonged to a
certain pilgrim club of which the priest was
president.

They appeared with an extra jinrikisha
carrying a Saratoga trunk of indispensables.
To be fair to the sex, as it shows itself in
Japan, it should instantly be said that in
this case the baggage was not chargeable to
it but to the god's delight in pageantry, as
interpreted by the Nichiren sect. The trunk
proved to contain several candles, some *sakaki*, a *gohei*, two large lumps of rice-paste
known as *kagamimochi*, or mirror-dough, va-

rious other objects of bigotry and virtue, eight volumes of scripture, vestments, rosary, and ecclesiastical trappings for the priest. He, and not the women, was the object to be arrayed ; they, poor things, remained modestly clad in dull indigo blue.

After all these articles had been unpacked and the priest had made a shrine of some of them and had put on the rest, he faced the altar and began to pray. He prayed a long time, an elaborate and beautiful chant in keeping with his clothes. A regrettable absence of finger-charms was made up for by the ingenious way in which he managed to read through the whole eight volumes of scripture. For want of a more consecrated expression it may be known as the way of the concertina, and is as useful as it is artistic. It was made possible by the mode of binding the books. Like old Japanese books generally, each consisted of a single piece about fifteen yards long, folded for the sake of portability into pages, the ends only being fastened to the covers. Holding them farther apart at the top than at the bottom, he let the pages slowly cascade from his left hand into his right, accompanying himself thus on the holy harmonicon to the chanting of a portion of its contents by heart. The fair ones chorused him at a respectful distance in the rear.

After thus adroitly disposing of his chief devoir, the priest repeated several remembered prayers, not on his rosary, but, as it were, to it. For in the possession ceremony the Japanese Buddhist uses his rosary not as tally to his prayer, but as musical accompaniment to it. As he prays he soothingly strokes it, and it purrs with the gratified responsiveness of a cat.

All this lasted a long while, but the sights and the sounds beguiled the senses to the forgetting of time. When the priest had prayed, in all conscience, enough, he turned at right angles to his former position, and beckoned to the maiden to approach and seat herself opposite to and facing him, sideways, therefore, to the altar. She then folded her hands and closed her eyes.

First he sprinkled her all over with a shower-bath of sparks from a flint and steel ; after which he repeated in a soporific way several monotonic chants, and watched the effect. When he judged her numb enough

he put the *gohei*-wand into her hands and
continued intoning, his own hands making
musical monotone meanwhile on his amber
rosary.

Possession came on gradually ; the *gohei*
behaving in a becomingly lady-like way, but
otherwise as usual. It slowly rose to her
forehead, and on reaching it began to shiver.
The maiden's eyes stayed closed.

The priest then asked what questions I
would like to put to the god. Some doc-
trinal points occurred to me, the priest acting
as spokesman. The god and the priest were
pleased with the answers ; I was not, their
conventionality veiled in vagueness failing
to commend itself. Then the god indulged
in some gratuitous prophecy, not subsequently fulfilled. He kindly foretold that a
week after my return to America I should
lose a large amount of money I had loaned.
I thanked him for this information, thinking
it unnecessary to inform him that I had no
money out on loan at the moment, which is
perhaps why I never lost it. But I realize
that the fault was mine. Had I been a
Japanese the chances are overwhelming that
most of my property would have been lent ;

and in that case I should undoubtedly have lost it. This is about as near as I ever came with the gods to successful prophecy. And yet to divine would seem to be of the very essence of divinity.

Altogether the most interesting feature of the case, psychologically, was the great ease of possession, due, as I am convinced, to the sex of the subject. In possessions by the Nichiren sect the god prefers women for embodiment; the only exception being the occasional employment of children as divine subjects. For in this sect men are never possessed.

At another *séance* by the same sect, four priests and a woman took part. There were no finger-twistings, and the service generally was short and simple. A hanging scroll of Kishibojin was suspended in the recess of honor ; while below it a small altar, over-laid with rich brocade, stood flanked by two *gohei*-wands. The principal priest put on white silk robes, and the woman a white cotton surplice. At first she sat disinterest-edly to one side.

At the close of the preliminary service the chief officiator beckoned to her to take

A BUDDHIST DIVINE POSSESSION

her seat; this she did, passing through the
row of priests with the customary respectful
symbolic scooping of the hand, and sat down
in the midst with her back to the altar. She
closed her eyes; the priest made the sign of
a Sanskrit character on each of her palms,
and then, taking the two *gohei*-wands, put
one into each of her hands. This duality of
divine descent was the most interesting
feature of the affair. Twitching ensued almost instantly, and was kept up a long time
while the officiator (*shugenja*) prayed on. At
the close of it the priest asked the god's
name, and then interviewed him. Then,
after permission had been asked by the
priest, the god condescended to interviews
with the rest of us. Replies would have been
made in any case, the priest said, but it
would have been rude to the god not to have
first obtained his consent. The subject was
quite insensible to pins stuck into her neck,
but objected at first to having her pulse felt,
pulling her arm away as if annoyed, till she
had been assured that it was all right by the
priest. Her pulse proved a trifle faster than
in her normal state (110 as against 100), but
decidedly weaker.

Although this is my first mention of pins, I hasten to add that I had already tried them with like innocuous result upon the sterner sex, and I desire to add in self-defense that it was the god, not the woman, that was pricked.

After speaking, the subject lapsed into a comatose condition, but could be roused by being addressed. When the priest had finished with her he took the wands from her hands, not without difficulty, they were so cataleptically clenched, and somewhat irreverently rolled her over on her side, like a doll, into a corner, where he left her to wake, while he and the others finished the service. By the time they were done she came to of herself.

The facing of the possessed — from the altar or simply sideways to it — is a matter dependent on the particular priest and upon the character of the god expected to descend. If the god be of more importance he sits *ex cathedra* as it were; if not, simply *ex parte*. This relative disrespect shown by the Buddhists to the possessing gods will be discussed later.

Such are the phenomena of god-possession

as practiced by the Nichiren sect. The
Shingon sect indulges in a somewhat similar
cult, of which I have been told by its priests,
but which I do not happen to have seen. The
Tendai practices the cult but little, the other
sects do not practice it at all. These definite possessions must be carefully distinguished from Buddhist meditation, which
also eventually lapses into trance. The first
may be defined as a change of one's personality into another's; the second as the etherealization of one's own. In Japan the Zen
sect are the greatest adepts in thus losing
themselves. Meditating one's self into protoplasmic purity is a specialty of the Buddhists consequent upon the essential tenets
of their religion, and has only a distant kinship in common with the purely Japanese
Buddhist trances I have described.

VII.

Oldest of all and yet youngest of any of
the Japanese possessions are the pure Shintō
ones. For they took place in the far past,
and then did not take place again till the
other day. They form the most interesting
branch of the family, because the most un-
conventional members of it.

In virtue of being a part of pure Shintō they are necessarily resurrections; although reckless believers now insist that they were always practiced in secret during Shintō's unfortunate unpopularity. If this be really the case, it is a sad instance of keeping a secret too well. For there is no mention made of them during the middle ages. But in a sense they never lapsed. For they survived in Ryōbu — from whose destruction they have phœnix-like emerged, as faithful reproductions of the prehistoric practices as is possible. Being biblical in character, they are invested with a certain archaism that imparts to them all the more seeming sanctity.

The personal auxiliary rites are few and simple; such being explained away on the score of purity. The pure Shintōists are so pure, so they themselves say, that they do not need them. The striking parallelism of this to the Shintō explanation of its lack of a moral code — that only immoral people need moral laws — is instructive. Nevertheless it is quite true that the more faith the less formulæ.

The finger-charms, decidedly the most

weird of the Ryōbu rites, are reduced to such very low terms as hardly to appear. Of purification prayers only those of pure Shintō origin are recited. Those of Ryōbu fabrication, such as the *rokkon shōjō no harai*, being carefully ignored.

On the other hand, the impersonal part of the service is elaborate. It has all the formality of the usual state function, for it is nothing more nor less than a divine banquet, with the god himself for after-dinner speaker. The dinner is all-essential to the affair, as it is to all Shintō rites. For the Shintō practice of dining its deities is not confined to the ceremony of possession. Wherever the gods are invoked, for any cause whatsoever, they are induced to descend by the prospect of a dinner. A repast stands perpetually prepared on all Shintō altars ; shrines being, to put it irreverently, free-lunch counters for deity, while every Shintō service is but a special banquet given some particular god. One comes to conceive of a Shintō god's life as one continuous round of dining out. To induce an after-dinner mood in a god whom one wishes to propitiate is doubtless judicious.

The rite is, of course, the apotheosis of primitive hospitality. With civilization, however, the divine dinner has, like mere mortal ones, taken on a most tedious etiquette. It consists now of six or seven courses, each of which is ceremoniously long in the serving. The priests, who are the waiters, are all most beautifully dressed, and stand drawn up in a properly impressive row. After a sort of grace, said by the chief officiator, the priest at the lower end of the line hands in, from the refectory behind the scenes, the first of the holy platters, which, with a long, deep bow, he passes up to the next man in the line, who passes it to the third, and so on till it reaches the chief priest, who places it reverently upon the altar. Each dish is thus solemnly offered up to the god and deposited upon the shrine in turn. The dishes consist of almost everything edible, and, considering that much of the food is raw, of everything inedible as well. Wine especially is always on the table, for the gods are anything but teetotalers.

So far as records and traditions make it possible, the aboriginal cult is reinstated. Even the archaic instruments of miscalled music, actual heirlooms, some of them, it is said, in the high-priest's family, are played upon by their modern descendant as they were by his mythologic forbears, that the unchangeable gods may still be pleased. In fact, the whole action is as nearly as possible as it would appear could one be transported a couple of millenniums into the past.

The trance itself is likewise different from its Ryōbu relative. It is more natural and more free. The possessed is not fettered to the conventionality of the Ryōbu forms. He sits, stands, speaks more spontaneously, and generally behaves himself with more of the self-prompting a god might be expected to possess. This, however, is in the believer's eyes of less consequence than the knowledge of the scriptures he displays. In proportion as he is able to elucidate the meagre accounts in the Shintō bibles, does he prove his superior divinity. That the subject has been well trained in this old folk-lore, does not, to the pious, constitute a *propter hoc* in the matter.

VIII.

Perhaps the most curious phenomenon of the pure Shintō possession-cult is the Kwancho's kindergarten. This is a Sunday-school of a unique kind, held by the high-priest of the Shinshiu sect every other week-day throughout the year, vacations excepted. The instruction is eminently practical, for it consists in teaching nothing less than the art of temporarily becoming god. It is the most esoteric of all the possession practices. To its exercises I was never permitted to bring another foreigner, my own purity just sufficing to admit me.

The school is composed of two classes, a boys' class and a girls' class, made up of the most pious young people of the parish. The boys' class is held first. The pupils begin by taking post in a row at the farther end of the main temple room, while the high-priest faces the altar and conducts a service in which the pupils join. Then he seats himself on one side and nods to a boy to come forward. The boy advances, squats in a divine attitude before the altar, and closes his eyes. After some subdued prayer the priest rises, puts the *gohei*-wand into the boy's hands, and, resuming his seat, plays sweetly on the sacred flute, exactly as you shall read of its being done in the Kojiki; which is not a surprising coincidence, since the action is copied from it. On advanced pupils the effect is almost instantaneous. The boy goes into convulsions, raises the *gohei* to arms' length above his head, brandishes it maniacally in the air, and while still doing so rises to his feet and proceeds to dance madly about the room. In the course of his divine antics he contrives to part with the *gohei*-wand, which he hurls inadvertently into a corner. He then enters upon several gymnastic exercises. First he turns somersaults promiscuously all over the floor. Then a low table is brought out by some of the other pupils and set in the middle of the room, and over this, directed by taps on it from the Kwancho, the possessed somersaults in every possible direction, following in a definite order the compass points. The table is then turned on its side, and he repeats his series of tumbles. The same is next done with the table turned bottom side up; and so forth and so on in pretty much every other position of the furniture. A pupil will sometimes turn thus some seventy somersaults in the the course of one trance. Against the wall stands a ladder, up which the entranced next climbs to the cornice, clinging to which he makes the circuit of the room. Not infrequently he wanders by the same means round all the neighboring apartments. After descending again by the ladder, he performs upon a horizontal bar.

Or he stands on his head up against the wall, first in one corner of the room, and then in another, until he has made the circuit of it, interpolating between times somersaults at his own sweet will. The curriculum varies with the pupil. Though of the same general character for all, it differs in detail for each. But each pupil repeats his own performance exactly, night after night, improving on it through a gradual course of trance-development.

With the girls the action is fittingly less violent. They do not journey along the cornice, but they do turn somersaults over the floor. Their specialty, however, consists in dancing dervish-like round and round the room. The waltzing they keep up indefinitely until stopped by the priest.

All these actions of the pupil mean something. The dance is the facsimile of the one that the goddess Uzume-no-mikoto performed in the first recorded possession. Somersaulting over the floor represents the natural revolution of all things; while somersaulting over the table denotes visits paid to the upper and the under world. Standing on one's head in the corner with one's legs straight up against the wall implies possession by the spirit of a climbing plant.

Before one pupil has finished, a second is started on his career, and then sometimes a third, which, considering the violence of their actions, very decidedly peoples the apartment. The girls are as decent as dervishes, but as to the boys, dancing dervishes are orderly, intelligent members of society by comparison. It is irresponsibility let loose. For they hurl themselves about the apartment with as utter a disregard of others as of themselves. Yet, though they often collide, they seem to regard each other as strictly inanimate things.

Though it is doubtful if they see at all, it is certain that they can hear the Kwancho, who occasionally warns them to be careful.

With the exception of thus occasionally addressing them and of tapping the table or
the wall, he does not direct their movements
in the least.   Such half-way stage between
hypnotic and possessed action is an interesting thing in itself.

The subject's pulse is accelerated and
weakened, so far as I could discover by feeling it immediately afterward.

Though adepts quickly fall into the state,
it takes practice to attain to pious proficiency, several sittings being necessary before the pupil is possessed at all.

IX.

We now come to the subjective side of the
trance, the first point being the getting into
it ; the cause, that is, as distinguished from
its occasion.   Entrance is effected, in fact,
in the simplest possible manner.   It consists
in shutting the eyes and thinking of nothing.
From the moment the *nakaza* takes the
gohei-wand into his hands, at which time it
will be remembered he closes his eyes, he
makes his mind as much of a blank as he can.

The ability to think of nothing — not the
simple matter even to the innately empty-

headed it might be imagined — has been increased by the previous etherealizing process of the austerities. The routine ritual indulged in just prior to the act, or rather the non-act, furthers this pious result. The repeating of the purification prayers has become so purely mechanical a process that saying them is tantamount to not thinking. *Nakaza*, quite unmindful of the doubtful propriety of the remark, have informed me that the two are the same thing. They do not think of anything, they say, after they have once sat down to the ceremony, though they are, patently, as busy as they can be reeling off the prayers. So true is this that a *nakaza* will at times begin to go off inopportunely in the midst of the preliminary rites and have to be brought back from his divine digression by a rousing cuff from the *maeza.*

Some *nakaza*, in order the easier to enter the trance, rest one end of the *gohei*-wand upon the ground, and, leaning forward, throw their weight upon the other, pressed against the forehead at the base of the nose between the eyes. The act is thought to be helpful to a speedy possession. It is an interesting fact that this *zone hypnotique* should have been discovered experimentally by the Japanese long before the thing was scientifically known to Europe. Not all subjects, however, make use of it. Some simply rest one end of the wand on the floor and then lean upon it; some do not even rest it on the floor, but hold it before them in the air. These various devices are matter of traditional practice with particular pilgrim clubs.

Easy as vacuity gets to be to those who can give their whole mind to it, the acquisition of such capacity is by no means an instantaneous affair, as the history of one earnest applicant for inanity from his first failure to his first success will suffice to show.

After having duly reduced himself by protracted austerities to sufficient abstraction, he was set one evening in the *nakaza's* seat. Ranged round him sat the regular company incanting. He closed his eyes and the *'gohei-*wand was put into his hands. From that moment he tried to make his mind as blank as possible. The result the first evening was simple nausea. It is not, perhaps, to be wondered at, that his first dose of divinity should disagree with a man.

The man's second attempt the following evening led to a like sickening result, but the unpleasant effect was a thought less acute. So it was on the third evening and the fourth, and in this half-seas-over state between man and god he continued to remain for fifteen consecutive nights, the nausea less at each repetition of its cause. At last, at the fifteenth sitting, his perseverance was rewarded. He entered the holy ring as usual and remembers hearing the others repeating the prayers fainter and yet more faint, like singers departing into the distance, and then he was aware of being rudely and irrelevantly shaken by the rest. They were bringing him to. Possession had been like the unconscious dropping off to sleep; coming to himself again like waking in the morning, only that he felt dull and tired. He was told by the company that he had nodded, brandished the wand, and become perfectly rigid.

Subjects, when catechized more curiously as to the feeling of lapsing into the trance, indulged in variously opposite analogies. One likened it to the sensation that creeps over a man after long immersion in the hon-

orable hot water, a luxurious soaking in a
bath of the parboiling temperature of one
hundred and ten degrees or more Fahrenheit;
a simile by some degrees too ardent to convey much idea of insensibility to Europeans,
but which commends itself as expressive to
Japanese. Another individual said it felt
like going up in a balloon. This daringly
inflated simile turned out a pure flight of
fancy, as on further questioning it appeared
that the speaker had never been up in one.
But, inasmuch as his audience had not either,
his definition was considerably more definite
than if he had made ever so many ascents.
Λ third man averred that it was like being
drowned and then being brought to life
again; a clever hit, this, though I have no
reason to suppose that he had had, any
more than the other, personal experience of
his comparison. Still another described all
sounds as seeming to go a long way off;
while a last adept said that when he lapsed
into the supreme of meditation, a condition
akin to that of being possessed, ordinary
noises ceased to be audible, and yet in winter he could hear the water freeze.

Of the trance itself most, if not all, of the

possessed remember afterwards nothing.
One man indeed said that it was like dream-
ing, only more vague, — the dream of a
dream, which certainly is very vague, indeed.
Even here I think he mistook the feelings
fringing the trance state for the trance state
itself. For certainly the average good *nakaza* is quite emphatic on the point, and this
particular man was not a specially able specimen.

All agree in the sense of oppression which
is their last bit of consciousness before going
off and their first on coming to. It is for
this the *maeza* slaps the *nakaza* repeatedly
on the back at and after the moment of waking. The throat is so throttled that unless
this were done the water could not be swallowed. As for the water itself, it is taken
for much the same reason that some people
take it when about to swallow a pill, to over-
come, that is, the involuntary contraction of
the glottis.

Possession begins, they, say, at the *gohei*.
The hands that hold it are the first parts of
the man to be possessed. In the incipient
cases they are all that are visibly affected.
As the control deepens the cataleptic condi-

tion creeps, on like paralysis, till it involves all of the body not actually in use by the god.

Possession ends much as it begins. The subject's arms and hands are the last part of him to lose their induced catalepsy. After the man is well waked and to all intents and purposes himself again, it is difficult to take the wand away from him. Only after being rubbed and kneaded will the fingers let go their hold.

In the trance itself the anæsthesia is usually marked. I have repeatedly stuck pins into the entranced at favorably sensitive spots without the god's being aware of the pricks. In some cases, however, where I had otherwise no reason to suspect fraud, the pin was felt. So that apparently want of feeling is not invariably produced in the state; but it is certainly a usual concomitant of it.

The pulse is quickened to a varying extent. This appears to be rather a symptom of the entrance into the state than of the trance itself, and is doubtless due to the exertion and excitement of the preliminary rites. The significant symptom of the actual possession is the pulse's very decided weakening. The performers themselves state that it stops. It comes very near it. I have explored the wrist of an entranced during possession for a long time only to find an occasional flutter. But the most important feature of this failure of the pulse consists in the way in which it keeps step inversely with the rise in the activity of the possession. The pulse grows feeble in proportion as the trance action grows strong, and tends to go out completely when possession attains its height. When the subject falls forward into his comatose condition the pulse returns. The performers themselves are perfectly aware of this reciprocal relation between the man's vitality and the god's. When the entranced's pulse was being felt I have known a whole company to redouble the energy of their incantation in order thus to keep the possession at its height and so cause the pulse to go out.

During the height of the possession the subject's body is in constant subdued quiver; evidence of the same nervous thrill that produces the initial spasm. Not till the comatose condition comes on does this cease.

And it is capable of being revived to greater or less fury by reincantation, at any moment.

At the time the subject consigns himself to vacating his bodily premises he shuts his eyes, thus closing the shutters of the house his spirit is so soon to leave; and the blinds stay drawn till the spirit has passed away and the coming on of the spasm indicates the advent of the god. At his entrance the eyelids are, in some cases, raised again (*gambiraki*), revealing that glassy stare peculiar to the trance; in others they still remain drawn. Which they shall do is matter of tradition in the subject's pilgrim club. If the eyes open — as also doubtless if they do not — the eyeballs are rolled up so that the iris is half out of sight; the lids quiver but never wink. By those who open their eyes, the not doing so is denounced as conducive to shams. It is certainly easier to sham with the eyes shut, if indeed the peculiar look of an entranced's eye can be counterfeited at all. Nevertheless, such as shut their eyes to the act deem their way equally convincing.

Beside opening or not-opening his eyes in the trance, dependent upon the habit of his club, the subsequent action of the possessed

is otherwise conventional. The behavior of
one god bears a striking family likeness to
that of another. Each begins by brandishing maniacally the *gohei*-wand, and after sufficient flourish brings it down to the commanding holding before the brow which
betokens that he is ready to be interviewed.
He is then invariably first asked his name,
which would seem to be a polite formality,
since god-experts say they can tell which
god has come by the manner alone in which
he brandishes the *gohei*-wand. Gods are as
easily told apart as men, when you know
them. Their general resemblance is due to
their divinity ; their slight individuality is
their own.

The conventional character of the actions
of the entranced is of course no sign of
shamming. To mistake such for fraud is to
be one's own dupe. His actions are but the
unconscious assimilation of precedent become stereotyped into trance habit, just as
artless a thing as any every-day habit. One
might make a more serious mistake and take
for necessary symptoms of the Japanese
trance these mere adventitious adjuncts of it,
due to auto-suggestion at first and then per-

petuated unintentionally, as the Salpétrière
did with those it first innocently induced in
its hypnotic patients, and then as innocently
marveled at afterward. Some symptoms,
nevertheless, are quite universal — those
connected with the *gohei*-wand. The way in
which this is treated is common to pure
Shintō, Ryōbu-Shintō, and Buddhist performance alike, the action only differing in
degree. On the other hand, the tying up of
the legs of the entranced is essentially a
Ryōbu practice, not being a detail of the
higher forms of pure Shintō possession nor
of that of the women subjects of the Buddhists.

Shamming is not so important a matter as
it might seem, because of its ease of detec-
tion. Shams there are in plenty, which is
scarcely surprising when we consider the
great vogue the act of possession enjoys.
But such are easily exploded. An unexpected pin in a tender part of the possessed's
body instantly does the business. For a
god is sublimely superior to being made a
pin-cushion of, while a mere man invariably
objects to it. The difficulty, indeed, lies not
in detecting the counterfeit but in failing to

detect the reality. To a sufficiently incred-
ulous eye the sham very rarely masquerades
successfully, while the genuine article, if very
perfect, often seems too good to be true.
Especially is this the case with woman.
One doubts her divinity at the time only to
realize afterward that he has done the lady
an injustice.

Though the god in these incarnations is
thus born, not made, he has after birth to go
through a natural process of development to
reach his full capabilities.

His gradual self-education would be interesting to witness did it not take so long.
The history of a boy about ten and a half
years old whom I was privileged to observe
in the course of his divine education will give
some idea of the laboriousness of the process. He began practicing to be possessed
on July 17; that is he was then first set in
the *nakaza's* seat, and the *gohei*-wand put into
his hands while he shut his eyes and tried
to make his mind as blank as possible. This
performance he went through five times
every day from that time on, twice in the
morning and three times at night. It was
at the end of August when the god at last

descended and possessed him. At first the
god did nothing but brandish the *gohei*-
wand. Gradually he learned to grunt. When
I first saw the boy in the latter part of
September, the god had got far enough
along to grunt quite imposingly. I saw him
again on October 28. The sounds had taken
on some form. He could then articulate so
that you thought he spoke what it was your
fault not to understand. By the middle of
November, I was told, he would speak distinctly.

The development of the voice is always
an acquired art; dumb possession preceding
the ability to converse in the trance. It
takes the god no inconsiderable time to
learn to talk. When he does do so the
tone is peculiar. It is not the man's natural voice, but a stilted, cothurnus sort of
voice, one which a god might be supposed
to use in addressing mere mortals. It
would be theatrical were it not sincere.
It is the man's unconscious conception of
how a god should talk, and commends itself
artistically to the imagination.

The possessory gods present certain interesting characteristics. In the first place they

are of either sex. This follows from the fact
that in Japan sex suffers no social restric-
tions among the gods, as in olden times it
suffered none among men. Goddesses are
both numerous and influential. Practically
the highest god in the Shintō pantheon is
a lady, the Sun-Goddess Ama-terasu-o-mi-
kami. The earth deity worshiped as the
principal god at the second Ise shrine is
also a goddess. For in Shintō is realized
the idea of the advanced woman's right's
wife, who, on sending her husband shop-
ping one day to match a piece of ribbon,
said to him, as a parting injunction, " If you
are in doubt, pray to God, and She will help
you."

Woman continued a power after she had
ceased to be divine. Japanese history boasts
of several empresses who, chivalry apart,
have played on the whole its most promi-
nent parts. The Empress Jingō is perhaps
the most striking figure in the imperial line,
not excluding her son, who was canonized as
the god of war.

When it comes to possession it is therefore not surprising that femininity should
be found to have a hand in it. In the olden

time both possessors and possessees were
notably of the sex, as we shall see when we
come to examine the Shintō bibles later.

Nowadays possession is chiefly confined to
males on both sides.   Still there are plenty
of exceptions in both parties to the business.
It is not uncommon for a goddess to descend
sandwiched in between a lot of gods.   In
such event the voice of the entranced changes
to suit the sex.   The sex of the subject does
not seem to signify ; goddesses not being
particularly partial to men, nor particularly
averse to their own sex.   Male deities usually descend upon both sexes indifferently,
simply because they are more numerous
than female ones.

Sex, however, is not surprising in divinity.
But there is one point about these possessory
gods in which they come much nearer being
unique, and in which they are certainly not
specially feminine — in their willingness to
share their subject.   Shintō possessions are
remarkable for the multiplicity of gods that
deign to descend in one and the same trance.
Such divine copartnership is of course successive, since otherwise it would not be personal possession at all, but a mere composite

blur of divinity, quite unrecognizable for anybody in particular. The communistic character of the possession is as singular as the
constituents to it are many. Rarely does
one god monopolize the trance. Usually from
three to a dozen descend in turn. As each
descends, the activity of the possession rises
from lethargy to somnambulistic action ; the
possessed acts, speaks, is the god. Then,
when the god departs, he sinks forward into
a comatose condition from which the next
god rouses him. Each god stays but five
minutes or so, and this five-minute rule in
speaking produces a wave-like rise and fall
in the character of the possession, by which
it becomes possible to count the number of
the divine visitors.

Contrary to what might be thought probable, the same god very rarely, if ever, returns in the same trance. To have come
once, instead of being reason for coming
again is reason for the reverse, which cer-
tainty shows a praiseworthy regard on the
part of the god not to monopolize his subject.

Although neither the subject nor any one
else knows beforehand what particular gods

will descend in any one trance, a certain
clique of gods usually frequents any one
man.   What the divine set shall be depends
upon what gods the man is intimate with in
his normal state.   One man's familiar spirits
will thus consist of the various Inari, gods
of agriculture ; another's of defunct and dei-
fied *gyōja,* pious hermits who lived much in
the mountains, and are particularly familiar with the peaks ; a third's of the higher
Shintō divinities.   Each is visited by his intimates ; his pious proclivities determining
with whom he may stand upon calling
terms.

Such an impersonal thread of godhead
upon which each particular god's personality
is strung, running in this manner through
the trance, reveals very strikingly the peculiar characteristic of these people — their
impersonality.   It shows how deep ingrained
that impersonality is, that after his sense of
self has entirely left the man, the essential
quality of that self, its lack of it, still lingers
behind.   It reminds one in a serious way of
the problem of the sand-bank with the hole
in it.   The sea comes up and washes away
the sand-bank ; does the hole remain ?   Here

apparently it does. For though vacuity
alone is left to be filled by deity, the form
of that vacuity reappears in the god. The
mould is still there to shape the new tenant
after all that was moulded in it has crum-
bled away.

So closes my presentation of the phenomena of this strange possession-cult. Before
passing on to interpret the noumena behind
them, there remains to be given some account of a custom intimately associated with
them, the pilgrim clubs. After that properly comes the proof of their essentially
Japanese character. But I cannot take my
leave of the phenomena themselves without
hoping there may linger with the reader
some impression, however faint, of the
simple beauty of the Shintō faith. For in
an emotional sense it is the very essence
of what makes far-eastern life so fine.
Mere outline of a faith as Shintō at first
sight seems to be, on closer study it proves
to be something little less than grand
in its very simplicity. Truly it needs no
formal priesthood, no elaborate service, no
costly shrine, for it has as visibly about it
something better than all these — its very

gods. To Shintō they are always there; and the great cryptomeria groves no longer seem untenanted, the plain, bare buildings no longer lack a host; for at any instant they may be pervaded by a presence, the presence of the incarnate spirit of the god.

PILGRIMAGES AND THE PILGRIM
CLUBS.

I.

EVERY traveler in Japan will have been struck by a singular yet well-nigh universal appendage to the country inn : a motley collection of cloths dangling from short fishing-poles stuck into the eaves in one long line before the entire inn-front. Unlike as they otherwise are, the greater part agree in displaying at the top the conventional far - eastern symbol that passes for a peak.

From their general shape, size, and stamping, the stranger will take them, at first blush, for the towels of the guests hung out in all innocence to dry, though their inordinate number slightly tax the credit of even Japanese tubability. Sojourn at the inn, however, will shortly dispel this illusion by showing them to be fixtures, a permanent part of the real estate of the establishment.

Forced to change his idea as to their character, the unenlightened will next conceive them to be some novel inn allurement, a sort of preposterous bait of landlord ingenuity, dangled thus to catch the public eye. Secularly speaking, both inferences are correct. For they were towels, and are bait, but not of landlord invention. They are the *ho-no-tenugui* or gift towels of the pilgrim clubs.

Once they were quite simply towels, bestowed ingenuously upon the inn as tokens of favor by clubs that chanced to put up at it and be pleased; just as ladies in tourney times cast their hand-kerchiefs to their knightly choice. Not having handkerchiefs, the Japanese presented as keepsakes their towels instead, rather the more romantic souvenir of the two.

But towels they are no longer. Time has raised them above domestic service. They are now a sort of club advertisement and guide-book combined. For though they are presented to the inn, they are presented for the benefit of those presenting them. Each bears conspicuously the club name and address, and is left with the landlord to be displayed for sign to subsequent brethren that this is where the club puts up. It is the inn asterisk in the pilgrim Baedeker.

The pilgrims are very free with these certificates of club satisfaction. On any fairly good inn you shall count from fifty to an hundred of them, and with hostelries of exceptional entertainment the inn's eaves fail to accommodate all its pious indorsements, and stout poles planted in the street in front fly the overplus. Landlords spare no pains to display them, for the pilgrim patronage is individually not unlavish, and collectively is enormously large.

The sight of such banner-bedizened inns will probably be the foreigner's first introduction to Japanese pilgrims, unless the equally striking spectacle of itinerants distinguished by — and well-nigh extinguished under — huge toad-stool hats have already caused him to mark such plants as men walking. Once recognized, he will find both phenomena everywhere, for they form a regular part of the scenery.

Now some of these pilgrim clubs turn out to play a most important rôle in god-possession, being, in fact, clubs for the purpose. Some general account of them becomes, therefore, germane to our subject.

To one of a poetic turn of thought the very name Shintō or the "Way of the Gods" pictures one long pilgrimage from earth to heaven. But such poesy is after all profane, the "way" here being as unvividly viewed by its followers as are the thousand and one other ways of the world by those who pursue them. Nevertheless, pilgrimages are more than foot-notes to its creed.

Probably at no time and among no people have pilgrimages been so popular as in this same nineteenth century in Japan, temporary excitements like the crusades excepted. Even the yearly caravan of the Mahometan world to Mecca, though it draw from greater distances and be invested with more pomp, does not imply so complete a habit. Every Japanese is a pilgrim at heart, though every summer fail to find him actually on the march. Poverty compels him to do his plodding at home. Want of funds alone seems to stand in the way of the nation's taking the road in a body from the middle of July to the first of September. As it is, the country's thoroughfares at that season are beaded with folk wending their way to some shrine or other.

Now there are three points worth noting about these pilgrimages. The first is that the impulse to them is emphatically of the people. Like so many Japanese traits, art for instance, the pilgrim spirit is not an endowment of the upper classes, but the birthright of everybody. Indeed, it is chiefly the simple who go on pilgrimages, the gentle not being sufficiently given to walking.

The next feature is their purely national character. Their patronage is quite insular. Their goals draw no devotees from *outre mer.* Buddhist though some of them be, no contingent ever crosses from China or Korea to visit them. On the other hand, to the more famous of them pilgrims flock from all over Japan. Men from one end of the empire meet there men from the other, and from all points in between ; a fact which in the eyes of the pilgrims adds greatly to the pleasure of the pilgrimage, since socially it is journeying the whole length of the land by only going part way. Regard for the smaller shrines is naturally bounded by a narrower horizon. But considering that till within ten years the means of conveyance were one's own feet, the attraction of even these lesser load-stars is felt surprisingly far.

That the pilgrim spirit is thus in a twofold
sense wholly national, — first in the sense of
only, and then in the sense of *all*, — implies
one important fundamental fact : that Japanese pilgrimages are not of Buddhist but of
Shintō origin. It is the first hint of the ground-
lessness of the Buddhist claims to spiritual
ownership in the mountain-tops, all of which
they assert they first made accessible to
mankind. But in spite of the very catholic
character of the pretension, the right to such
eminent domain grows airier and airier the
closer we scrutinize it. The Buddhist idea,
like the early Christian, seems to have been,
when confronted by a strong popular superstition : Baptize it at once.

The third peculiarity about these pilgrimages consists in their being probably the
most unreligious in the world. Speaking
profanely, they are peripatetic picnic parties,
faintly flavored with piety ; just a sufficient
suspicion of it to render them acceptable to
the easy-going gods. For a more mundanely
merry company than one of these same pilgrim bands it would be hard to meet, and to
put up at an inn in their neighborhood is to
seem bidden to a ball. They are far more

the "joly compagnie" of "fayerie" Chaucer
tells us of than the joyless "lymytours" that
displaced it.

The Japanese go upon pilgrimages because
they thoroughly enjoy themselves in the process, the piety incident to the act simply re-
lieving them from compunction at having so
good a time. Sociability is the keynote of
the affair from start to finish. To pool one's
pleasure is always to increase it, and for a
Japanese to pool his purse is matter of as
much account. For a Japanese is not only
poor, but impecunious. His personal property of impersonality is only matched by the
impersonality of his personal property. For
what a Japanese appears to possess is, ten
to one, borrowed of a friend, and what he
really owns pledged to a neighbor. He is,
in short, but a transition stage in one long
shift of loan. We talk of our far-reaching
system of mercantile credits. It is financial
self-sufficiency beside the every-day state of
far-eastern affairs. Everybody there lives
as a matter of course upon somebody else.
To these states of mind and money are due
the founding of the pilgrim clubs.

The pilgrim clubs (*kōsha* or *kō*) are great

institutions in numbers as well as in other
things.   Indeed they are numerous beyond
belief.   Collectively they are said to com-
prise eighty per cent. of the entire population of the empire, a statement I accept only
at a popular discount.   Their individual
membership consists on the average of from
one hundred to five hundred persons apiece.
Some clubs are smaller than this, and of
some the membership mounts into the thousands.   The *Tomeye kō*, the largest I know
of, has about twelve thousand men enrolled
in it.   That these are drawn chiefly from
the small tradesman and artisan class speaks
for the hold the habit has on the people.

Ladies are quite eligible for election and
even for office in these clubs.   The wife of
a tobacconist with whom I am acquainted is
actually the head of a sub-sect, which com-
prises several clubs; and the husband is
an enthusiastic club-man in one of them.

The constitution of the clubs is delightfully simple.   The club charter is obtained
from the head of the sect by some energetic
individual of the society-founding propensity,
who collects about him a few friends and
incidentally appoints himself to the club pres-

idency, becoming what is called its *sendatsu.*
When not thus self-appointed, the president
is elected by the brethren for his piety,
which is another name for the same thing.

Besides their simplicity, one great charm
about these clubs is their cheapness. Whatever may be argued by domestically inclined
individuals against clubs generally on the
score of expense, these at least would hardly
seem open to the charge. For the initiation
fee is from three to five cents (five to ten
sen), and the dues from two thirds of a cent
to a cent and a third (one to two sen) a
month, according to the club. And yet the
president of one of them once told me that
the principal item in his club's running expenses was the cost of dunning the members
for their dues. So lamentably lax in paying
its debts is humanity the world over. But
indeed it was a serious matter, for it
amounted, it appeared, to a fifth of the gross
receipts. His club consisted of five hundred
members each of whom was supposed to pay
eight cents a year into the club treasury ;
which sum it took eight dollars to collect.

When his club obligations have finally
been discharged, the member receives a

ticket (*kansatsu*) with the name of the club
and of the sub-sect to which it belongs inscribed on its face, and the name of the
member and half the stamp of the club seal
on its back. The other half remains in the
registry books, of which the ticket is a slip.
The ticket constitutes a certificate of membership to all whom it may concern, inn-
keepers principally.

Forgetfulness to discharge one's club dues
is the less excusable in the face of their being
of the nature of gambling debts. For after
the cost of collection and the other running
expenses have been deducted, the remainder
is raffled for by the members, and pocketed
by the lucky winners through the club
treasurer, for pilgrimage purposes.

Once a year, about three weeks before the
pilgrim band is to start, the lots are drawn,
and in the drawing everybody who has paid
up participates except the winners of previous pools. They are barred, to give the
unlucky a chance, till each shall have had his
journey apiece. Thus are the inequalities of
fate corrected and all eventually made happy
at the club expense.

The dues being so modest, the percentage

of prizes is necessarily small ; only about three members in a hundred being annually recipients of the club fund. Paucity of prizes doubtless conduces to remissness in paying up ; and even rotation in eligibility, just though it be, does not add to the desire of past beneficiaries to make present, personally unprofitable, disbursement.

The fortunate winners are held to be especially invited of the gods to visit them. The club fund is turned over to the club treasurer for their benefit, and the others heartily envy them their lot.

The envy is chiefly pecuniary. For though the god is supposed through the lots to show a pleasing preference for the winner's company, he is not considered averse to self-invited visitors. Any one who wishes to join himself to the pilgrim company may do so at his own expense; and very many avail themselves of the privilege.

On the day appointed for the start, the god-chosen and the self-invited rendezvous at what stands to the club for club-house, and thence sally forth under the guidance of their revered president. This individual, being presumably the holiest man in the club,

if not the actual author of its being, is
clothed from the start with a certain fatherly
prestige. His importance is heightened by
the fact of his having made the pilgrimage
several times before. Indeed, he goes usually
every year, and paternally expounds the won-
ders of the way to the brethren, who listen
agape and retail it all in their turn to a no
less spellbound audience at home. For, like
the month of March, though in another way,
they come in like lions who went out like
lambs.

The worthy man is not only the head but
the only dead-head of the party. He alone
pays no scot. There are thus more substantial benefits accruing to the post of club
president than simply a cicerone's gratified
sense of importance. That he does not have
to pay reminds one of directors' cars at
home. However, so holy a person is otherwise superior to money considerations; the
purse being carried by the *tori-shimari-nin*
or treasurer.

The treasurer is the club's man-of-affairs,
of very small affairs indeed. The Japanese
are not above a monetary system which
descends in decimals to the thousandth part

of a cent, and, what is more surprising, they keep accounts to the like infinitesimal figures. Small wonder that neither arithmetic nor trade have charms for them. To such microscopic quantities the club treasurer is no stranger. Nothing is too minute to figure in his cash-book, from a fresh pair of straw sandals at a cent and a half a pair to a pickle or two at next to nothing. To the bill for which, lilliputian in all but length, the innkeeper with due solemnity affixes his seal.

In spite of the infinitesimal values of the separate items of the expense, the sum total invariably causes the club fund to fall short, the deficit having to be made up out of the individual pockets of the pilgrims. Unlike the club dues, this does not seem to be begrudged, the fact being that a pilgrimage is altogether too delectable a thing not to render those who indulge in it blind to its cost.

In addition to the president and treasurer, there are other officials known as *sewanin* or help-men, officers whose principal duty would seem to be helping the president dun members for their dues.

The pilgrim clubs find no counterpart in China. They are therefore not an imported institution, but a custom indigenous to Japan.

II.

Japanese pilgrimages are of two kinds, the distinction being matter of topography. For though some pilgrimages are Buddhist, some Shintō, a much more fundamental point about them is the character of the country concerned — whether they are made to the lowland shrines or to the sacred summits.

In importance, the Shintō pilgrimages come first, measuring importance by patronage. Half a million folk, it is estimated, make the journey to the shrines at Ise every spring, and ten thousand climb Fuji every summer. Of the ten modern Shintō sects, all but two are addicted to going upon pilgrimages, and each has its special great goal, as well as innumerable minor ones. These goals are the spots dedicate to their special gods. Of the two sects without goals, one is a sort of government bureau, and is consequently sedentary. The other would seem to be in the act of evolving the pilgrimage habit, for it has pilgrim clubs which, however, go no whither. Of the other eight, three are devoted to Ontaké, two to Ise, two to Fuji, and one to Izumo. Sects do not mix goals, but it is quite permissible for individuals to mix sects. So that persons of advanced pilgrimage proclivities can indulge them to any extent without too tiresome repetition.

Pilgrimages to the lowland shrines and to the sacred peaks differ in several important respects ; in sex, to begin with. For femininity has always flocked to the one, and, until western ideas broke down all the proprieties, was debarred the other. This was no matter of physique, but of piety. Woman was altogether too godless a creature to tread such holy ground as the peaks; an odd assumption, to our thinking, since woman with us, when not superficially godlike, is pretty sure to be godly. But the other side of the world thinks otherwise. It was considered favor enough to permit her to climb three quarters way up, where she was obliged to stop; which must have been considerably more aggravating than not to have been allowed to climb at all.

Proof, however, that this was an invidious

distinction, and that woman is by nature no less devout in Japan than elsewhere, is the way in which she tramps to the lowland shrines, and has a radiant time of it the whole distance. To see her trudging sturdily along, beaming at the least provocation, the very impersonation of vacant good-humor, does one good like a gleam of sunshine. Sometimes she dutifully follows in the wake of her lord and master; sometimes she shuffles along in the exclusive society of her own sex, chattering continuously upon nothing at all. But she is always perfectly happy and apparently never tired. She knows no nerves.

To the great Shrines of Ise it is the fashion for pilgrim clubs to go composed entirely of pilgrimesses, maidens of Kyōto and Osaka, who make the journey in bands of from fifty to a hundred, taking with them only one man, or two, to do the heavy work; veritable bouquets of pretty girls.

Stranger still, to our notions of propriety, little girls of eleven or twelve will surreptitiously club together and slip off some fine morning all by themselves on a tramp to the shrine. There is at first some slight alarm when the disappearance is discovered. But the very inquiry that raises anxiety soon lulls it by revealing similar bereavements among the parents' particular friends. Then the financial accomplices to the deed, kind-hearted neighbors, wheedled by the children into loaning them the necessary funds, come forward and own up, now that the borrowers are beyond recall. But, indeed, so soon as the cause of the flight is known, there would seem to be no thought of fetching back the fugitives. On the contrary, their act is deemed eminently praiseworthy, which strikes one as perhaps illogical. But religion covers a multitude of sins.

The parental heart is not set quite at rest, however, till other pilgrims returning from the shrine bring word of the waifs ; one has met the little girls disembarking at Yokkaichi, another saw them at the Ise inn. All report the truants quite well and happy, as if children at mischief were ever otherwise. Then, with palpitations of pride, the parents make great preparations against their return. Elaborate these are, for honor enough, apparently, cannot be done the young scapegraces. Long before they can possibly arrive, their relatives go out to meet them many miles down the road, and then wait sometimes several days at a convenient village till the band heaves in sight. The girls are received with praise instead of blame, and amid great rejoicings escorted into town; a reception which conduces to recurrence of the escapade.

Each lowland shrine has its special festival season, although it may also be visited advantageously at other times. Pilgrimage to the shrines at Ise is made at the time the cherries blow. Then the great highways that lead thither are as gay with pilgrim folk beneath as their flower aisles are bright with blossom overhead. The progress of each band is one long triumphal march. As it nears an inn where it purposes to spend the night, runners are dispatched ahead to notify the place of its coming, which instantly becomes all bustle to receive it. Hastily donning their best clothes, the maids and other servants scamper out to meet the band and escort it in with festival pomp. A feast follows in the evening quite as spirituous as spiritual, pointed with pious song right secularly sung. At the end of it there is something very like a break-down by the whole company, maids and all. The pilgrims rising, make a ring about the maids in the middle and then walk round and round chanting the Ise hymn, while the maids join lustily in the chorus. In this unpuritanical fashion is each evening brought to a close.

Upon their departure the next morning the pilgrims present everybody with souvenirs of themselves : the inn with the club banner and the maids with their club visiting-cards. Especially is the president to the fore with this charming attention. Both kinds of keepsakes are carried in large quantities by the band, and distributed unstintedly. For not to scatter such mementos of themselves along their route would be, in pilgrim estimation, to travel in vain. The landlord beams on the threshold, and the maids, all smiles, attend the band some distance out, and then throw good wishes after it till it disappears down the road.

But the supreme moment is when the company reënters in triumph its native town. Careful account has been kept of its whereabouts, and just before it is due horses strangely and gorgeously caparisoned are sent out to meet it. On either side the horses' necks are stuck long bamboo fronds, from which hang scarfs of gayly colored crape. Each horse carries a rich riding saddle, to which are fastened two paniers, one on either hand ; each steed thus seating three persons apiece, one astride in the middle, and two asquat in the baskets on the sides. With the steeds are sent personal adornments for the pilgrims ; hats made of flowers (*hanagasa*) and gayly embroidered coats, beside cakes and coppers for scattering to the crowd. Thus accoutred, rollicking along and strewing the largess as they pass, the pious pilgrims make their entry home. That evening a banquet is given them by their relatives and friends, regardless of expense, like to some coming of age in the gay middle ages. *Saké* and merriment flow without stint, and not till the next day do the pilgrims sink back again into private life ; holier folk, however, ever after.

III.

More serious matters are the pilgrimages to the peaks. The seriousness shows itself on the surface in the matter of dress. For according to the character of the pilgrimage is the character of the costume worn by the pilgrim. To the shrines in the plain, the thing to wear is the height of holiday attire; for the peaks, on the other hand, the consecrated dress is as plain as possible.

Theoretically, the costume of the ascensionists is pure white or pearl-gray, according to their sect or pilgrim club; practically it is a grimy dirt-color in both cases. For it is never washed, the travel stains being part of its acquired sanctity. Its hue, self-effacing to begin with, is thus further rendered by nature self-obliterating. It becomes, therefore, doubly expressive of a proper blankness within.

It begins with a huge mushroom hat made of wood-shavings cleverly plaited, held on by a complication of straps. Natural deal-color is deemed in this connection as holy as pure white, since both are attempts at colorlessness. Under this hat, umbrella, or parasol, for it is most serviceably all of them as occasion requires, the pilgrim wears a handkerchief in fillet round his brow. A long white tunic comes next, which theoretically is the pilgrim's only garment, except of course the ubiquitous loin-cloth. Practically he usually has on something beneath it, first in the shape of a shirt and then of tight-fitting trouser-drawers. The tunic is thoroughly stamped with ideographs; some of them being the names of the gods of the mountain, some those of the pilgrim club. Girdling this is a long belt-sash, round which often runs a row of transmogrified Sanskrit letters, quite illegible to the wearer or to any one else, so caricatured have they been by successive ignorant transmission. Their illegibility of course enhances their religious effect ; just as the word "amen" sounds incomparably holier than "so be it." White gaiters, white cloven socks, and straw sandals complete the more intimate part of the costume. The gaiters are sometimes lavender for the ladies.

But the most peculiar portion of the dress is the wing-like mat (*goza*) which the pilgrim wears over his shoulders by a strap across the breast. As it extends beyond his arms on either side and flaps in the wind as he walks, it gives him an ostrich-like effect at a distance, and what I conceive to be a seraphic one nearer to. At all events, it is the nearest mundane attempt at angelic representation. What is even more saintly, it is quite without vainglorious intent, being simply a combination waterproof-coat and linen-duster. It is also, very conveniently, both a carpet and a bed.

Quite as inseparable a part of the pilgrim is his staff. This is sometimes round, sometimes octagonal, and is branded with the name of the peak, and stamped in red with the sign of the shrine at the place where the ascent is supposed to begin. The imprint further takes pains to state whether the pilgrim came in by the front door or by the back one, mountains usually having both entrances, the original path being considered the front approach. The staves are counter-stamped again at the summit; the holy seals effectually silencing all skepticism on the pilgrim's return, and permitting his imagination freer play in the domestic circle.

Somewhere about his person each man carries a kerosene-looking tin can in which to take home the holy water, a specialty of sacred peaks. With sublime superiority to detail it cures all ills, irrespective of their character.

In his right hand the leader of the party holds a bell which he rings as he walks; others often do the same. The tinkle of this bell, together with the chanting in which all join, imparts a fine processional effect to the march, very impressive to less pious wayfarers.

Up their sleeves or tucked into their girdles the pilgrims carry *gohei*-wands, rosaries, and other tools of their trade; together with the indispensable pilgrim banners, badges, and the club's visiting cards. Of earthly baggage they have none. The reason for this has a moral. It is done to ingratiate the gods, because of the greater peril of pilgrimages to the peaks. The gods are supposed to have a fancy for such ascetic attire, and to protect themselves against the dangers of the ascent the pilgrims take particular pains to propitiate the gods; a reason kin to that the little girl gave for omitting her prayers in the morning, though she said them scrupulously at night; that she needed

THE LEADER OF A PILGRIM BAND BLESSING THE HOLY WATER

God to protect her while she was asleep, but that she could look after herself in the day-time.

If the costume seem somewhat destitute of comfort, the mountain itself is not. The traditional ascetics are described, indeed, as having made the ascent on single-toothed clogs, which certainly sounds difficult, and was thought a particularly meritorious thing to do. Its merit lay in thus avoiding crush-ing stray beetles, it is said. But the moun-tain knows such rigorous single-mindedness no more. Nowadays the ascent is specially convenienced for the comfort of the pious climbers. Every sacred peak is well rib-boned with paths which are all thought-fully beaded with rest-houses at intervals suited to the weakness of the flesh. A care-taker inhabits each of these hostelries and dispenses tea, cakes, water, and other fare to the exhausted, besides providing *futon* and such-like necessaries for spending the night. In the season the huts are crowded with pilgrims. Nominally there are always ten of them on every path from base to summit; one at the end of each section into which the path is fictitiously divided. The parts go

by the rather surprising name of "gills"
(*go*) ; the first "gill" being just within the
mountain's portal, and the tenth welcoming
the pilgrim at the top. Amid much that is
passing strange in the Japanese method of
mountaineering, this startlingly liquid measure for a painfully waterless slope is perhaps
the strangest; for it is not the rest-houses
that are so designated, but the path itself
with what, considering its distressingly dry
condition, must be thought very ill-placed
humor. In explanation it is said that mountains are likened to heaps of spilled rice,
the measure being one for both rice and
liquids, and reckoned at a *sho*, or three pints,
quite irrespective of size. The length of the
path, by an easy extension, is called a quart
and a half, and then divided into tenths, each
of which becomes a gill.

Shrines beside the path are almost as numerous as rest-houses. Temples also are
not wanting. There are several at the bottom, one at the top, and often others between, for though there be few on the flanks
themselves, the foot of a mountain is of indefinite length. Untenanted by priests, they
all stand open to the public, and the cords of

their bells hang in mute invitation to the pilgrim to call upon the god.

But most peculiar and picturesque of the features of the way are the *torii* or skeleton-archways that straddle the path, Japanese colossi of roads. There are many of them for every shrine, the outermost placed at a seemingly quite disconnected distance away from what it heralds. The several passes known as *Torii tōge*, scattered all over Japan, are all so called from such portals erected on their summits to sacred peaks visible from them in clear weather. One of the most important is the *Torii tōge* on the Nakasendō, through whose arch the pilgrim, as he tops the pass, catches his first view of Ontaké, a long snow-streaked summit, seen over intervening ranges of hills, thirty-five miles away, as the crane flies, or would fly, were he not practically extinct in Japan. This is the outer portal of all ; after this the pilgrim finds gateway after gateway across his path, till the last ushers him on to the holy summit itself. Distrust of his own purity prevents the pious from actually passing under them on the ascent, and he modestly goes round them instead. On the descent, holiness conquers humility.

Shrines, rest-houses, and portals make breathing spots for the pilgrims, which the church instantly turns to business account, for the church is not above trade. In its hands, faith very properly becomes a marketable commodity. In return for ready money it barters its salvation in the shape of charms. These are usually small pieces of paper stamped with the names of the gods, and sometimes lithographed with rude portraits of the same, manufactured by the million and sold for a cent. With such popular prices, sales are enormous, and booths under the charge of holy salesmen do a continuous business from morning to night, for no pilgrim passes on his way without buying his charm. Some of these (*mamori*) guard one against special catastrophe, disease, or misfortune; some bring particular good luck, such as a prolific propagation of one's silkworms; others are cure-alls and universal protectors. Charms are religion's epigrams; packet essences of truth, potent for being portably put. When the pilgrims get home, they pin them upon the lintel of their outer doors, and few doors in any Tōkyō street but are placarded with them.

The pilgrims are much given to chanting as they march. They do it as naturally as some people whistle. The Ise bands go rolling along to the enlivening cadence of the *Ise ondō,* and to many more special odes set to what with good will passes for music. It is rhythm on the road to song, a caterpillar stage in the art of melody, lacking as yet transformation to the winged thing.

The chants consecrated to the peaks are more truly processionals. Common to all of them is the stirring refrain *Rokkon shōjō; Ōyama kaisei,* chanted antiphonally in two tones, the second about a fifth higher than the first. Literally, the meaning of the refrain is : May our six parts be pure, and may the weather on the honorable peak be fine. But the words are mystic to most of those who repeat them. The first half is a portion of one of the purification prayers, the *rokkon shōjō no harai,* the second a part of a prayer for fine weather. It is, so I am informed, simply invaluable in dispelling mist.

Unlike the gods of the lowland shrines, which have each their special reception days, the gods of the peaks are all of them at home to mankind at the same season — midsummer. This is very considerate on their part, since to visit them at any other time would be troublesome. In consequence, in Japanese eyes, an ascent out of season is not only impious, but actually impossible. Every year, about the 20th of July, takes place what is known as the mountain-opening. At that time, all over Japan, the mountain-paths are repaired, the huts unbarred and put in order, and the peaks climbed with great pomp for the first ascent of the season. The peaks then remain open till about the 5th of September, when they are again deserted till the next July.

In this manner the "Goddess who makes the Flower Buds to blossom" receives her worshipers upon Fuji's crater-crest, to which a temple just without, known as the Goddess' Welcome, ushers them up. Other gods and goddesses are similarly visited upon their special peaks. But on all but one the eye of faith alone perceives them; only on one are they incarnate in the flesh.

IV.

For there is one mountain that makes bourne to a farther journey than any possible to the feet. Ontaké is goal to the soul's pilgrimage into the other world. For Ontaké is the mountain of trance. To its summit pilgrims ascend, not simply to adore but to be there actually incarnate of the gods. Through the six weeks in which the gods deign to receive man, divine possessions daily take place upon it. Furthermore, it is the only peak in Japan where, of the spot's own instance, such communion is thought to occur. It is what the Japanese call the great original (*hon moto*) of trance ; other peaks, such as Ōmanago near Nikkō, getting their power by direct spiritual descent from it.

In keeping with the character of the peak, is the character of the pilgrim clubs that climb it. The Ontaké clubs differ from all their fellows in being divine-possession clubs. To become entranced is the club occupation. Instead of simple prayer-meetings in their dead season, these clubs hold regular *séances* for the purpose of being possessed, *séances* which they turn to very practical ends. For they direct all the important affairs of their lives by such revelation. Once a month they hold communion of the sort, and every midsummer as many of them as may travel to Ontaké for a yet higher spiritual flight. The thin, pure air of the peaks is conducive to ethereality, and Ontaké is furthermore invested with faith's most potent spell. If to have faith as a grain of mustard seed can remove mountains, it is not easy to set bounds to what a mountain of it might not be able to do.

Each club is a divine dramatic company in itself, containing all the performers necessary to a possession. Only in very small clubs is such organization lacking. But as in this case their president is often president of some larger club, the loan of a *nakaza* is easily managed. For the president borrows of himself in the one capacity what he needs in the other.

Very large clubs contain several such companies. There may be as many as fifteen *nakaza* in a club, and twice that number of *maeza*. There is no rule in the matter. But except for exceptional cases of *esprit de corps*, many *maeza*, or *nakaza*, in one club do not

A PILGRIM CLUB ASCENDING ONTAKÉ

apparently make a happy family of it, finding divided prestige disagreeable. So, like queen bees, they swarm with their following and found a new club. Such fission is one mode of club generation. Another is by the spontaneous generation from the fertile brain of some energetic individual spoken of above.

Once started, each club is a spiritual law unto itself — a possession Salpétrière perpetuating its own peculiar practices. For it educates its own *nakaza* under the tuition of its *maeza* and the previous *nakaza*. The tuition is one long process in purification. A man begins as a simple member, gradually rises to a lower part in the function, and, if proficient, may eventually rise to be a god-possessed. The outward ceremonies are of course consciously copied, the inward initiative quite unconsciously conformed to.

When one subject has thus educated his successor he retires from active practice, becoming what is called an *inkyo-nakaza*. An *inkyo*, lit. a dweller in retirement, is a singular Japanese conception. It denotes a man who has abdicated all earthly cares, duties, and responsibilities in favor of his

son ; a man professedly gone from the world
while still patently in it. This is a state of
existence immaterial enough, but to be a
retired potential god would seem a doubly
etherealized idea. Nevertheless the thing
exists, and in case of sickness or other incapacity on the part of the *nakaza*, the man
who represents this abdicated embodiment
of immateriality performs in the other's
place.

The chief difference between the various
schools of divinity consists in the opening
or non-opening of the eyes of the possessed
during the height of the trance. But all the
other actions of the possessed during the
trance are likewise stereotyped. His whole
behavior in it is no more nor less than a
bundle of hypnotic habits. The mechanical
raising of the *gohei*-wand to his forehead,
the peculiar frenzied shake he gives it, the
settling of it again to a statesque imperative
before his brow, are all but so many cases of
unintentional artificiality. This is particularly discernible in the difference between
the simpler attitudes of the Ryōbu trances
and the more elaborate poses of the pure
Shintō ones. The Buddhist feminine fash-
ions, again, are different from either.

To be a club *nakaza* is pretty hard work. He must be possessed at least two or three times a month, and may be called upon to be somebody beside himself much oftener. It depends upon how much divination work there is to be done. This work is of two kinds. There is first the regular routine business of the club in the way of prophecy : the foretelling of drought, storms, earthquakes, and other general catastrophes affecting the interest of the club. Some clubs have to interview the gods once a month on such matters ; others manage to get along on two questionings a year, at the two great semi-annual festivals. This is probably due to club-temperament, just as it suffices some people to ask a question once for all, while others have to be perpetually putting it under indistinguishably different forms. In addition to this routine work there are the inevitable extras : the unavoidable illnesses, to be cured by divine prescription, and incidentally any other misfortunes to which flesh is heir, all of which the god is expected to relieve on application. Between these various duties the god, and incidentally the poor *nakaza,* is kept pretty busy. To be so frequently divine has its drawbacks. Except for his *succès d'estime*, a *nakaza* must wish at times that he were merely mortal. Even in all the club diseases, to be both doctor and patient, which is what it amounts to, is no slight strain on the poor man's constitution.

The god's conversation, though not superficially brilliant, is tolerably to the point, and certainly suggests intuition at times, though I know no cases of a very startling nature. The best instance I witnessed was the divining by the god of the pain in the leg of a friend of mine, to which, since the man was unknown to him and betrayed the fact by no outward sign, there was no visible clue.

The prophecies are not striking, though quite satisfactory to the club. They are religiously recorded on slips of paper and filed in the club archives. So that one may find there what the club's history was, or should have been, month by month in the past. The prophecies are laconic and indefinite enough to figure in the predictions of the "New England Farmer's Almanac;" a lack of precision which does not detract from their chance of verification.

Other-world work is apparently quite compatible with hard work in this. One of my special friends, the *nakaza* of the August Dance Pilgrim Club is a case in point. His club communes once a month and his duties begin as soon as ever the monthly business accounts are settled. He then comes in for a series of possession engagements. Indeed, if you apply for a sitting you will find his time taken up ahead in a way to suggest more earthly callings. In addition to all of which he works like anybody else at his regular trade, and is a strong, hearty young fellow in spite of his being a god so goodly a fraction of his time.

Thus, humble though their active members be, the Ontaké pilgrim clubs furnish society not to be found in any other clubs on earth : the company of heaven is to be had for the asking. For the Ontaké pilgrim clubs are the only clubs in the world whose honorary members are, not naval officers, not distinguished foreigners, not princely figureheads, but gods.

THE GOHEI.

IN the beginning of this account of Japanese divine possession I stated that it was of Shintō origin, and I promised later to justify the assertion. The time has come to fulfill that promise. Having seen that esoteric Shintō is esoteric, it becomes pertinent now to show that it is Shintō.

To prove this initially was anything but the forthright matter it may seem. For the establishing of the genuineness of the act of possession was child's play beside establishing the genuineness of the possession of the act. At first glance the latter was as prettily mixed up an intellectual lawsuit as one could buy into. Nobody really knew anything about the case, and those who confidently ventured a verdict did so in suspicious accordance with their special interest;

while as for general principles, so far as they proved anything, they turned out to prove what was not true.

Two claimants presented themselves for possession of the cult, Shintō and Buddhism. That the cult was chiefly practiced by neither, but by a third party well known to be illegitimate, called, with a certain pious duplicity of meaning, Both, — such being the literal rendering of the term Ryōbu, — did not simplify matters. For the hybrid Ryōbu, having candidly confessed its illegitimacy, dumbly refused to confess further on the subject.

The importance of the inquiry quite transcends the question of creed. Did it not do so, we might safely leave it to the zeal of church polemics. But it is not simply a question of religion ; it is a question of race. For if the thing be Shintō, it is purely Japanese ; if Buddhist, it is but another bit of foreign importation. In the one case it possesses the importance that attaches to being of the soil, in the other merely such superficial interest as attaches to soiling, — matter of much less archæologic account. The point thus possesses ethnic consequence.

Direct inquiry elicited worse than igno-

rance; it evolved a peculiarly mystifying
doubt. For the priestly evidence was bit-
terly baffling. No sooner had one man con-
vincingly told his tale than another came
along with an upsettingly opposite story.
The sole point in which the tellers substantially agreed lay in ascribing it pretty unan-
imously each to his own particular faith.
The Shintōists asserted that it was Shintō;
the Buddhists that it was Buddhist; while
the Ryōbuists ascribed it at times to the one,
but more commonly to the other. A few
humble brethren modestly admitted that they
did not know.

The only fact that emerged tolerably self-
evident from this bundle of contradiction
was that somebody had stolen the cult from
somebody else, but as to which of these rep-
utable parties was the reprehensible robber,
and which his unfortunate victim, the poor
investigator was left sadly at a loss to discover.

Where doctors of divinity disagreed in this
alarming manner, it seemed hopeless to try
to decide between them. Under such weighty
counter-assertions one's own opinion swung
balance-wise to settle at last to the lowest

level of equi-doubt. And there, so far as mere human help could go, it might have stayed forever in indeterminate suspension.

At this critical dead-point in the investigation, when any advance toward conviction seemed an impossibility, a bit of circumstantial evidence suddenly presented itself to turn the scale. I say presented itself, for it was not through the deposition of either contending party that it came into court. It wandered in one day unexpectedly, and proceeded quietly to give most damaging testimony in the case. Indeed its evidence was crucial. Oddly enough, this circumstantial witness appeared in the shape of what stands to Shintō for crucifix — the *gohei.*

The acquaintance of the *gohei* is among the first that one makes in Japan. The startling zigzags of that strange strip of white paper, pendent at intervals from a straw rope lining the lintel of some temple-front, instantly catch the eye with the realistic suggestion of lightning. Indeed, so far as looks go, the thing might very well be a flash of that hasty but undecided visitant of the skies, caught unawares by some chance, and miraculously paper-fied. For striking

enough it still is. And that its discontinuities
of direction can all be fashioned out of one
continuous sheet remains one of those hopeless mysteries of construction kin to the
introduction of the apple into the dumpling,
till one has actually seen the sheet cut and
folded into shape before his eyes.

Specimens enough, however, he is sure to
see, first without and then within the temple building. As it drapes the entrance,
so it hangs in holy frieze around the holiest
rooms, appearing at every possible opportunity, till, finally, at the very heart of the
shrine, it stands upright upon a wand, the
central object of regard upon the altar.

But it is by no means confined to the
temples, the *miya* and the *jinja*, plentifully
as these are dotted over the land. Almost
every house has its *kami-dana* or Shintō-
god's shelf, a tiny household shrine, the glo-
rification of some cupboard or recess. And
there in the half-light stands the *gohei* again,
there in the heart of each Japanese home.

It is no more confined to an indoor life
than man himself. You shall meet it abroad
all over the land, in the most unexpected
nooks and corners. The paths that lead so

prettily over Japanese hill and valley are set with wayside oratories and before many of them stands a *gohei* on its stick, sometimes quite humanly housed under a tiny shed, sometimes canopied only by the sky and the stars. Thoroughfare, field, and forest know it alike. Now it marks a quiet eddy in the tide of traffic of a bustling town, and now, the long year through, it points the bleak summit of some lonely peak that only in midsummer knows the foot of man.

Welcoming anchorite to the mountaineer, it is no less the farmer's friend. In fact it is peculiarly addicted to agriculture. When the growing rice begins to dream of the ear, it makes its appearance in the paddy-fields, stationed here and there among the crops, keeping an overseer eye upon them from the top of a tall stick.

But strangest post of all, you shall chance upon it some fine day riding in festival procession, perched in solitary grandeur upon the saddle of a richly caparisoned horse.

In short, it is omnipresent, this Shintō symbol.

Its religious significance it would be hard to overestimate. It is to Shintō what the

crucifix is to Christianity and a great deal
more ; one of those symbols which modern
defenders of the faith take much pains to
assure you is only a symbol, and no pains
whatever to prevent the people from worshiping as a god. As Shintōists are not so
much distressed to harmonize their beliefs
with science, being as yet unfired by the
burning desire to know the reasons of
things, they make small distinction between
the *gohei* and the god. In many cases they
make none at all.

For there are two kinds of *gohei ;* the one,
the *harai-bei* or purification present, and the
other, the *shintai* or god's body. The first
has for analogue in Christianity the crucifix.
It is the universal Shintō symbol of conse-
cration. Wherever you meet it you may
know the spot at once for holy ground dedicate to the god ; and specimens of it may be
seen in profusion about any Shintō temple.
They are the *gohei* that first greet the devotee, pendent from the sacred straw rope
upon the lintel of the temple door ; and
they are the *gohei* that festoon the building's
eaves and make frieze to the holier rooms
within. It is they also that in the possession

act inclose the place of the god's descent and sanctify it to his brief habiting. In short, wherever a *gohei* is hung up you may know it for one of the purification kind.

To the second or the god's body variety belong all such as are stood upright upon a wand. The *gohei* that makes cynosure upon the temple altar is of this kind and so is the one so daintily domesticated in the family cupboard at home. So also are those met with in the mart, on the mountain-top, and amid the paddy-fields. Last but most important of all these vicarious emblems of deity is that which is clenched in the hands of the possessed during the possession trance.

They are called the god's body, not because they are permanently god, but because they may become his embodiment at any moment. The little that we know of the evolution of the *gohei* will help explain what is supposed to take place. Its name signifies cloth, *gohei* meaning august cloth or present ; the former meaning having in course of time developed through a whole gamut of gifts in the concrete into the latter meaning in the abstract. For the *gohei* is the direct descendant of the hempen cloth hung on the

sacred *sakaki* (the *Cleyera Japonica*) in present to the gods. A relative of this its ancestor may still be seen in Korea in the
shreds of colored cloth attached there to
the devil trees ; a shift of devotion which
need distress no one, since devils and gods
are always first cousins in any faith.

From hemp its material constitution
changed successively first to cotton, then to
silk, and finally to its present modest paper,
a transformation of substance quite in step
economically with the progress of the arts.
As to its color, the earliest mention of it —
in the Kojiki, recorded therefore as early as
anything in Japan — tells of two kinds, one
dark blue, the other white, used together.
Nowadays it is almost always the plain
white of ordinary paper. But occasionally
gohei of the far-oriental elemental colors,
yellow, red, black, white, and blue, may be
seen in a row, a cosmic quinquenity of the
five elements, wood, fire, earth, water, and
metal.

Cloth it was, clothes it has become. For
in form it now symbolizes the vesture of the
god. Falling in spotless folds that spread
out on either side about the wand, it suggests,

even to the undevout, the starched flounces
of some ceremonial dress. In the Ryōbu
variety the central connecting link is raised
upright in the midst, clothes-pinned upon
the stick ; owing to its cut, it flanges out a
little toward the top, which does for the divine neck and head. In the purer Shintō
form the top piece is bent down over the
rest, symbolic of a more perfect pose.

On occasion the god deigns to inhabit this
habit of his. Such embodiment, indeed, is
graciously taking place every day at any
Shintō temple. To say that it takes place
at the god's pleasure, however, is to put it
flatteringly to the god ; for it really happens
at the will of the worshiper. Every prayer,
even the merest momentary mumble, involves incarnation of the *gohei* by the god,
and at a moment's call. For before he begins his prayer the worshiper claps his
hands. This is a summons to the god to
descend ; a like signal bids him depart. At
any popular shrine there is thus a continual
coming and going on the part of the god ;
which seems understandable enough until
one attempts to understand it. For what
happens when two persons call at overlap-

ping times upon one and the same god, so
that one worshiper bids him be gone while
the other would still have him stay, is not
strictly clear.   But such complications confront the too curious in all theories of anthropomorphic gods, especially when their
worshipers are on intimate terms with them.
I merely suggest it here as a problem in
higher esoterics.

Cases of incarnation where the god may
be supposed more nearly to suit his own
convenience are those of the *gohei* of the
paddy-fields.   These are divine scarecrows,
or rather scare-locusts, those pests of the
paddy-field farmer.   They are scarecrows,
however, in an occult sense, for in spite of
resembling gods as monstrously as the more
secular monstrosities do man, it is not their
looks which the locusts do not like, but their
disposition.   And, to judge from their general
employment, they appear to do as effective
police duty in frightening off insects as those
about the temple do in frightening off imps.

Another instance of the *gohei* incarnated
of the god is where it is borne in festival
procession sitting upon the sacred horse.
This animal, usually an albino, is the god's

steed of state, kept for the divine use in the
sacred stable, an adjunct to all well-appointed
shrines. For in these festivals it is no stick
that rides ; the god himself sits in the saddle. It is the god's chosen way of appearing
in public. In no other way, indeed, does the
god ever leave the temple. The prurient
may possibly detect some inconsistency between this statement and the one made
above to the effect that the god is always
coming and going ; but it should be remembered that in no cosmogony is consistency
expected of spirits. Besides, to go out in
state and to go out incognito are two very
different things, even in the case of royalty.

All these are examples of quite invisible
possessions. Though the god be there, the
undevout would never know it. But there
are sensible possessions of the *gohei;* cases
where the incarnation of the god may be
both seen and felt. It will be remembered
that the first sign of the coming on of the
possession in the possession trance is the
shaking of the *gohei*-wand. So spontaneous
does this shaking seem, that it is no wonder
it should be thought so in fact. The *gohei*
shakes, believers say, because the god de-

scends into it, and it quivers yet as passing through it he slips on into the body of the man. Without its mediation possession would not take place. The *gohei* is thus a sort of spirit lightning-rod to conduct the divine spirit into the human one. It is not, therefore, without a certain poetic fitness that it should look so like lightning.

Another case of its visible possessions, one where it plays a more autonomous part, is its christening power. A very curious custom this, and so far as I know one quite unknown to foreigners; so much so that more than one of my acquaintance who has had children by a Japanese wife have stoutly maintained that no such custom exists. It is a fact, nevertheless.

There are three methods of naming children in vogue among Shintōists. One, the most obvious and the least devout, is for the father to name the child himself. The next in an ascending scale of piety is for the father to select several suitable names and then submit the choice among them to the god. The way the god shows his choice is as follows : The father brings the child to the temple, and with him slips of paper in-

scribed with possible names. Three or five
is the usual number. The priest rolls them
up separately, puts them into a bowl, and
after due incarnation angles for them with
a *gohei* upon a wand. Whichever the *gohei*
fishes out first is the god-given name the
child is to bear ; a convenient custom when
a father is in doubt between the far-eastern
equivalents of Tom, Dick, or Harry. This
ceremony takes place when the infant is a
week old. It is not to be confounded with
the *miya mairi,* which takes place a month
after birth and is not our christening at all,
but akin to the Hebraic presentation of the
child at the temple. For at the *miya mairi*
the child, named some weeks before, is presented to its guardian god and formally put
under his protection. This style of christening is also largely performed by the pilgrim clubs.

The third method of getting the babe a
name is by possession pure and simple.
The *nakaza* goes into his trance, the god
descending through the *gohei,* and the *maeza*
asks the god what he will have the baby
called, to which the god makes reply. This
method of christening one's child is reputed

the most holy of the three, and is duly practiced by the ultra devout. Of the population
of Japan, about twenty per cent., it is estimated, are named thus by the *gohei* or the
god, — about ten per cent. by each.

From such many and various capacities
inherent in the *gohei* may be gathered the
part it plays in the thoughts of the Japanese
people. Indeed, it is all that is most Shintō,
and reversely Shintō is mostly all *gohei*.

It is, therefore, not surprising that in the
wholesale Buddhist spoliation of Shintō the
gohei should have been one of the few possessions which Shintō was able to retain.
Not that some of the Buddhist sects did
not flatteringly adopt it. The Shingon and
Nichiren sects have both been pleased to
find it useful, and have adapted it to suit
themselves, transforming it, for example,
from unpretentious paper into solid brass.
Nevertheless, its ownership is quite unques-
tioned. It is not only of Shintō creation, but
admittedly so.

II.

Now it was this *gohei*-wand that in conjuring up the god conjured up unexpectedly one day the spirit of the rite. Its exorcism was sorely needed, for in spite of boring the priests and even bothering the god on the subject, nothing but perplexity had come of the investigation, when one day it suddenly occurred to me that the *gohei* was always present at a possession; that in every instance this wand had been put into the hands of the man to be possessed preparatory to the possession, and that he had then held it through the trance. Other details had varied, but the wand was always there. I could recollect no exception to this rule. Having once been struck by the coincidence, I observed more closely, and to complete confirmation of my conjecture. At every function, whether at the hands of Ryōbuists, Shintōists, or Buddhists, there was the wand, constant as the trance itself.

Upon which I asked and got innocent admission from the Buddhists that it was a necessary detail of the rite, while from Shintō I learned the explanation of its presence.

The fact and its reason may be formulated together thus : The *gohei-wand is used in every divine possession in Japan, without exception, as a necessary vehicle for the god's descent.* Whether the possession take place by Shintō, Ryōbu, or Buddhist rite, in every instance the *gohei*-wand is put into the hands of the man to be possessed at the time the invitation to the god to descend begins, and through it is the god believed to come. It is *post hoc* because *propter hoc.* The *gohei* is thus the very soul of the rite.

To add argument to this fact savors of supererogation, for the crucial character of its circumstantial evidence is patent. As if, however, gratuitously to emphasize its importance, both faiths festoon the place where the descent is to be made with other *gohei*, pendent overhead, for purification. Both *haraibei* and *shintai* are thus present at the function.

Before the waving of this little wand, all the Buddhist pretensions to the cult pale to impalpable phantoms. Further discussion becomes suddenly vain. One cannot argue with a wraith; and if one think to strike insubstantiality, he is aware only of the void.

But as some good souls will still persist in believing in spooks, in spite of the failure of the not over-incredulous Society for Psychical Research to find a single really trustworthy specimen, it may be well to lay this ghost by a funeral logical rite or two.

To begin with, then, it is important to remember that to believers the means to a mystery is the mystery itself. For those addicted to such things do not follow them as sciences, but as arts. They have inherited the act embodied in certain actions, and the symbols in which it stands enshrined are to them essentials to its performance. From being so in act, they become so in fact. For so potent is faith, that to believe in a means as essential to an end is, by virtue of that belief alone, to make it so.

Now a mystery is not a thing a faith is in the habit of naïvely imparting to the first man it may chance to buttonhole for pious purposes, especially when it is a mystery of the utmost significance to itself. Every well-organized hierarchy has to keep up a certain amount of celestial exclusiveness for purposes of self-preservation. Just because by prolonged devotion it has secured

a distant divine recognition is no reason
why it should minimize this intimacy to others. Anteroom admission to the favor of
the gods is surely as valuable a privilege as
a like reception at the hands of the great
ones of the earth; and we all know what
lustre in their own eyes such threshold intimacy casts upon the favored few, even to the
extent of pretending to make light of it to
others. Now this divine intimacy is imposing enough in all conscience when it rests
simply on the word of the admitted. How
infinitely more so when confirmed by visible
action on the part of the gods themselves.
An introduction to such peculiar privilege is
not thoughtlessly to be given to everybody.
It will not do to present profane outsiders to
one's gods; still less thus to present one's
bosom foe. Such an act is nothing short of
sacerdotal suicide.

Yet something still more improbable the
Buddhists would have us believe. For they
admit getting the *gohei* from Shintō, and at
the same time they assert that they taught
that faith the possession cult. If so, then
they took three steps to their own destruction, each more trance-like, to say the least,

than its predecessor. First, they parted for no consideration whatever with a most valuable possession — simply inestimably so for purposes of conversion — to the very folk whom they were at the moment doing their utmost to convert. Next, they permitted these people, once taught, to substitute their own sacred symbol as conjurer in the supreme act, a concession which must speedily have induced complete oblivion that the cult itself had ever been a gift; and then, to cap the climax to their kind self-effacement, they actually adopted this, their proselytes' symbol, for exclusive use themselves. And then they ask the world to credit the account. One does not know whether to be the more astounded at the colossal coolness which can put forth such a tale, or at the amazing simplicity which can suppose others capable of believing it.

Were I merely making an argument in the matter I should here rest my case, the convincing character of this bit of evidence alone rendering any other superfluous. But as it is an exposition on which I am engaged, I go on to some more facts, all in the same line.

To a pro-Buddhist prejudice in the matter,
the first of these must prove a revelation
second only in surprise to the last.   It is
this : the very gods the *gohei*-wand summons
turn in its hands state's evidence against it.
For it is the Shintō gods that descend.   Not
only is it its own gods alone that Shintō
summons, but the Buddhists also call Shintō
deities, and of their own pantheon only the
lower, never the higher, members.   To explain this unusual fancy for their neighbors'
gods, combined with a relative disregard for
the company of their own, the Buddhists
allege the, to them, comparative unimportance of the cult.   Such indifferentism is
perilously near abandonment of their previous claims.   People are not given to detecting flatness of flavor in their own fruit.
If the practice be to them so unimportant
an affair, why indulge in it at all ?   Besides,
even this lame admission halts at summoning
the Shintō gods.   Doubtless it is most flat-
tering to the Shintō deities thus to be called
on for their opinion by professing outsiders,
but it would seem quite an inexplicable credulity on the part of the Buddhists to do so,
even among the politest people in the world.

III.

So much shall suffice here for the mute evidence of acts. But language has a word or two to say on the subject which, as a matter of courtesy, it may be well to admit. And first in the way of records.

The Kojiki and the Nihonshoki, known also as the Nihongi, are the oldest written records of the Japanese people. Compiled, the one in A. D. 712, the other in A. D. 720, they together constitute the Shintō bible, being different gospels, as it were, of much the same facts and fictions about the national past. Many of the fictions are doubtless founded on fact, though exactly how and even inexactly when, it would outwit mythology itself to state. There is at the beginning the usual attempt to make something out of nothing in order to account for the cosmos, much of which is probably Chinese. Then having got primeval chaos into something approaching order, the account gradually assumes consistency, till at last it becomes substantially history, of a far-oriental kind. As it begins with gods and ends with men, the evolution is not of the strictly sci-

entific kind, but rather a general devolution
in keeping with the doctrine of original sin.
During this abnormal development various
improbable events occur, some necessary to
it, some irrelevant. Of course the gods are
the *dei ex machina* in the matter; and it
takes a long time before the universe gets
into fairly passable running order, and their
presence can generally be dispensed with.
This dispensation, indeed, never wholly takes
place, and even after the world is going
along well enough of itself, and the gods
have formally left the field to their descendants, they are continually popping in and
out, just to be sure no mistakes are made.
One of their favorite methods of appearing
on the scene is to possess people. Such
manifestations of themselves were not, if we
are to trust the histories, very uncommon.
There are at least three recorded instances,
and, what is peculiarly to the point, these
are described with almost the exact detail
which distinguishes the possessions of to-
day; which makes the accounts peculiarly
interesting ethnologically. We seem to be
looking down that long vista of the past to
trances similar to any taking place about us
at the present time.

The first incarnation of which mention is made took place in the purely heavenly half of the history, at the time when the gods alone lived in the land. The occasion was the unfortunate withdrawal of the Sun-Goddess into a cave in consequence of the unseemly conduct of her brother, Susunao, or the Impetuous Male. This rude individual is the first recorded instance of the *enfant terrible*, and is not unhappily named, I think, to express the fact. He was subsequently banished to the moon for his improprieties. The displeasure of the Sun-Goddess was peculiarly distressing to the company of heaven, because her withdrawal of itself plunged them into utter darkness. They accordingly set about concocting a scheme to lure her out, the execution of which, as given in the Kojiki, reads as follows : —

"They hung all manner of things upon the tree : five hundred jewel-strings of brilliant bent beads to the top branches, an eight-sided looking-glass to the middle ones, and dark blue and white *gohei* to the lowest. Then his Augustness Jewel August Thing took an august *gohei* in his hand, and Heavenly Small Roof August Thing made repetition of some august (*i. e.* Shintō) prayers, while Heavenly Hand Power Male God was sent to hide beside the august door. Thereupon Heavenly Ugly Face August Thing, using a heavenly vine from the Heavenly Incense Mountain as shoulder-cord to tuck up her sleeves, and making herself a wig of the heavenly *masa*-tree, and tying up a bunch of bamboo-grass from the Heavenly Incense Mountain to hold in her hand, turned a cask bottom up before the door of the heavenly rock-house, and treading and stamping upon it with her feet became possessed (*kamu-ga-kari shite*). And clutching the clothes from about her breast, and pushing down the girdle of her skirt, she let her dress fall down to her hips. And the Plain of High Heaven resounded as the eight hundred myriad deities with one accord laughed. Thereupon the Heavenly Shining Great August Goddess, hearing the sound, cried out" — what is now immaterial, since her curiosity once caught, she herself soon followed.

The next mention of divine possession occurs in the Nihonshoki. It is recorded in the reign of the Emperor Sujin, a most unlucky monarch, with whom everything went

wrong. He naturally attributed this to the
gods, and determined finally to question them
on the subject. So going out into a certain
plain he collected the eight hundred myriad
deities, immaterially speaking, doubtless, and
asked to have his fortune told. Upon which :

"At this time a god descended upon the
princess Yamato-tōtōhi-momoso-hime-no-mi-
koto, and said (*kami-gakarite-iwaku*) : 'Why
is the Emperor troubled in spirit because the
country is vexed and there is no law in the
land ? If he diligently worship me and follow
my commandments the land shall rest in
peace.' Then the Emperor inquired and said,
'What god is it that thus instructs me?'
And the god answered, 'I am the god that
dwelleth within the boundaries of this land,
the land of Yamato, and my name is Omono-
nushi-no-kami.' Then receiving reverently
the instructions of the god, the Emperor
worshiped diligently according to his commandments."

A little after this, in the next reign, the
reign of the Emperor Suinin, we are told of
an image that was suddenly possessed by
the god whose image it was. This also is
out of the Nihonshoki : —

"In the third month, in the second year of the boar, on the first day, being the day of the monkey, the Emperor, taking an image of the Heavenly Shining Great August Goddess from the Princess Toyosuki-hime-no-mikoto, gave it to the Princess Yamato-hime-no-mikoto, and charged her, saying, 'Search me out a place where I may set up this image.' So the princess took the image and carried it first to Totanosasahata. And from thence she journeyed to the land of Omi, and, turning eastward, went by way of the land of Mino, till she came to the country of Ise. Then the Heavenly Shining Great August Goddess spake, and instructed the Princess Yamato-hime-no-mikoto, saying, 'This land of Ise, this land of heavenly breezes, this land of ever-curling waves, this sea-girt shore, is a delectable land. In this land will I dwell.' So, according to the words of the goddess, was a shrine built there to her in the land of Ise." In this way were founded the famous shrines of Ise.

But perhaps the most interesting of all the possessions mentioned in either of these books are the possessions of the Empress Jingō, recorded more or less in both.

The Empress Jingō was a good deal of a man. She was a great deal more of a man than her husband, though she was only his second wife. She was simply Empress-consort at first, eventually succeeding her husband, who died from want of faith, as will appear later. Masculine in character, she was most feminine in looks. The Nihonshoki speaks of her as exceedingly pretty and her father's pet, which latter fact proves to my mind that she was a woman of will, for I have observed that fathers are usually proud of daughters of decision. She it was who conquered Korea, in the histories at least, and did many other manly acts, besides giving birth to the Emperor Ojin, afterwards canonized as Hachiman, the God of War.

Apparently she was prone to being possessed, and ended by being quite intimate with deity. Her chronicle is a curious patchwork, pieced out, however, fairly complete between the Kojiki and the Nihonshoki. The Nihonshoki, after some Almanack de Gotha work introducing a few rather dry domesticities, simply kills her husband, without offering us any excuse for the deed

except the apparent unimportance of his life.
The Kojiki, however, condescends to tell us
how it happened : —

"Before that (referring to a digression
about a certain posthumous name of her son)
the Empress was divinely possessed (*kami-
yori tamaeriki*, lit. got-god-approached). At
the time when the Emperor, dwelling in the
Oak Temple in Kyūshiū, was about to make
war upon the land of Kumaso, the Emperor
played upon the august harp, and Take-no-
uchi-no-sukune went into the place of inquir-
ing of the gods (*saniwa*, lit. sand-court), and
inquired of them. Then the Empress, being divinely possessed (*kan-gakari shite*), informed and instructed him, saying, 'To the
west lieth a land full of all manner of precious
things from gold and silver upward,' etc., etc.
This glowing description, of which it were
needless here to quote more, referred of all
places in the world to Korea. It is perhaps
not matter for wonder that the Emperor
proved skeptical on the subject, and made
light of the divine information ; upon which
he was promptly killed by the gods for con-
tempt of court. After which the Nihonshoki
takes up the narrative, and tells us that the

Empress, who seems to have been a pious
person, was much grieved at the Emperor's
sudden taking off for doubting the divine
word, and resolved, woman-like, to know
about those jewels, a resolve she carried
out as follows: "Choosing a lucky day,
she went into the purification shrine and
became possessed (*kannushi to naritamo*).
And this was the manner of it: Giving orders to Take-no-uchi-no-sukune, she caused
him to play upon the august harp, and
calling Nakatomi-on-ikatsu, the August Attendant, she made him the inquirer of the
god (*saniwa to su*). Whereupon he placed
a thousand cloths and rich cloths upon the
top and bottom of the harp, and besought
the god, saying: 'The god that spake on
a former day to the Emperor, instructing
him; what god was it? I would fain know
his name.' Then when seven days and seven
nights had passed the god answered, saying "
— first what his abode was, and then what
was his name, and then, in reply to further
questionings of the *saniwa*, Nakatomi, gave
instructions for conquering Korea, which
had been his object from the beginning.
The Empress being a very devout body, and

possibly being influenced slightly by the
glitter of the prospective jewels, acted on
his instructions, and with complete success.

Here, then, we have accounts of possessions long pre-Buddhist ; their very accounts
being practically pre-Buddhist themselves.
For the Kojiki and the Nihonshoki were
written less than one hundred and forty
years after Buddhism came to Japan, too
short a time for it to have draped old
legends with its own detail. Besides, there
is not the slightest suspicion that it ever
tried to do so. The accounts read as real-
istically Shintō as one could have them do.
What is more, they read, barring a few
archaisms, as if recorded of to-day. In
skeleton the modern procedure is all there.
In these old Shintō biblical narratives you
see the same features that you mark in the
Ryōbu-Shintō trances now. The conserva-
tism is quite far-orientally complete, which
is another proof, not only that the thing is
Shintō, but that the Buddhists brought with
them from China nothing akin to it. For
we may be sure the gods would not have
been behind their people in the great national trick of imitation, and had there been

any foreigners to copy they would assuredly have copied them, and not have stayed starchedly Shintō to the present day.

In addition to the interest of the records themselves, the verbal evidence of these records is interesting. The words describing the possessions are all pure Japanese. Many of them are yet comprehensible, being in a way grandfathers to the modern terms. *Kami-gakari*, of which *kamu-gakari* and *kan-gakari* are euphonic forms, means god-fixed-on. An intransitive verb, it shows the spontaneity of the act. This spontaneity of deity is further dwelt on by tradition. In those good old days the gods descended, it is piously taught, of their own initiative, and not as now because importuned of man. Such seems a true mirror of the fact. For at first the act must have been fortuitive and sporadic. It could only have been later that men learned to lassoo deity at will. The modern term *kami-oroshi,* causing the god to descend, marks the subsequent business stage of the practice. Indeed, this domestication of deity, this taming of once wild trances, is not the least peculiar attribute of the far-eastern branch of the subject.

Among every people divine trances have taken place, but to make of the accidental and fortuitous the certain and the regular, to develop the casual communion into a systematic cult, shows a degree of familiarity with the subject peculiarly Japanese.

The word *kami*, which appears both in the ancient and modern expressions, is highly suggestive. For *kami* refers exclusively to Shintō gods ; Buddhist gods being always known as *hotoke*. *Kami* originally meant, and in certain uses still means, "top," or "above," and therefore was applied to the supreme beings. It is the same *kami* that figures in *kami* the hair of the head or topknot, and that appears in the expression *o kami san*, your wife, lit. Mrs. Upper, used when addressing the middle classes. Even its sinico-Japanese equivalent *shin* shows the same significance. For it never referred in China to the Buddhist gods. The two characteristics of which it is composed mean "declare, say ; " whereas the character for *hotoke*, a Buddhist god, means simply "not man." Whether trance-revelation lies hidden in this "declare, say," is another matter.

Another word in the bibles is worth a

note, the word *saniwa.* The characters with which it is written mean "sand - court." What that means has nonplused the commentators, as Mr. Chamberlain tells us. It has not foiled the priests. They explain it satisfactorily, if perhaps ex-post-factorily, as the god-interviewer, what is now commonly called the *maeza.* The explanation of the priests is at least explicable. For "sand-court" has the same impersonality about it, the designation of the place in lieu of the person, which is so curiously conspicuous in *maeza,* the seat-in-front. That it appears to make nonsense in personal English does not imply that it makes nonsense in impersonal Japanese.

I will now give, from the Nihonshoki, two or three accounts of *Kugadachi,* or the Ordeal by Boiling Water, which will show that the miracles are as old as the incarnations, and as purely Shintō. The first of these ordeals was undergone in the reign of the Emperor Ōjin, son to the Empress Jingō.

" In the ninth year (of his reign), in the spring, in the fourth month, the Emperor sent Take-no-uchi-no-sukune to Kyūshiū to take account of the people. Now at that

time Umashi-uchi-no-sukune, the younger
brother of Take-no-uchi-no-sukune, wishing
to rid himself of his brother, laid charge
against him before the Emperor, saying:
'It has come to our ears, O Emperor, that
Take-no-uchi-no-sukune is desirous of possessing Japan, and goeth about secretly to
stir up the people of Kyūshiū against the
Emperor. Then, when he shall have es-
tranged the land of Kyūshiū and called in
the Three States (Korea), he purposeth to
seize upon Japan.' Hearing these words,
the Emperor sent a messenger to Take-no-
uchi-no-sukune, to put him to death. Then
Take-no-uchi-no-sukune made answer to the
messenger, saying: 'I am not double-minded,
but true to the Emperor whom I serve.
What is, then, the crime of which I am ac-
cused? And if guiltless, why should I suffer
death?'

"Now there was living in Iki a certain
man named Ataeno-maneko. This man
greatly resembled Take-no-uchi-no-sukune.
And being troubled in spirit that Take-no-
uchi-no-sukune should be put to death without just cause, he said unto him: 'All Japan
knoweth thee to be a true man and a faithful

one to our Lord the Emperor. Now, therefore, fleeing hence secretly, get thee to our
Lord the Emperor and justify thyself before him. And furthermore men say that
I greatly resemble thee. So, therefore, in
place of thee, will I die, and thus show all
men that thy heart is pure before our Lord
the Emperor.' Whereupon he slew himself
with his sword.

"Then Take-no-uchi-no-sukune was sad at
heart, and, secretly leaving Kyūshiū, took
ship and came round by the southern ocean
to the port of Kii, and landed there. And
from thence he came, after much trouble, to
the court of the Emperor, and told the Emperor concerning his innocence. Then the
Emperor, perceiving some evil thing had
been done, called both Take-no-uchi-no-
sukune and Umashi-uchi-no-sukune before
him. Thereupon each told his own story,
and there was no way to tell the true from
the false. Then the Emperor commanded
that prayer should be offered to the Heavenly Gods and to the Earthly Gods, and
an ordeal by boiling water made (*kugadachi seshimu*). Whereupon Take-no-uchi-no-
sukune and Umashi-uchi-no-sukune went

together to the banks of the river Shiki and
performed the ordeal (*kugadachi su*) ; and
Take-no-uchi-no-sukune was justified by the
gods.　Then Take-no-uchi-no-sukune, taking
his sword, struck down Umashi-uchi-no-
sukune, and would have slain him, but the
Emperor commanded that he should be par-
doned and handed over to the Arae family
in Kii."

The next example occurred in the reign of
the Emperor Inkyō.　"In the fourth year,
in the autumn, in the ninth month, being the
year of the snake, on the first day of the
month, being the day of the bull, the Emperor gave instructions and commanded, saying : 'Anciently were the people ruled in
peace, and family names were never confounded, but now in this, the fourth year of
our reign, do the lower and the higher
among the people contend with one another
in the matter, and the people know no peace ;
either, peradventure, making mistake, have
they lost their proper family names, or else,
taking of forethought names above their station, they have turned them to their own
use ; and there is no law in the land.　Now,
perchance, it is we who are lacking in wis-

dom. How, then, may we correct our mistake? Do you, attendants, taking counsel
together, advise us in the matter.' Then the
attendants, with one voice, answered: 'O Emperor! if pointing out the mistakes and cor-
recting the wrong, the Emperor settles this
matter of family names, we, even risking
death, will tell the Emperor the truth.' So,
in the year of the monkey, the Emperor
gave instructions, saying : 'The Lords, High
Dignitaries, and other officers, down to the
governors, have together made answer, and
said: Verily the generations of the Emperor and the generations of his people are
both likewise descended from heaven. Yet,
since the day when the three bodies (heaven,
earth, and humanity) were one, many years
have passed, and from one name now many
descendants have spread abroad and taken
many family names, and it is not easy to tell
the true from the false. Therefore, let all
the people bathe and purify themselves, and
let each take oath before the gods to perform the ordeal by boiling water (*kugadachi
su*).' So the priest gave orders, saying,
'At the end of the hill called the Amakashi
hill, let an iron pot (*kugae*) be placed, and let

all the people be collected and gathered together there. Then shall they that speak the truth pass through the ordeal unharmed, but they that speak lies shall surely suffer.'

"Thereupon all the people tying up their clothes by shoulder-cords and going to the iron pot performed the ordeal by boiling water (*kugadachi su*). And those that spake the truth were by virtue of their verity unharmed ; but those that spake lies suffered. Therefore did the rest of the liars greatly fear and run away before ever they came to the hill. And from that time family names settled themselves of their own accord, and there was not one liar left in the land." A result which doubtless satisfactorily accounts for the present almost painful veracity of the Japanese people.

At the dawn of history, then, we find both possession of things and possession of persons already a part of the nation's mythologic heritage. Almost as soon as the gods were they began thus to visit one another. Then so soon as their earthly descendants appeared upon the scene they proceeded to visit them. Deity and humanity have continued on calling terms ever since.

Thus we see, first, how crucial, and then how exhaustive, is the proof that this divine possession cult is purely Shintō, and that all the Buddhists have done is to set upon it in the most conclusive way the seal of their appreciation. It pains me to prick this Buddhist bubble, blown of filching other people's soap. But I feel the less compunction about doing so for the fact that Buddhism has enough beautiful ones of its own fashioning, round and perfect philosophic films that catch and reflect the eternal light in iridescent hues sufficient to charm many millions of men. Emotionally its tenets do not at bottom satisfy us occidentals, flirt with them as we may. Passivity is not our passion, preach it as we are prone to do each to his neighbor. Scientifically pessimism is foolishness and impersonality a stage in development from which we are emerging, not one into which we shall ever relapse. As a dogma it is unfortunate, doing its devotee in the deeper sense no good, but it becomes positively faulty when it leads to practical ignoring of the mine and thine, and does other people harm.

THE SHRINES OF ISE.

Y first meeting with the gods, upon the top of Ontaké, had been strangely unexpected ; my last sign from them was destined to be no less so. It took place in an utterly dissimilar yet even more improbable place — the Shrines of Ise.

If, when buds first stir with dreams of blossom amid the forbidding April of our New England year, a man could quietly be spirited away from doubt, delay, and disappointment to a certain province of what is still old Japan, he would find himself in what he would take for fairyland. Over the whole countryside and far up its background of hills glow cloud-like masses of pink-white bloom, while upon all the country roads carnival crowds of men, women, and children journey gayly along, chanting as they go, beneath the canopy of blossom. It is the great Shintō pilgrimage to the Shrines of

Ise that he is gazing on, made every spring by three hundred thousand folk at the time when the cherries blow.

Up the winding street of the town of Yamada, the house-eaves on either hand one long line of fluttering pilgrim flags, the gay throng wends its rollicking way, and, crossing a curved parapeted bridge, enters a strangely neat park in the centre of a little valley shut in by thickly wooded slopes. At the farther end of the open an odd sort of skeleton arch makes portal to a carefully kept primeval forest. Through this ghost of a gateway the pilgrims pass by a broad gravelly path into a natural nave of cryptomeria, the huge trunks straight as columns and so tall that distance itself seems to taper them to where their tops touch in arch far overhead. Down aisles of half light on the sides show here and there the shapes of plain unpainted buildings, with roofs feet-deep in thatch, and curiously curved projecting rafters ; while under the great still trees the path winds solemnly on through a second portal, and then a third, to the foot of a flight of broad stone steps, up which it ascends to a gateway in the centre of one side of a plain wooden palisade. The gateway's doors stand open, but a white curtain, hanging from the lintel in their stead, hides all view beyond.

In front of the curtain lies a mat sprinkled with pennies. Before it each pilgrim pauses, lays aside his staff, takes off his travel robes, and tossing his mite to lie there beside its fellows, claps his hands, and bows his head in prayer. Then, his adoration done, he slowly turns, takes up again his robe and staff, and goes the way he came. For this is the goal to his long pilgrimage.

That curtain marks his bourne. Beyond the veil none but the Mikado and the special priests may ever go. Yet every now and then a gracious breeze gently wafts the curtain a little to one side, and for an instant gives the faithful glimpse of a pebbly court, a second gateway, and, screened by pale within pale of palisades, more plain wooden buildings with strangely raftered roofs, reputed counterparts of the primeval dwellings of the race. And this is all that man may ever see of the great Shrines of Ise, chief Mecca of the Shintō faith.

If with the mind's eye the pilgrim penetrates no farther than his feet may pass, he may well say with the disappointed tourist whom Chamberlain quotes in the guide-book, in warning to such as would visit these shrines : " There is nothing to see ; and they won't let you see it."

II.

Indeed, materially, there is little within save the eight petaled mirror, known by tradition to be there, emblem of the Great Goddess of the Sun.

But there is something there not yet down in the guide-book ; not even fully appreciated by the priests themselves. For revelation comes only to those who stand ready to perceive it. It chanced to me in this wise.

Never having made the pilgrimage to these famous shrines, I was minded, after my intimacy with deity, to do so ; and, accordingly, under the kind auspices of the high-priest of the Shinshiu sect, was properly accredited to the priests.

The Shrines, technically so called, consist of two congeries of temples inclosed by elaborate series of palisades and bosomed in grand old parks. One is known as the

Gekū or Outer Temple ; the other as the Naikū or Inner Temple ; in ordinary parlance, the Gekūsan and Naikūsan.

An immemorial tradition requires that all the more sacred buildings shall be torn down and exactly rebuilt again once every twenty years. For this purpose each is provided with an alternate site which, similar to and by the side of the one occupied at the moment, awaits, vacant, its turn to be used. There are three such sites at each shrine ; one belonging to the main temple and two to smaller temples a short way off through the woods.

The two main temples are dedicate, that at the Naikū to Ama-terasu-o-mi-kami, the Sun-Goddess, and that at the Gekū to Toyo-ake-bime-no-kami, the goddess of food. Formerly the Gekū was dedicate, as Satow, who made a study of non-esoteric Shintō, tells us, to Kuni-toko-tachi-no-mikoto ; both the former and the present incumbent being deities connected with the earth. With these chief gods are associated several subordinate divinities. At the Naikūsan these are : Ta-jikara-o-no-kami, the strong-hand-great-god, he who pulled the Sun-Goddess out of the cave whither she had retired displeased ; and a divine ancestress of the Imperial house. At the Gekūsan they are Ninigi-no-mikoto, grandson to the Sun-Goddess and ancestor of the Mikado, and two deities who accompanied him when he descended from heaven to rule over the earth, that is, Japan.

Of the lesser temples nothing is said in the guide-book, because next to nothing was known about them. Even the custodians themselves are not aware of all they guard, though they know sufficient to have put any one who had had knowledge of Shintō's esoteric side upon the discovery. But this side, as we have seen, was not suspected.

Now, it happened in the course of my visit that, under the guidance of the priests, we came through the wood upon one of the two smaller temples, and I asked them what it was called. Ara-mi-tama-no-miya, they answered, the Temple of the Rough-August-Soul. Having some acquaintance with the ways of the gods, I began to suspect, only to have my suspicions verified. The Rough-August-Soul turned out to be the rough spirit of the Sun-goddess, — not her usual spirit, they explained, but her spirit when she possesses people. Once, they said, she had possessed a daughter of the Imperial house, many centuries ago, upon this very spot. Here, then, was a strange temple, indeed ; a temple dedicated to a possessory spirit; possibly something without a counterpart on earth, save for another like it at the Gekūsan, which I found in the course of the same day.

To the Ise priests all this was but a half-understood tradition. For their sect is esoteric no longer. They know nothing personally of the practice of possession. All the greater their unwitting witness to the fact ; and to the still more important fact which this one proves. For it proves that in early days the possession cult was common to all Shintō, and not as now the heirloom only of certain sects.

So completely was possession once an integral part of the Shintō faith, that it erected these temples to the possessory spirits. Nothing could well testify more deeply to belief in their existence, and nothing seem to bring them home more closely to their devotees than this fashioning of an earthly pavilion for their temporary sojourn. Among all the strange details of this god-possession cult, this, perhaps, is the strangest — these temples to possessing spirits.

NOUMENA.

I.

HAVING seen these spirits, the next thing is, if possible, to see through them. For after establishing first their existence, and, secondly, their identity, it becomes interesting to know their essence. In order to discover this, we may best begin by considering our own spirit or self.

The idea of self, religiously known as one's soul or spirit, presents itself to us under three aspects: as a feeling about ourselves; as a feeling about others as affecting ourselves; as a feeling about others independently of ourselves. The first we call the sense of self; the second, the personality of another; the last, simply a man's individuality.

Now, to begin with, every one has a private conviction that his sense of self is as strong as any one else's, just as he is pri-

vately persuaded that his feelings generally
are as praiseworthily poignant as his neighbor's. Nevertheless, his equally infallible
estimate of others may hint to him that
this is possibly a pleasing personal delusion,
since in those about him he perceives very
clearly that in strength of selfhood man
varies markedly from man. Some men affect him instantly and indescribably as of
strong personality ; others as of a feeble
one. Scanning them critically for objective
proof of this subjective feeling of his toward
them, he finds in their behavior unmistakable signs that it is founded on fact. He
notices that the feeble brother unconsciously
plays chameleon to all he meets, while the
positive person seems largely sufficient unto
himself. In short, it becomes perfectly apparent that men differ as much in selfhood
as they do in, say, artistic taste.

Just as men of any one community differ
thus among themselves, so whole communities contrast with one another in the same
way. The French and the Anglo-Saxons
offer us an instance at our very elbow.
What is more, both sides to the antithesis
recognize the difference perfectly, and apply

derogatory epithets to it in the other. *Ce grand original d'Anglais* heartily despises those monkeys the French, and knows not at which he stands the more aghast, the awful sansculottism of their institutions or the shocking manner in which they unbosom themselves to the first comer.

Another generic instance is even more ready to our hand. We do not have to go abroad to find it. For it is found world-wide in femininity. So universal is it, and so bound up with the question of trances, that it deserves mention here ; especially as I do not recall having seen it scientifically recognized. It is this, — that self is what, psychically, peculiarly distinguishes the sexes. In woman there is a comparative absence of Ego.

With regard to a want of it in woman, doubtless there are persons who will promptly and indignantly deny the fact ; certainly all those who are trying their best to-day to make of woman an inferior kind of man may be trusted to do so. But woman is altogether too valuable as she is to be thus disposed of, and it is precisely in her relative lack of self that her value lies. This it is that makes her the almost unmitigated blessing she is. For it is in her direct relations with man that this quality of hers comes out conspicuous, first as wife, and then as mother.

To how many men, I wonder, did it ever occur what an upsetting sensation it would be to change one's name at marriage. To be known by one name, to speak it, hear it, write it, read it, from the time one first remembered one's self, through all those years when habits are formed and crystallized, and then, presto! to be known by, speak, hear, write, read, another one ever after. Such metamorphosis would certainly give self-centered man a shock. Yet the fair sex take their maiden electrocution without a quiver. Nevertheless, words are very telling things. It is compliments, not good-will, that pay us the most poignant after-calls; just as it is insults, not injuries, that stick. All the more so, then, in the case of that word which of all words is most one's self. To change that would, to hardened man, seem dangerously like parting with a part of himself.

Precursor of change it actually proves to be with woman. Change of name, to which the maiden takes so kindly, turns out but exponent of the change of thought in her that follows it. To a great extent the wife merges her self in her husband's. She adopts his interests, acquires his dislikes, echoes his opinions. In the usual case, his intellectual property, in short, becomes hers. As a small offset, doubtless, to these acquisitions, her material property became his.

She shows the same self-obliteration as mother. A woman lives for and in her offspring in a way quite impossible for a man. A father may care as much for his children, but he cannot sink his own personality in theirs as a mother may and does. Her thought centres in them as naturally as his centres in himself, with a like absence of all intention in the process.

Thus in both of the two most important relations of her life a woman shows a disregard and a sacrifice of herself which finds no corresponding counterpart in man. Man praises her for it, which is tantamount to praising her for being a woman. For in her the action is neither noble nor ignoble; it simply is. It is also simply normal that man should appear a very selfish animal by comparison.

Noticeable as these differences in the self are, they are as nothing compared with the contrast that confronts an Anglo-Saxon in the Japanese race. Its indirect manifestations are so striking that they have found embodiment in aphorism. The well-worn epigram that the Japanese are the French of the far East really rests on this. So does, also, the less trite one that Japan is the feminine half of the world. For her delicacy, her daintiness, and her dignity instantly suggest to our more coarse, more direct, more original mind something of the fair sex. An etiquette of soul, I can hear some one phrase it. Certainly in emotion both go through the world gloved, but the resemblance rests on something below the surface. Very different as are femininity and far-orientalism in most things, there is strangely enough in both a relative absence of self.

Japan is at present engaged in making the resemblance evident in an interesting if objectionable manner. When a woman once lets go her old rules of conduct, she will go pretty much any lengths in the new. Just as a fine woman will make even fine men blush, so a low one will stagger even her

male associates. Impulse possesses her for
its own. There is in her a capacity for self-
abandonment to an idea impossible to man.
Lady Macbeth, once started, outdoes my
lord in crime. She knows no hindering
regard for self, no ghostly shapes of other
thoughts to rise and cry to this one "Halt!
enough!" So Japan. Decorous as was old
Japan, young Japan, inoculated of foreign
fancy, will cause even the rough and ready
foreigner to start. Just as politeness stood
personified — one may almost say petrified —
in a Japanese gentleman of the old school,
so rudeness incarnate jostles you in his son.
A greater contrast could scarcely be offered
than that between the pageant of an old-
time Japanese setting out upon a journey
and a modern Japanese arrival from one by
train; the polite eternity of self-deprecatory
bows of the one, the scramble for the wicket
of the other, where man, woman, and child
bump and hustle their neighbors with an
indifferent rudeness that, in any more personal land, would cause several free fights on
the spot. That it does not do so here shows
that though politeness has gone, personality
has not yet come. Indeed, the impersonal

character of the hustle is something which may be felt; for it is as devoid of subjective sensibility as of altruistic regard. Impersonality stands patent in the very touch of it. It seems subtly to embody the distinction hinted at in the injunction of the topical refrain, "Don't push; just shove."

II.

Furthermore, this selfhood is a force. We feel other people's personality in direct effect upon ourselves, and we perceive and, in a way, even feel the effect of our personality upon others. We also notice similar inter-effects between two third persons. Like all other forces, this force acts inevitably, often quite unconsciously; and fatally produces its results when not opposed by counter forces. Married couples give us striking every-day instances of it. The happy pair grow monotonously like each other, even to the extent of acquiring a certain family resemblance. The wife becomes a replica of her husband, and the husband, to a certain extent, a duplicate of his wife, although the effect is more marked on the woman. As the world is constituted, it is fortunate for domesticity that mutual transformation is the rule, since otherwise it may be doubted if the divorce court would be the exception.

But such inter-affection is no monopoly of matrimony. Each one of us is continually impressing, or being impressed by, others in proportion to the strength of our respective selves. Originality marks the height of the one, imitation the depth of the other. The action is commonly unconscious at the time, and only recognized afterwards. The fact is that character is contagious. All men go through life more or less inoculated thus of others. Boswell's very acute case of Dr. Johnson, pathologic as it was, is but an aggravated instance of what is not without a parallel about us every day. Plenty of men contract effective admirations, which they carry with them more or less through life. And we none of us wholly escape contagion, both good and bad. Whence the importance of carefully choosing one's friends. For to have a sufficiently violent attack of one person insures, for the time being, practical immunity from another. To such an extent are we all chameleons in mind.

That one self has this effect on its fellows hints at a common essence pervading them all. ˎIt suggests one great impersonality of spirit underlying our several personal embodiments of it, a certain cosmic, communistic character for the soul. It is fortunate there is such mutual influence between men. Were it not so, this isolated globe would be a still more isolated spot; love would instantly fly out of the window, and friendship itself be put out of doors.

Minds differ greatly in their power of thus impregnating other minds. But it is especially a quality of the male mind as compared with the female one. The one is original and forceful; the other receptive and self-adapting. The one imitates, the other adopts.

Personality, or a man's mental force upon his fellows, is also in a way measure of the mental energy of the man.

For we meet personalities that repel us as well as ones that attract; personalities, even, that do not affect us beyond a recognition that they are, and that they do affect, our neighbors. We are, therefore, conscious of personality as such; in some sort, we even gauge its amount.

Now the faculty of being influenced by other people the Japanese possess to a marvelous degree. Fundamentally unoriginal, they have always shown a genius for self-adaptation. They are at present engaged in exemplifying their capacity upon a wholesale national scale.

It is hardly exaggeration to say that Japan at this moment is affording the rest of the world the spectacle of the most stupendous hypnotic act ever seen, nothing less than the hypnotization of a whole nation, with its eyes open. Forty million of folk there are now innocent freaks of foreign suggestion. It is not simply the imitating of foreign customs, but the instant unassimilated character of the invitation that stamps the national state of mind as kin to hypnosis, and gives to both their cousinly touch of caricature. The new idea is adopted with little or no attempt at adaptation. Such sublime disregard of congruity shows the hypnotic completeness with which it is received. In consequence, Tōkyō is now one vast public platform, in which nature is giving an exhibition of ideal force. Combinations in costume as beautifully incompatible as any the hypnotized subject can be induced to adopt are at large on its streets, worn in the two cases from the same motive, unreasoned response to stimulus from without ; whence the irrationality of the result. Nor do the other subjects see anything ludicrous in it all.

The action may be said to begin, but by no means to stop, with costume. Customs, from top to toe, are undergoing the same foreign-motived transmogrification. The imitation pot-hat and accompanying aura of billycockism sit no less comically upon a *kimono* and cloven socks than does a modern Tōkyō court of justice upon an old-fashioned Japanese case.

Hypnotoidal imitation is no new trait of these people. They showed the same proclivity in just the same way more than a millennium ago. China was the operator then, as the western world is the operator now. Susceptibility to suggestion lies at the root of the race.

III.

Not only can one self thus sway another, but from prehistoric times men have believed that one self could actually oust another and act in its stead. The dispossessing self has been variously deemed a deity, devil, or disembodied spirit — embodied spirits being apparently less eager to leave their quarters. But whatever its moral character, it has been held to be every whit as existent as the poor devil it dispossessed. Among all peoples we have instances of persons thus possessed by gods, goblins, and others, instances cropping up all over the world, from the earliest ages down to the present day. The character of the possessing spirit has, however, varied with singular complacency to suit the opinions of the persons it possessed. In a simple society that favored the idea, the visitant has boldly proclaimed himself a god; in communities where this assumption was considered arrogant, he has contented himself with the more modest rôle of devil; while, finally, in these latter days, he has been fain to put up with being the spirit of an Indian brave or other worthy too insignificant to dispute.

It is scarcely surprising, perhaps, that these possessing spirits should have seemed actual beings, seeing that to common sense they are such, inasmuch as they rigorously pass all the tests by which we cognize personality and know one man from his neighbor, just as rigorously as the unfortunates they dispossess. This seemingly astounding statement is easily shown to be undeniable. Not only to the simple, superficial eye do the manifestations comport themselves like distinct personalities; they do the like when gauged by all the criteria we are wont to apply. For how do we know people about us for distinct individualities? We know them psychically by the fact that each seems conscious of himself and of his own emotions, thoughts, and memories, as being his own, and as not being anybody else's. The same is true of these spirits. Each is evidently conscious of itself, and conscious of the distinction between itself and all other selves, the man, in whose body it is, included. It has its own emotions which are not his; its own thoughts, which are not his; its own memories, which are not his. It not only denies that it is he; it really knows nothing of all those states of consciousness which alone are he. Except as an outsider, it neither knows him, nor he it.

It does not, of course, follow from the undeniable fact of its distinct psychical existence that it is either a god or a devil. To jump to this conclusion is a quite unwarrantable assumption of divinity. But the immateriality of the god does not invalidate the actuality of the so-called spirit. Because Smith may erroneously be called Jones, does not jeopardize the existence of Smith, though it may considerably imperil the existence of Jones.

The reconciliation of these two separate selves consists, as we shall see later, in a certain denial of self altogether.

Now, besides revealing so much, common to all manifestations, these Shintō ones reveal indirectly considerably more. In the first place, they disclose the fact that the Japanese race is very easily possessed. They do this, first, by their amount, and secondly, as significantly, by their character.

Their quantity we have seen to be something enormous. It is safe to say that no other nation of forty millions of people has

ever produced its parallel. For not only is
each form surprisingly common, but there
are such a surprising number of forms.
There is intentional possession, and possession unintentional; possession by the mediation of the church, and possession immediately by the devil; beneficent possession by
dead men, and malevolent possession by live
beasts. There is, in short, possession by
pretty much every kind of creature, except
by other living men.

This omission is highly significant. For
it shows that no Japanese personality of itself
has proved potent enough thus to affect its
fellows; from which it instantly follows that
the great extent possession has reached in
Japan is not due to an excess of personality,
but to a lack of it. As collateral evidence of
this, is the fact that mesmerism, hypnotism,
and the like, were unknown in Japan till
introduced there by the western world; ab-
sent, not from dearth of subjects, but from
dearth of hypnotizers.

Even more subtly significant is the quality
of the possession. Fortuitous, of course, at
first, god-possession in Japan has passed
from the spontaneous into the systematic

stage. From being wild, the possessing
spirits have become tame. Deity has been
domesticated. Originally a voluntary act of
god upon involuntary man, possession has
become practically an involuntary divine
acquiescence to human constrainment. The
lightning, in short, has been turned into ser-
viceable electricity.

This constrainment of deity is no new
thing there. It had already come about in
prehistoric times, as the Kojiki and Nihonshoki show. Since then it has been more
and more systematized till it has now grown
into a regular business, done as a matter of
course. Comment on this is needless.

The trance itself tells the same story, in
the ease with which the possession is effected. For the closer the normal state lies
to the abnormal one, the less the wrench in
passing from the one to the other, and the
more seemingly natural the latter when entered. Now compared with mediumistic
trances, the Shintō possessions are decent,
gentlemanly affairs. There is, indeed, the
initial throe and the subsequent quiver, but
the one is not an epileptic portal to a general epileptic appearance throughout, which

so disgusts a looker-on in possessions by mediums. The Shintō gods may be dull, but they are at least decorous, whereas the mediumistic spirits are most undesirable company. And this in spite of the fact that in America the subjects are usually women, from whom one would expect more ladylike behavior.

For to be easily controlled abnormally is as much a characteristic of woman as to be easily influenced normally. Spirits apparently have always been perfectly aware of this. From the earliest times they have shown a pardonable preference for possessing her. The divinely inspired prophetess was a regular appurtenance of ancient religions. And that the spirits are still as partial to her as ever is shown by the present preponderance of female mediums. For that the female monopoly of the business is due to natural capacity, and not simply to surplusage of the sex, is hinted at by the host of shams which the apparently lucrative character of the business is able to support.

Hypnotism tells the same story. In spite of authoritative statements to the contrary, women are naturally more hypnotizable, than men. That the opposite has been stated to be the case would seem to be due to the not uncommon fallacy of not sufficiently simplifying the experiments. For there are two factors that enter into the result beside the skill of the operator : the natural capacity of the subject and the degree to which he is made unconsciously to coöperate to his own suppression. Indeed, just as no one may be hypnotized against his will, so in all cases the subject really hypnotizes himself. The art of the operator simply consists in getting him, more or less unwittingly, to do this. The greater the natural aptitude of the subject, the less the art necessary in the operator. To get the best experiments, therefore, we should eliminate as much as may be the latter's skill. The tyro of an hypnotist is thus the man whose experiments are really to the point ; and every tyro in this art of recreating personality knows that, unlike the original creator of it, "his prentice hand" he tries on "woman," not "man," because thus he stands the greater chance of succeeding.

Woman's superior capacity for being possessed shows itself even among the Japanese.

The Nichiren Buddhists, with praiseworthy astuteness, employ women as vehicles for the divine descent for this very reason, and the resulting trance is so easily entered as sometimes to pass counterfeit for a sham.

The French display a like proneness to altro-possession. Had they not been relatively easily influenced, Mesmer would not have failed of a livelihood in Vienna to become the rage in Paris; nor would Charcot and Nancy have been the pioneer names of modern hypnotism. For an art does not become the vogue among those who have no natural aptitude for it. Nature divorces such incompatibility of temper. Priority of practice is thus the best proof of fitness.

Now it is these same three classes of mind, the far-oriental, the feminine and the French, different as they otherwise are, that we saw to be relatively so impersonal. Personality, then, appears to be the opposite pole to proneness to possession. Spirits of this world and of the next would seem to have a reciprocatory action in their possession of the human body; the more man the less god. This suggests that the qualitative difference between selves is in some sort a quantitative one. Self would appear to be a something capable of more or less; inasmuch as a man who is not much himself at most finds it more facile to become some one else on occasion; an instance of the general principle that it is easier to introduce a substance into a comparative void than into space already occupied; and this in fact is what I conceive happens; not materially, but kinematically. For though we do not here introduce matter, we do, as I shall hope to show, introduce motion.

IV.

To do this we must again have recourse to ourselves, and diagnose, if we may, our own spirit.

Now on looking into ourselves to see what ourselves may be, of what are we made aware? For my part I am conscious of a kaleidoscopic series of thoughts. These successive dissolving views of mine seem to me to have about as much inter-connection as kaleidoscopic combinations generally, and I seem to have about as much influence over their appearance as I should have over those of that delightful but unpredicable instrument, if by attention I could induce it to evolve along some slightly definite line. In other words, I am conscious at first sight of what we call ideas and will, and that the latter has a certain limited effect upon the former.

My next discovery is that this power of my will is not a directly creative force at all. Not only can I acquire no new mental property by simply willing to have it; I cannot even lay my hand on what is already my own, when I would. For I can neither think a new idea by direct exercise of will, nor can I directly recall a memory when I please. All I can do is hold on to, or let go, what my stream of thought is kind enough to present me with. By choosing to attend to any particular idea that chances to come along, I allow that idea to beget others after its kind; an opportunity of which it instantly avails itself. If I pay no attention to it, it promptly goes out. And this is absolutely all I can do. In this pitifully feeble fashion I manage to live, move, and have my being in the firm belief that I could do almost anything if I pleased.

Will then, consists in the exercise of

selective attention. I choose to attend to one thought rather than another, and then I do attend to it. But though will in action is thus all selective attention, all selective attention is not will. For on further scrutiny of my stream of thought I am made aware rather startlingly that will meddles with it uncommonly little. Observation shows me that the like is true of my fellows. Indeed, the greater part of all our lives is made up of will-less action, of simply thinking the act and then doing it without any exercise of will at all. Yet we are not conscious of being our own on-lookers merely. On the contrary, we feel very poignantly that we live in this pageant that unrolls itself before the mind's eye. We feel this because selective attention is busy all the while, whether we will or no, and we are quite aware that it is thus at work involuntarily.

In the case of this involuntary attention, the power behind the throne seems to be quite simply the interest the particular idea possesses for us. If the idea appeals to us, we attend to it in spite of ourselves. We can, indeed, often catch ourselves led pleased captive thus to some fascinating thought, remonstrating impotently as it drags us after it. It rivets, as we say, our attention.

In short, involuntary attention is simply the dynamic outcome of the idea. The idea results as fatalistically in turning and fastening our attention as a bright object does in rotating the fovea upon itself, or as the percussion of the cap does in the discharge of the gun.

Now voluntary attention appears to differ from the involuntary kind not the least in attent, but only in intent. We seem in the latter case to choose which idea we shall press upon, the consequent pressure proving quite similar in both.

In our search for the noumenal, then, in what we call will, we are driven back upon the act of choice alone.

Now when we search for the cause of our choice we always bring up against some determining thought. Whenever we succeed in overtaking that will-o'-the-wisp, our own will, and triumphantly clutch it, we find invariably that we have caught — an idea. Why am I willing to write these words, when as a matter of fact I am tempted to lie on the grass and gaze into the drifting islands of cloud? Because I decided yesterday that I would — an idea — or because it will be pleasurable later to have done so — an idea — or simply to prove to myself that I have a will — an idea again sarcastically bobbing up. Every time that I' think to have closed upon that elusive force, the will, I find myself left grasping a palpable idea.

Yet we call ourselves conscious of the autonomy of our will. Nor will I yet say that we are not. What I will say is that we should be just as conscious of the fact were the fact not so. For that only is not free which is determined from without. Now whether the will were a noumenistic *primum mobile*, or a mere dynamic outcome of the idea, it would in either case be determined from within and would necessarily, therefore, seem free.

But we may go further. Whatever will be, it is dependent for its existence in consciousness upon the existence of ideas. This is palpably instanced every day of our lives. For we are constantly conscious of ideas without will; we are never conscious of will without ideas. Further yet, in these will-less yet conscious times, we are quite aware of ourselves as being ourselves. Will, there-

fore, except as included in the ideas, is not
of the essence of the Ego. For a thing
which only pays us visits in this manner
and is distinctly recognized as doing so can
be no indispensable part of that innermost
something each of us calls " I."

Lastly, will appears to be quite uncomplex-
ioned. Nobody pretends that his will differs from his neighbor's, except in strength,
that is, in amount. It differs in its application, but not in itself. It works in one man
on one thing ; in another, on another : but
that which works seems essentially the same
in both. Will acts, in short, like any other
impersonal force. Either, therefore, will is
the I only as included in the Idea, or it is
in no personal sense the I at all.

Now the method of getting into the trance
state has something very apposite and important to say about all this. For the entrance to that peculiar condition lies through
an abnormal use of selective attention. By
keeping the attention fixed long enough on a
very insipid idea, or, better yet, upon nothing
at all, out go both ideas and will ; that is,
will can inadvertently bring about its own
extinction when intent upon the extinction

of something else, namely, an idea. But of this truly astounding performance on the part of the will we need not go to trances to become astonished witness. For each one of us has experience of it, as a matter of fact, whenever he falls asleep. In lapsing into our nightly unconsciousness, it is our ideas that seem to go out directly, our will only seeming indirectly compelled to go with them. Baron Munchausen lifting himself up by his pig-tail is child's play to this self-extinction of the will, if will be in any sense the self.

V.

Having thus eliminated will from any intrinsic participation in the self except as included in the idea, we have reduced self to ideas. Of what ideas, then, is it made up? Clearly not of the simple main idea of the moment. No one ever mistook his idea of a beefsteak for himself. But one's train of thought is not wholly composed of beefsteaks or philosophy, or any other chain of single thoughts. For first it is a palpable fact of consciousness that the object of consciousness is complex. Take the simplest act of discrimination, for example. The Irishman who said he could tell two brothers apart when he saw them together, unwittingly hit the psychologic bull's-eye. For the only conceivable way of telling two things apart is by thinking them together. But the momentary me is more complex than this. There are, in the first place, a host of fainter ideas or suggestions of them, which the main idea drags up, attached to it, and secondly, there are the fading forms of previous ideas and the brightening forms of coming ones, side by side with the culminating thought of the moment. For it is no less a palpable fact that ideas take time to develop into distinctness, and even more time to fade again into oblivion. Dissolving views upon our cortical screen, the last grows ghostly as the next takes shape, and lingers some seconds ere it vanishes quite. It is this corona of past, present, and nascent thought, limning the central idea of the moment that gives that idea its setting, and us our sense of self.

As a proof of this, an idea of our own which came to us unhaloed, however brilliant it may have been, is often subsequently recognized so little for our own that at times we feel conscientious scruples about claiming it. Such self-abnegation fortunately, perhaps, is rare. For an assumption of probability induces us instantly to appropriate whatever has not upon it the stamp of another. Nor is there a more poignant chagrin than to awake suddenly to the knowledge, through some casually resurrected detail, that our yesterday's self-imputed epigram had been previously told us by Jones. Another's seal consists in those, often almost indescribable, concomitant details in which the foreign idea comes to us fringed, its setting in short. This differs entirely from the setting that surrounds our own self-suggested thoughts. At the time we heard the epigram, which we subsequently so sadly mistook, we were conscious not only of hearing *it*, but of *hearing* it; afterwards this acoustic aura faded out, and therefore when the idea reappeared it bore no identifying tag, and we insensibly took it for one of our own. For though our own thoughts come to us as a rule quite differently fringed by a halo of their own, they sometimes have little or none, and the in-

stinct of possession causes us to impute all
such to ourselves — until increasing exacti-
tude teaches us distrust.

VI.

Now of what do ideas consist? They
consist, apparently, of molecular motion. An
idea, in short, is a mode of motion ; another
form of that fundamental, seemingly protean
thing.

But to see this we must first be sure just
what we mean by an idea. Now we mean
in ordinary parlance by an idea a conscious
pulse of thought. A mere reflex action we
do not associate with any idea. We even
speak often of having acted from impulse as
opposed to having acted from thought, and
hold ourselves largely irresponsible in consequence. Now all such unconscious brain
action, whether it be so-called reflex action,
or so-called instinct or impulse, there is, in
the present state of our knowledge, little
difficulty in conceiving to be a mere mode of
motion from one end of the chain to the
other. Suppose, for example, I am walking
along the street, and an inadvertent gnat
runs full tilt into my eye. The eye instantly

closes, and proceeds to weep copiously, while still remaining tenaciously, much too tenaciously, shut. Indeed, I have considerable trouble in opening the eye enough to get the insect out. Here the collision of the insect starts motion in the nerves that convey their wave of it to specialized ganglia, from which it wakes other ganglia that send word down to the eyelid to close. And the stupid eyelid obeys its immediate message to my great annoyance. Now this seems a perfectly clear case of machinery, one that works inevitably and certainly. If I can manage to induce another gnat to repeat the thoughtlessness of his predecessor, the performance of my eye will be also perfectly reproduced. I recognize this action for a bit of machinery so thoroughly that I do not identify myself with it. On the contrary, I am annoyed at the stupidity of the eye in persisting so obstinately to stay closed when, if it would but open, I could soon get the insect out. In like manner, instinct and impulse, in their turn, start trains of automatic action. Indeed, all unconscious cerebration can be thus explained on general mechanical laws. In similarly explaining other brain processes, the difficulty comes in with consciousness.

Consciousness is still held by most people to be a noumenon or noumenal phenomenon; mind being conceived by them to be something quite apart from brain, and this in face of the self-evident concomitance of the two. Now when we scan this distinction for an underlying difference, we find it to be due solely to man's desire for distinction. To put it unflatteringly, it is nothing but part and parcel of our innate human snobbery.

Darwin's doctrine was held for many years by most religious folk to be impious, and is still so held by a few of them. It was thought to deny a special creator. What it really denied were special creatures. So far as God was concerned, all it did directly was to remove him to a proper height above his handicraft; it was man whom it treated with scant respect by linking him with the brutes. Darwin committed the unpardonable sin of recognizing his own poor relations. The justice of such recognition has now nearly universally been conceded, and to-day practically nobody disputes the essential kinship of all living things. But the snobbish instinct that opposed it still survives, as it is bound to survive so long as we remain

largely creatures of instinct. For under a
better name this instinct is nothing but a
subtler part of the instinct of self-preservation, the instinctive holding to all that makes
for our individuality and the like antagonism
to all that threatens it. Materially, this
prejudice in favor of ourselves is now conceded to be misleading; yet it still survives
immaterially, that is psychically, in our unnatural divorce between brain and mind. For
not to have them two makes us one with all
the rest of the universe. Whether we suppose mind to be matter or matter mind,
we become in either case part and parcel
of the material world; and so tenaciously,
though unconsciously, do we hold to our supposed superiority to the rest of the universe,
that we refuse to recognize the relationship.
We are very loath to admit that we are kin
to stocks and stones and other reputed sense-
less things. This is the gist of the whole
matter. Thought we deem to be something
grand, while chemical action strikes us as
ignoble; although the one is every whit as
inscrutably potent as the other. It is because we really know nothing about the essence of either that we dare decide so defi-

nitely between the evolutionary merits of
the two.

Incidentally it is somewhat amusing to notice how thoroughly irreligious this supposed
religious view is. For what warrant has
man to prescribe laws to an omnipotent creator and to turn up his human nose at one
mode of creative action as unworthy to be
used in his construction. The dualistic assumption thus carries with it, both scientifically and sentimentally, its own disproof.

The truth is that the only logical explanation of matter and mind is that the two are
one ; and that the life-principle of the whole
is some mode of motion. When we have,
as we say, an idea, what happens inside us
is probably something like this : the neural
current of molecular change passes up the
nerves, and through the ganglia reaches at
last the cortical cells and excites a change
there. Now the nerve-cells have been so
often thrown into this particular form of
wave-motion that they vibrate with great
ease. The nerves, in short, are good con-
ductors, and the current passes swiftly along
them, but when it reaches the cortical cells,
it finds a set of molecules which are not so

accustomed to this special change. The current encounters resistance, and in overcoming this resistance it causes the cells to glow. This white-heating of the cells we call consciousness. Consciousness, in short, is probably nerve-glow.

Now we know by experiment that the heat of the hemispheres rises while conscious processes are going on, and does not rise to the same degree when processes of more reflex action are taking place in them. Furthermore, we have reason to think that the molecular action of the cortical cells must be of the same nature as that which takes place in the nerves, since by mere repetition of the action the one develops into something indistinguishable from the other. For at each repetition of any brain action, consciousness of it grows less, till finally we cease to be conscious of it at all; that is to say, the molecular change occurs with ever-increasing ease till at last it comes to be performed quite automatically and quite unconsciously.

Phenomena of both normal and abnormal states of consciousness hint that this theory is correct, as I shall now try to make evident.

That an idea is a force that shows itself as a mode of motion is borne out, to begin with, by the fact that its action conforms to that of all the other forces we know, in being, first, inevitable, and secondly, impersonal. This, so long as we regard ideas only in bundles, as my mind or your mind, is not apparent, but becomes evident so soon as we analyze mind into its successive simple parts, ideas, and consider them.

Some years ago, Carpenter came across what he regarded as an astonishing abnormal mental phenomenon. It was this : that at times the mere thought of a bodily movement was able of its own instance actually to bring that movement about. Lotze improved upon this by showing that the phenomenon occurred with much more commonness than was supposed. Finally the discovery was made, scarcely second to any in this age of discoveries, that this startling phenomenon was no abnormality at all, but the normal function in all its primitive nudity ; that every motor-idea, that is, every idea of a bodily movement, instantly produces that movement when not inhibited by other ideas.

William James tells us that the instance
that first convinced him of this general law
was the way in which he eventually got up
of a morning.   In due course after waking,
the thought came to him, "I must get up."
But this idea instantly suggested the inad-
visability of doing so.   The bed was too
cosy, the world too cold.   So he lay where
he was.   How, then, did he ever get up?
Consciously, he never got up at all; the first
thing he knew, he was up.   He had fallen
into a revery upon the day's doings, when
suddenly the idea that he must lie there no
longer popped up again, and at that lucky
instant, before it could start objection, had
started him.

Introspection will soon yield any one
countless instances of the same thing; but
it is introspection of the second order of
difficulty.   One cannot simply stalk out into
his thought preserves and pot his instance;
the fugitive character of the action obliges
him to take it on the wing.   For to catch it
stationary, is, by its very nature, impossible.
So soon as one thinks about his thinking,
he is, *ipso facto*, engaged upon a different
thought, namely, the thought of thinking,

a very different thing from simply thinking the thought; and the second idea inhibits the action of the first. The only way to become aware of what one seeks is, by a process akin to the optical trick of detecting a very faint star, to look a little off it with the mind's eye. One has to play detective on one's self; by sly show of inattention, to fool one's self, as one would fool another into being unsuspiciously natural. He will then detect instances by the gross. All his impulsive actions will give him more or less complete examples of it. The expression "to go off at half cock" is nothing but an unappreciated recognition of these very things.

After thus recognizing it in one's self, he will perceive it in others. Any nervous man is a perfect museum of specimens. While he is listening to you, or even talking himself, his eye will fall upon a paper-cutter upon the table, and out goes his hand to play with it; or, a book strikes him as being misplaced, and he must needs set it right; or, he sees his pipe, and forthwith proceeds to fill it; and so forth and so on. Each new idea instantly produces in him its fatalistic effect.

The reason we are not directly conscious of this force of our ideas is that one idea rarely has free play. A second idea starts to act before the first has finished and more or less inhibits the first's action, thus complicating the problem. If motions generally were not complex, no science would be needed to unravel them.

So much for motor-ideas. But beside motor-ideas, there are other ideas not concerned with action at all, but with thoughts as such; ideo-ideas, we may call them. In James's matutinal experience, the idea of rising, instead of rousing him, roused first the idea of not doing so, by spontaneously calling up the consciousness of his cosiness, and this, doubtless, prompted the happy thought of a like snug inclosing of his last psychic find in some pithy phrase, and that brought up the subject of embalming generally, which reminded him that life was fleeting, whereupon it flashed upon him that he would better be up and doing, and up he got.

If thoughts did not thus run their own trains, we should be simple automata, void of memory, and incapable of reasoning; nature's puppets at sensation's string.

As one ideo-idea thus gives rise to another, so it may rouse a motor-idea which generates bodily movement, and the circle be complete. Some motion happens inevitably in every case, were it only the inevitable dissipation of its energy in the form of fatigue or general bodily excitement.

VII.

So much for the inevitable character of the action. The impersonality of it is, on scrutiny, no less apparent. For, personal as an idea seems to be in its manifestation, such association turns out to be purely fortuitous. Not only is an idea competent quite alone to institute another idea or a bodily movement in the man himself, — it will do precisely the same in another person. There are all degrees of such inter-individual action, from the most partial persuasion to the most complete control. Its most startling examples are afforded by hypnotic subjects, who, at a word from the operator, act with even more than normal energy. But the same effect, less extravagantly accomplished, may be witnessed in every-day life. In certain heavy or preoccupied states of mind, a person will obey, automatically, a word from another, to be astonished the next instant at having done so.

A like effect, in a partial form, is taking place between all of us all the time. The so-called personality of a man is nothing but the inter-individual action of his ideas upon other people. In its least complicated forms we are quite aware that it is merely the idea that acts, while the action is as often unconscious as conscious. Insensibly a man finds himself reproducing the ideas of those about him. Especially is this the case where fundamental sympathy exists between him and his causative, and preëminently so when that person is the woman he loves. At times he startles himself by tones and gestures which he recognizes as hers, and then glows all over at the reflection. With corresponding annoyance will he catch himself reproducing the tricks of manner of some one he cordially despises. In the one case, the background ideas help as a mordant to set the dye; in the other, the ideas themselves prove catching enough.

The fact is, that ideas are as catching as scarlet fever. We can no more escape hav-

ing them enter our minds than we can escape
having material germs enter our bodies. And
the only preventive against instant and indiscriminate imitation is constitutional mental
energy. For, in normal states, the mind
lies open to any action from without; any
foreign idea finds instant access through the
usual sensational channels, and at once proceeds to work, the possibly baleful effects to
the host of such indiscriminate hospitality
being tempered by the simple choking upon
the premises of disagreeable outsiders after
admission. The measure of success which
the intruder achieves is determined by the
amount of opposition it arouses. The more
vacuous the host, the more the stranger has
his own sweet way. In hypnotic subjects,
where the mind is otherwise blank, any idea,
if once introduced, receives actually more
honor than it is accustomed to at home. A
consideration, this, of the proverbial prophet
kind, paralleled by the greater respect a
policeman inspires in small boys who are
unacquainted with him, or by the way in
which a newspaper's editorials impress a
simple public for their apparent impersonality. For the idea of another's personality

instinctively rouses opposition; while, contrariwise, that of one's own inspires one's self
with distrust, so essentially modest is man.
But with the hypnotized, personality in both
phases lies dormant. For, in the hypnotized
mind, when abandoned to its own devices,
activity is nil. Hypnotic subjects, when left
to themselves, and asked of what they are
thinking, usually reply: "Of nothing."

VIII.

Ideo-ideal activity is a higher and later
stage in the progress of mind evolution than
motor - ideal action ; response to objective
stimuli preceding the subjective action of
the mind upon itself, as the development
from amœba to man testifies. Although the
protozoön doubtless has consciousness of a
rudimentary sort, by which he differentiates
his own absorbing person from his no less
engrossing food, his brain is his belly, and
his one idea a kind of conscious digestion.
His mind is a process of nervous pepsia,
which, thanks to evolution, has unfortunately
become nervous dyspepsia in such men as let
their thoughts follow the same line ; so true
is it that what is one creature's meat proves

another's poison. As we rise in the scale of animal life we find more and more complicated reaction upon stimuli from without; then, finally, rudimentary reasoning. But even animals gifted with this last capacity usually prefer to keep their minds as empty as possible. The idyllic stupefaction of the cow in the stall, or of the dog upon the hearth-rug, betrays the vacuity which is theirs so much of the time, and into which they contentedly fall when not pricked to action by sensational spur. This beatific inanity of the brutes is close of kin to the Buddhist height of holiness, — Nirvana.

When we come to man we find that even that so-called reasoning animal thinks as little as he may until pretty well up in the line of development. He is for the most part content to let circumstances pull the sensational trigger and make snap-shots at life. Even when he takes to thinking, it is thinking for things' sake that he usually indulges in. Thinking for thinking's sake is the employment of the highest few.

As a side light upon this we notice how, when a person becomes weak from some drain upon the system, he grows less and less self-controlled and more and more automatic to both sensations and foreign suggestions.

Now clearly the amount of inly initiated activity measures the individuality of the man. For chance of change is greatly increased if, in addition to outer impressive diversity, inner diversity have a hand in the matter. The more individual a man already, the more individual is he bound to become, and as the rate of change depends on the change already effected, individuals must grow ever logarithmically apart. Marriage may retard this, but it may also accelerate it; and the last is undoubtedly its normal result. Otherwise, why has nature departed, in the propagation of the species, from the good old protoplasmic practice of identical fission.

Less self and greater facility in becoming another, impersonality and proneness to possession, should therefore be found together. And it is to be noticed that as development proceeds, nature gives with the gift of selfhood the means of guarding it. For the same increase of mental activity that constitutes the increased individuality enables the individual to maintain that individuality from disastrous attack and destruction.

IX.

Before applying these principles to an explanation of the trance, let us see whether they explain that seeming inexplicability, the uncommon impersonality of the Japanese mind. If a lesser mental activity be the cause of a less differentiated individuality, signs of that lesser activity should otherwise be patent. Now when we look for them we find such signs to be numerous.

As a friend of mine once put it epigrammatically in the heat of the moment, a Japanese does not think. Allowing for pardonable exaggeration due the occasion, he really hit their state of mind on the head. Specific evidence of the fact confronts one at every turn.

One may, if he will, begin at the top, with lack of originality leading off the list, but instead of beginning at the top, he may as well begin at the bottom and mark the absence of reasoning there.

If in any western land you hail a cab and jump in without a word, the cab-driver before setting out will ask you where you wish to be taken. Indeed, this seems so self-evident a preliminary to driving you anywhere at all, that it sounds supererogatory to chronicle it. But attempt the same thing in Japan. At any of the treaty ports jump into a jinrikisha as if in a hurry, and say nothing. Five to two off goes your man at a dog-trot for a couple of hundred yards; then he suddenly slackens, stops, turns, and to his surprise, though not yours, inquires where you wish to be taken. Not till then did the idea strike him that he did not know his destination. He had at first acted on the impulse your jumping into the jinrikisha had given him, to go; the afterthought of whither had not occurred to him. His first idea had instantly translated itself into action before it could wake a second thought.

Instances of this in more complicated form are to be met with, of course, the world over. Witness the adventure of the shop-girl to whom darts in through the door an urchin with the announcement: " Marm ! your little boy has just been run over in the street !" The poor shop-girl drops everything, rushes from behind the counter, bolts out of the door, and gets a couple of steps down the sidewalk, when she suddenly stops, throws back her head, and with a laugh blurts out: "What a fool I am! I have n't any little boy! I'm not even married!" The rascally urchin had sprung his mischievously explosive idea by hinging it upon the great instinct of maternity latent in every woman, and the idea had passed into the act before the rest of the brain was roused to inhibit the impulse.

The next occasion afforded the stranger of remarking the Japanese want of reasoning will wait upon him the moment he gets his eyes open to the numberless opportunities he offers the natives to cheat him; opportunities of which they naturally avail themselves, a kind Providence having provided strangers for that special purpose. But he will find some slight compensation for all he may be eased of by noting the inadequate manner in which Providence, doubtless with an eye to humor, has fitted these folk to such god-given avocation. For the essence of successful deceit lies in the apparent truthfulness of the false. The one should be a good counterfeit presentment of the other; otherwise it is useless. To carry conviction, a story must be above conviction itself. For the art of lying consists in consistency. The Autocrat's dictum, "Be not consistent, but be simply true," if reversed, would make a good motto for lying, "Be not true, but be simply consistent." Inasmuch, therefore, as facts conspire against the liar, it is the part of a long-headed man to think out his whole story in advance. But this these brachycephalic people never do. When caught and arraigned, a non-committal "Don't know" keeps their counsel, and lack of self-consciousness keeps their face. But so soon as ever·they adventure themselves upon a story, which sooner or later is bound to happen, they are gone. Their tale never holds together, because never carefully concocted beforehand to do so. It is suggested piecemeal on the spur of the moment, and consequently comes apart as easily as it was put together. One's facile satisfaction at thus exposing the culprit is marred only by the culprit's entire lack of discomfiture upon exposure.

But daily intercourse with these people will furnish many pleasanter instances of the same artistic thoughtlessness. Servants will follow with most exemplary fidelity any routine set them, and then become hopelessly lost when occasion arises that calls for reasoning; occasion consequent not upon foreign semi-domesticated ideas, but upon ones of broadly human intent. For that European customs should be taken topsyturvy is matter of course. For your untutored "boy" to put the buttons in your shirt regularly outside-in every morning, or to hand you your waistcoat invariably inside-out, is simply the inevitable, if sad, consequence of generally antipodal habits. But pure forgetfulness of a duty and subsequent instant unassumed contrition at sight of its object, a not uncommon episode in far-eastern housekeeping, knows no particular country, and yet seems peculiarly at home in Japan; the pathetic repentance turning the tragedy of your wrath into its own farce.

Now when we rise from these daily discoveries to a more bird's-eye view of the Japanese character, we observe the same quality of mind otherwise patent. In the first place, the lack of originality of the Japanese is very striking after one has got over one's first dazzle at strange antipodal sights. The student finds that what he at first took without question for the product of home construction, in truth came originally from abroad. They were adopted, and then adapted, these delightful ways of doing things. Modification of foreign motif, modification always artistic, and at times delightfully ingenious, marks the extent of Japanese originality. Now absence of originality is but another term for absence of innate activity of mind. For the one is father to the other. But when energy to coruscate is lacking, action continues in the easier round of routine. Only in more evolved minds do ideas bud in profusion, and they do so just in proportion to the degree of development of the mind. So that a superior mind is not only ahead in the race, but is advancing at a proportionally rapid rate; a fact which offers small consolation to those who happen already to be behindhand.

A general incapacity for abstract ideas is another marked trait of the Japanese mind. This, joined to a limited reasoning power, has made would-be far-eastern science as funny as far-eastern art is fine. Before the nation went to Dame Europe's school, its criticism

was comic. Far-oriental treatises read ex-
cellently well in spots, from such antipodal
point of view; the very dry desert of thought
being occasionally relieved by unintentional
oases of humor. The commentators give us
admirable instances of this : one of them
gravely explaining Shintō's lack of a moral
code by the conclusive statement that only
immoral people need moral laws ; while
another in all seriousness derives *neko*, a
cat, by a kind of protoplasmic fission and
subsequent amalgamation from the first syl-
lables of *nezumi konomo*, words which translated, signify " fond of rats," which is much
as if one should assert " poet " to have been
evolved by a sort of shorthand from " potential etymology."

Indirect evidence of the same lack of ideal
activity is shown by the uncommon imita-
tiveness of the race. For to have a foreign
idea act with the imperative instancy observable in Japan argues a dearth of native
incumbents to dispute it possession. You
shall soon be given plenty of instances of
this proclivity, of a personal nature. Indeed,
this sincerest kind of flattery eventually
grows just a trifle flat from mere excess of

expression. It begins at home and spreads out into the farthest suburbs of your polite acquaintance. You begin to be aware that you are setting the fashion in things below as well as upon the surface. Not only do hats, the facsimile of your own last purchase, suddenly make their appearance upon the heads of your friends, but even your momentary tastes wake instant echo in the crania underneath. " It is very odd," one of my very nicest far-eastern familiars was never tired of saying to me as he suited the action to the word, "how I like whatever you like." This will sound of course like the simple quintescence of exquisite far-oriental politeness. But observation will show you that it is in truth something deeper. You will be convinced of the genuineness of the appreciation after you have been sufficiently its victim.

As for your household, your peculiarities diffuse themselves subtly through it to be reproduced some fine morning in surprisingly incongruous settings. Your " boy," so soon as ever he contrives to get into the coveted foreign garb, appears before you strangely appareled, not simply in reproductions of your habiliments, but clothed upon with your mannerisms and fitted with your very gait; his evident innocence of intent alone convincing you that this is not all some put-up caricature. Never had you full conception of how peculiar your peculiarities were till you saw them donned by another. Indeed, the reproduction of yourself is carried so far that from being putative father of your whole household by patriarchal custom, you begin to question whether in some antipodally *ex post facto* fashion you have not become its father in fact.

Lastly, the decorous demeanor of the whole nation betrays the lack of mental activity beneath. For it is not rules that make the character, but character that makes the rules. No energetic mind could be bound by so exquisitely exacting an etiquette. It must inevitably kick over the traces now and then till little or nothing of them were left. This a Japanese not only does not do, save as motived to foreign ways, but left to himself would have no desire to do. The stately quietism of all classes of old Japan is due, not to forms that make for tranquillity, but to that innate tranquillity of mind that

fashioned the forms.   Among this stately
people there is less activity of mind needing
constantly to be curbed,   It shows itself before long-continued habit can have set its
seal upon the man himself.   He inherits it
with the rest of his constitution.   In Japan
the very babies are unconscionably good.

X.

We now come to a consideration of the
trance.   To this sleep and dreams may make
a fitting word of introduction.   For the phenomenon of sleep and dreams are kin enough
to those of the trance state to entitle this
night side of our nature to be called the
normal trance.

There is a curious rhythm in our conscious
life of which both the occasion and the cause
is cosmic.   Our spiritual life, in contradis-
tinction to our bodily existence, is made up
of disconnected bits, whose conditioning is
emphatically of the earth, earthy.   It is indeed worth noting, that our minds should
thus in a sense be more mortal than our
bodies.   For once during every rotation of
the earth consciousness is snuffed out like
the candle we extinguish to help us to the

act; and though some men be so strong that they can sit up all night occasionally, they cannot continue to do so for many nights together.

This nightly good-by to self and surroundings would certainly prove startling were it a thought more rare. As it is, so little are we disturbed at the idea of it that we actually assist at our own apparent annihilation. We not only put ourselves to bed, but usually to sleep every night. We help nature close our eyes, and compose what is left of our minds to absolute inaction. To a certain extent we thus hypnotize ourselves nightly. Indeed, as our minds grow less active with years, some of us find no difficulty in performing this feat in the daytime.

All of which shows that the force which runs the brain machinery is regularly exhausted by action, and has to be as regularly recruited by rest. For that the force has the power to store itself up again is proved by the fact that we ever wake.

So soon as mental activity has thus been reduced to a minimum, and we are sound asleep, the potential begins to rise. Debarred from flowing, the stream of thought proceeds to accumulate a head for the next day. And in this manner the potential continues to rise till it has reached so high a point that a tap from some sensational stimulus suffices to start action once more, and we wake. Doubtless we should eventually wake of our own motion if we lay in a sensational vacuum. Practically this event rarely happens, because sensations of some sort or other are always knocking at our mind's door. But a less and less obstreperous one suffices to call us as time wears on. A knock that would have passed unnoticed in the middle of the night easily rouses us in the morning. Once started, the machinery is not long in getting into full swing.

At least this is what happens in the perfectly balanced mind, that character so comfortable to himself, and so disappointing to his more enthusiastic fellows. In ideal equipoise the whole mental energy, potential or actual, ceases approximately together, and starts again together. All of us, however, have probably been abnormal enough at times to have dreamed dreams. Now dreams are interesting things; interesting not only for what they show us, but far more interesting for what they intrinsically are. For they are twilights of thought, the dawn glimmerings of inner light before that be risen above the horizon of full sensibility. This half-way state of mind throws not a little light on clearer states of consciousness by comparison.

Dreams betray a midway condition of mental activity, where action has reached the point of conscious internal, but not yet of conscious external, discharge. Our dream-life takes place in an ideal world within, upon which any outer sensation is permitted to enter only under some disguise. Whence the visitant came we are not aware, for we only take cognizance of it after it has donned a transformation to suit the mental scene it finds there. Our body may perchance turn over in bed, but in consequence we gracefully float from the top of a precipice to the bottom, and find ourselves unharmed.

The next peculiarity idiosyncratic of dreams consists in their seemingly irrational irrationality. In our dreams the most unlikely people do the most impossible things, in the most easy, credible manner. A thread of apparent causation connects one act with the next; and the phantasmagoria rolls cheerfully on, breaking all the dramatic unities in its passage, in the most natural way in the world.   In our deeper dream states the whole seems real; it is only in our less dense ones that wonder begins to mingle with the show, as a looker-on, who doubts without exactly disbelieving.   We have a dim sense that all is not right without quite realizing that anything is wrong.

Now the explanation of this seems to be that in dreams our thread of thought is comparatively fringeless.   Motion in the mind is confined largely to one line, a very crooked line, but a simple one.   As the current passes along, each idea starts the next, the one most easily associated with it at the moment, without rousing much in the way of side ideas to play critic to its creations and throw unpleasant doubts upon its credibility.

Such action as this shows that the whole brain is not yet roused to that pitch of potential where motion takes place with normal ease.   The current encounters inertia in its passage, and in place of spreading into side tracts is confined to the easiest path of discharge. But that there should be any current at all proves that some part of the brain has risen to the necessary pitch of possibility before the rest of it. Now what part has done so, and why?

If we consider the motifs of our dreams we shall find them, when not directly traceable to boiled lobster, to be due to the play either of very habitual ideas or of ideas that had last preoccupied us before we fell asleep. The lover dreams of his mistress, the merchant of his transactions, the scientist of his discoveries. Each dreams after his kind, because the habitual idea is in action so much of the time that its train of cells has become specially permeable to the current and vibrates upon slight provocation. For the same reason, the idea that preoccupied us before we fell asleep is the one which, from having just been in action, is easiest set in action again.

The motion once started passes out along those associated channels which, under the then conditions, offer least resistance to its passage. But as the brain, as a whole, is still sluggishly inert, the current rouses no side motion to speak of in the process.

The result is rather a lightning-like zigzag through the mind than a general illumination. This accounts for what we call inconsequently enough the inconsequence of dreams. For dream inconsequence really means too absolute ideal consequence. Each idea fires the next, and only the next. That we believe everything that comes along, and see nothing odd in so doing, shows that side considerations are not roused. For it is our side-thoughts that cause us to comment upon our leading ones. In dreams we are for the moment men of one idea, with the usual monomaniacal result. Purely sensational starting-points, *à la* lobster, rouse in the same way such simple dream trains that, destitute of their accustomed fringe, we fail to recognize them for the sensations they are.

In our deeper dreams we have not even those adumbrations of other thoughts which so commonly give us ghostly warnings in our waking state. This makes us fall easy dupes to the deception. For where only one idea exists it must inevitably seem true for want of possible contradiction. It simply *is* till it is contradicted. As we get nearer the waking point, the inertia grows less till side motion starts and summons obscure shapes of thoughts to hint dimly at delusion.

This theory as to what consciousness is affords explanation of another peculiarity about dreams which seems at first to defy comprehension, and certainly is inexplicable on the ordinary dualistic theories of the thing — their vividness. It is matter of every-day notoriety that dreams are often extremely vivid, and commonly exceed in vividness like events of waking life. That they quickly fade out does not detract from the fact of their vividness at the time of their occurrence. Now the dualistic theories that consciousness is a thing apart from brain processes, its directing power, according to the spiritualists, and its complaisant handmaid, according to the materialists, neither of them can account for this. For if consciousness be, as William James would have it, a loader of vice in the game of life, she shows herself here to be an utterly unprincipled gambler ; inasmuch as in dreams she actively abets delusions in the most seemingly ingenuous manner, and *pro tanto* makes us go mad. Nor, on the other hand, can consciousness be mere concomitant of brain processes, for if we have here simply a case of increased current, why is not the rest of the brain roused, and if we have not a case of it, why are the ideas that are roused more vivid? That the dream current might occasionally be stronger than a waking one is possible, but that our dreams should usually seem more vivid than our every-day waking experiences, which is certainly the case, is to credit nature with a strange lack of economy in the running of our psychic affairs.

But there is a worse dilemma yet for the dualists. They stand confronted by this question: Why should consciousness be present as markedly both when we have reason to suspect the current to be strong, in times of passionate excitement, as when we have reason to believe it weak, in times of torpor? For of both these phenomena we have instances. In times of excitement, we strangely recall forgotten things; and so we do in times the opposite of excited. Extremes here emphatically meet.

But if consciousness be the effect of brain

friction, the heat, as it were, evolved by partial stoppage of the current, we see at once that this should develop both when the current is increased, the resistance remaining the same, and when the resistance is increased, the current continuing as before. We ought, therefore, in dreams, to find great vividness of impression side by side with no impression at all; which is just what we do find. Though the stream of thought in dream-states has probably less head to it, the increased resistance enables it to produce as much commotion. We may parallel the action by that of an electric current, which, when great, will make even a conductor of slight resistance glow, and when feeble, will make one of great resistance do the same. At present, this is merely a suggestive analogy; but it may turn out truer than we imagine.

The theory here advanced explains, therefore, the at first strange anomaly, that both an unusually strong current and an usually feeble one may alike produce an unusually vivid consciousness. For vividness follows either an increase in the current or an increase in the resistance.

Conditions of brain torpor other than dream-states display similar phenomena. For a general tiring of the brain is not the only way, as we know, of bringing brain torpor about. Many drugs will do it, probably by directly numbing the molecules of the cortical cells. Chloroform, laughing-gas, flowers at a funeral, will all temporarily take a man out of the world — to say nothing of the every-day effect of wine. But side by side with the general torpor these things induce, goes a heightened consciousness along particular lines, if it be no more than a consciousness of one's emotions. This chiaroscuro of consciousness has all the unreal reality of the lights and shadows thrown by a carbon point. Opium, for example, is delectable, not more for the peculiar ideas it gives a man than for the poignancy of them. And we all know, by observation, at least, how loving or quarrelsome men grow in proportion as they grow unreasonable, under the influence of wine.

Some dreams we remember after waking. If we did not do so, to a minimal extent at least, we should not know that we had ever had them. Possibly, therefore, some vanish with the fashioning, or if afterward partially recalled, pass unrecognized for strange, inexplicable impressions. Those that we do remember we shall find are hinged on to our waking life by the continuance of an outer sensation common in part to both states. Were it not for such link, it would be mere haphazard if we struck them again. For their train of association is not one likely to recur under normal conditions.

XI.

But besides the daily running down of the whole brain machinery to sleep, due to the using up of the potential energy of the cells, or its slowing down artificially through the effect of certain drugs, it is possible to bring brain action to a dead point by a simple exercise of will. By shutting one's bodily eyes, or by keeping them fixed upon some uninteresting thing, while at the same time shutting one's mind's eye, or keeping it similarly fixed upon some insipid thought, brain activity may be brought to a strangely sudden stand-still. It is by this portal that the subject passes into the trance state.

Of trances, we may distinguish two kinds:

the hypnotic trance, and the possession trance. The two differ markedly, both in their physical and in their psychic symptoms; while at the same time bearing a strong family resemblance to each other. To an unsympathetic bystander, the subject of the one seems an idiotic automaton, while the subject of the other appears raving mad. We will take up the hypnotic variety first.

To an outsider nothing marks that critical point when the subject's statuesque immovability passes from the voluntary into the involuntary state. It simply was the one and is the other; a passing over as indistinguishable as the traveler's crossing the line, known only by the change of pole round which all things seem to turn.

If left alone the subject remains in his mummified state till at last he comes to of himself. If, however, while in the midst of it he be addressed by the operator, instantly certain striking phenomena follow. Out of a lethargy seemingly too deep for any stim s to stir, he suddenly responds to the operator's word with the instantaneity of mechanism. He not only wakes to life again, but as soon appears to a most peculiar phase of it. For though he responds to the hypnotist as if he had been simply waiting to do so, his immediate response made, he sinks back once more into passivity. His action would seem merely the effect of momentum impressed from without ; as if the hypnotist had given his mental machinery a shove which had carried him a certain distance, and whose impetus had then been gradually dissipated by the friction of the parts. This momentum gone, he becomes as before — inert. He possesses apparently no initiative of his own.

While the foreign momentum lasts he acts with a perfection of performance realized in some machines, but not by conscious man. What he does he does far better than the best of which he is capable in his normal state. And he hesitates at little or nothing. His action is kin to the somnambulists who will walk on ridge-poles and the edges of precipices without fear and without falling; only that whereas the sleep-walker does so of his own motion, the hypnotic subject does so at the suggestion of another. And the hint needed to start him is at times inconceivably slight. What a bystander on the alert quite fails to notice, the hypnotic subject, to all appearance sunk in stupor, perceives and acts upon at once.

Side by side in the hypnotized with such trigger-like action toward his hypnotist goes in the initial cases an utter deadness to everything and everybody else. For him nothing exists but his hypnotizer. Through this person's fiat, and only through it, may anything enter the subject's world. At a word from this man other things and other people are perceived, either when directly pointed out or when indirectly involved in the execution of the suggestion itself. They can also be made to remain incognito by the same process. Still further, imaginary things can be made to seem real to the subject; their non-existence in fact forming no bar to their existence in his conscious-ness. If the operator says they exist, for him they do exist. In the full hypnotic state this is no mere nominal acquiescence, for the subject will go on to detail their characteristics and retail their subsequent actions without further prompting, showing that to him they are thorough-going realities.

Now this abnormal action of the mind in

the trance state seems most explicable as follows. By the enforced inaction or induced tiring of the brain cells in action at the time of lapsing into unconsciousness, all activity in those cells ceases, while the rest of the brain, being inactive already and being shut off from outward stimulus, remains inert. Furthermore, the stopping of action in the cells acting at the time seems to bring the whole brain to the dead-point; which is logical since apparently it is only these cells that are vibrating at the moment. After the stoppage a time is necessary to raise the potential to the point of overcoming the inertia. Now if all the cells were at the same potential, this state of lethargy would continue till the whole brain eventually woke up. But the cells are not all at the same initial potential; some are nearer the activity point than others. Especially are two kinds of cells at a higher potential than their fellows : those connected with habitual ideas and those connected with ideas peculiarly poignant at the time. It is to the awaking to action of one of this latter class while yet the rest of the brain still stays torpid that the peculiar phenomena of the hypnotic trance are probably due. The initiation idea thus resurrected is the idea in the subject's mind that the operator will have a certain indefinite but all-effective power over him when he shall have lapsed into the trance. It is not necessary that this impression should reach the level of full belief; a bare fear that he may be thus controlled is enough. That the mere idea of it should be present to the person is all that is necessary. Now such idea is the last poignant idea in the subject's mind before he composes himself for the trance. Consequently, after he has entered the trance state it is this idea that is nearest the point of passing over into action and that, as the whole potential rises, passes over first. Thus it is the idea which the subject carries with him into the trance that becomes the dominant idea of the trance itself.

Now the fact that this idea alone is at the necessary potential to be stirred explains the insentience of the brain to all other stimuli. The brain cells connected with it alone are in a condition to be affected from without; all others are affected only as they are connected with them. Nor are these secondary ones as easily stirred by the first as they would be in normal life. The brain cells are all abnormally torpid. In consequence, as the motion passes along them very little side action is roused, and, as it is the ramifying side-thoughts that make comparison possible and constitute judgment, the hypnotic subject sees no incongruity in his actions and performs each with a self-abandonment to it that insures a perfection of performance unattainable in his complex normal state of mind.

The force of the habitual ideas makes itself felt by hindering and even preventing the performance of a suggested idea that conflicts with the subject's character. Indeed, other things equal, the grooves of temperament are followed by the train of thought. Less force is necessary to set them in motion. Not only is the subject's action under a suggested idea in keeping with his character, but it is impossible to get him to do things which are abhorrent to it. To induce a subject who is not essentially depraved to commit murder, for example, is practically beyond even the operator's power.

We have parallels to such semi-spontaneity of action of an habitual idea in every-day life. In a preoccupied state of mind we engage upon some act only to wake to find ourselves doing not the thing we started to do, but the habitual one. I knew a man who, having come home late and gone up-stairs to dress for a ball, which he proceeded to do mechanically, suddenly found himself in bed. The preparatory taking off of his clothes had started the machinery, which, in default of supervision, had run then itself and fatally done the habitual thing.

Of peculiarly poignant ideas we all know countless examples of the persistent manner in which they turn up in season and out of it. They are forever showing their faces amid the ever - changing crowd of other thoughts.

That the hypnotic subject seems to be on the lookout for everything connected with his hypnotizer is of course a purely uncon-scious one. It is paralleled in waking life by the exceeding sensitiveness of any acute idea to anything connected with itself. The lover, the politician, the burglar, are alive to actions related to their quest which to other mortals would pass unnoticed. We all catch our own name uttered in a conversation to all the rest of which we have been apparently quite oblivious. The exceeding sensibility of the entranced to the acts of the operator, joined to absolute insentience, so far as appears, to irrelevant matter, need not surprise us, since we are all hourly doing the same thing. It is only the degree of completeness with which it is done that differs sufficiently to startle us.

The relative sensibility of the hypnotized toward his hypnotizer, side by side with his complete insensibility toward all else, may thus be accounted for; but there is a further exhibition of sensibility that he shows which is as startling as it is inexplicable on the generally received theories of the subject. This is the surprising vividness of his consciousness of things of which he comes to have any consciousness at all. We have seen an adumbration of this in dreams, but in the case of the hypnotized it fairly rises into the region of the marvelous. Like dreams, it is evidenced by the general vivid character of the subject's experiences, but unlike them it is further borne direct witness to by mental acts so out of every-day experience as to lead hastily credulous persons to attribute them to some sort of supernatural power. For the hypnotic subject will display an amount of knowledge of which in his normal state he is known not to possess even the rudiments. Sometimes his apparently supernatural insight can be traced to the resurrection of memories faint at the time of their experiencing and long since lapsed; but sometimes it is due to the actual *ex post facto* creation of consciousness out of brain processes of which there was no consciousness at the time of their occurrence.

Now our present theory, whatever its merits or demerits may be, is at least able to give an explanation of this phenomenon. If consciousness be nerve-glow, a local molecular change of the cells due to a forced arrest of the neural current from temporary or permanent impermeability of path, it is precisely in the generally torpid brain of the hypnotic subject that it should be most acute. That his brain generally is torpid is shown by the fact that action does not spontaneously take place in it. When, however, a current is induced from the only starting-

point possible, the suggestion of the operator, and turned into the desired channel, it
traverses a path whose resistance is much
above the normal. Instead, therefore, of
gliding rapidly along, it soon expends itself
in overcoming the friction it meets, causing
in the process a glow of the successive cells
which we call consciousness. The current
tends, of course, to make the molecules of
the cells vibrate as they did before rather
than in some perfectly new combination, but
it finds unwonted difficulty in making them
vibrate at all. The result is that the old
combination of cell action is resurrected
with accompaniment of consciousness ; that
is, we have an idea where before we had only
its latent possibility. Whether this be the
revival of a lapsed memory, or the evoking
of an actual bit of brand-new consciousness,
is mere question of degree. The greater
the resistance, short of stopping the current,
the greater the current's, so to speak, creative power.

That this is due to the increased resistance, and not to an hypothetically increased
current, is further evident on considering the
alternative. For if the current were greater

than under normal conditions would be the case, it should both continue longer and rouse greater side action along its course. But, as we know, it does the contrary of both these suppositions. It speedily expends itself, and starts next to no side-thoughts in the process. It thus completely negatives an imputation of increased force.

Another general phenomenon of hypnosis proves the same relation of increased resistance to increased consciousness. As is well known, the events of the subject's normal life are both possible of recall and spontaneously remembered in the hypnotic state; while, contrariwise, the hypnotic life is entirely hid from the man's normal consciousness. Now this fact, instead of implying greater powers in the hypnotic state, as superficially viewed it seems to do, implies exactly the opposite. It is indeed but a more general instance of what we have just considered. For the permeability of a path depends, *cæteris paribus*, on the number of times it has been traversed. Now the hypnotic or possession paths, having been comparately little used, are relatively less permeable than the normal ones. Consequently an hypnotic path is not likely to be entered in the waking state, the current preferring its more habitual routes. Even if the hypnotic idea should reappear, it would probably fail of recognition in the broad glare of the normal state, since in the twilight of the trance its associations were too few and feeble to give it fringe enough for identification. For like reasons, even suggestion will fail to resurrect hypnotic ideas, or identify them if resurrected. The normal ideas, on the contrary, can be recalled in the hypnotic state, because, unless blocked by suggestion, their paths are the most permeable paths there. Consequently that the hypnotic life can be made to include the waking one, while reversely the waking life cannot be made to include the hypnotic one, instead of being proof of greater powers in the latter, is simply proof of less permeability of path.

XII.

From hypnotic trances we now pass to possession ones.

So far as the subject is aware, the portal to both is the same. In a quite unconsciously similar manner to that purposely taken by the hypnotic subject, the person to be possessed either shuts his eyes or keeps them fixed, while at the same time he fixes his thought on nothing. If he thus properly focuses both kinds of attention, he soon goes off.

In spite, however, of the apparent sameness of method employed in both cases, the subject's symptoms as he lapses into his trance, and his subsequent actions in it, differ radically in the two.

A throe marks the entrance into the possession trance, and a suppressed quiver accompanies it throughout ; the hypnotic trance is entered imperceptibly, and the subject continues apathetic till instigated to action by a word or sign from the operator. Perhaps the most peculiar physical feature of the possession trance is the rolled-up condition of the eyeballs, so rolled up that the iris is half out of sight. This position they hold throughout the trance, and the eye never winks, though the eyelids are constantly twitching. For the rest, their names sufficiently describe the two states, — the one subject seeming in truth possessed by a devil, while the other, if left alone, appearing to sleep as he stands. It requires, indeed, no faith in the onlooker to see in the one an alien spirit acting and speaking through the man. Such is the instant natural inference from his looks and behavior. On the other hand, the hypnotic subject can hardly be said to have either looks or behavior till commanded to have them to order by the hypnotist.

The one subject thus acts from spontaneous impulse; the other only of derivative accord. The next point of dissimilarity is that the sense of self differs entirely in the two. The possessed believes himself to be another person, the possessing spirit. The hypnotized continues to think himself himself unless told by the hypnotist that he is some one else, upon which he promptly conceives himself that other person.

In both trances such sensations only as are compatible with the hypothesis entertained by the entranced are allowed to enter consciousness. These are perceived with abnormal alacrity, so abnormal as to have suggested a possible explanation of clairvoyance. All irrelevant sensations are simply ignored. It is as if telegrams were constantly arriving to a man from all parts of the world, and he should leave all but those from Chili unopened on his desk. That the senses and the lower centres do their work perfectly, and that it is in the hemispheres that the messages are laid aside unscanned, is proved clearly by hypnotic experiments. For in certain cases the subject can be shown to have carefully distinguished two things first, in order subsequently to ignore one of them. These last sensations may afterward be recovered.

The same thing occurs in the case of the possessed. Violent sensations unconnected with the spirit of the trance, and even wounds inflicted in it, pass unnoticed. Pins stuck into the man are not felt by the god at all, though the pain of the prick continues sharp enough to be very disagreeably felt by the man on coming back again to himself. Yet when he does thus become aware of it he remains quite unable to assign its cause. On the other hand, sensations appropriate to the god may almost be said to be divined rather than ordinarily perceived, so alert to them is the entranced.

In neither trance, under natural, that is,

unsuggested, conditions, does the man remember anything of what happened in the
trance after he has waked up. In the case
of the hypnotic trance, a suggestion by the
operator during the trance that he shall remember it afterwards, will enable him to do
so. As to the possession trance, I am not
aware that it is ever remembered in the
waking state, though I believe this could be
done. Certainly it is not done in Japan.
The man knows nothing of the god.

Discontinuous, however, as the trance consciousness is from the normal one, in each
kind of trances its own consciousness is
continuous. The hypnotic subject remembers in subsequent trances what happened
in former ones. So does the god. Some
curious details of this I shall consider pres-
ently.

Agreeing thus as the two kinds of trances
do in so many respects, it becomes all the
more singular that they should differ so in
others, entered, as they both seemed to be,
by the same gate. In what, then, does the
difference consist? It consists, so I conceive, in the idea that dominates the trance.

To explain it, we must look a little back

of the immediate phenomena, for it is the power behind the throne of thought that does the business. Now in both trances the general state of the brain is the same. In both it is as a whole torpid, and in both action eventually takes place along certain isolated lines. The idea that first reaches sufficient potential to respond to an outside stimulus, or to stir of itself, is the idea that acts. This idea is the dominant idea of the trance.

We have followed this out in the case of the hypnotic trance. We shall now see that it applies equally to the possession trance, and that the intrinsic differences in the dominant idea of each account for the different phenomena.

Let us see what the dominant idea in each case is. The hypnotic subject enters the deadening processes leading to the trance with the idea — more or less definite, from a full belief to a bare fear — that in the coming trance the hypnotizer will have an irresistible power over him. That he will then lose his identity, will cease to be himself, is no part of this thought, except as unconsciously included in the power the operator may be able to exert. The person to be possessed, on the other hand, enters his trance under the firm conviction that he is about to become the god or the devil, or whatever else the possessing spirit is to be.

Now each of these ideas proves exponent of what happens in their respective trances. In the one trance, the subject acts like a mind-mechanism worked at the will of the operator; in the other, he acts, as the community considers, like a god.

That this is due to the dominant idea rising first to potential possibility, is more or less demonstrable phenomenally. In the possession trance we can actually see the increasing effect of this rise. The statuesque immovability preceding the trance is eventually shaken by a slight quiver, and gains till it culminates in the throe of possession. In the hypnotic subject, the rise is not directly evident. The character of the dominant idea accounts for this. The hypnotic subject is possessed by a purely passive idea, the idea of the eventual influence over him of the operator, which, as yet, is latent, and passes into action only on command. His dominant idea never thus quite peeps over the threshold of consciousness, but merely stands by to usher other ideas in. It gives them their pass, without which they would be refused admittance. In the spirit-possessed, action is spontaneous. There, the dominant idea actually takes possession of the otherwise vacated apartments of the mind and runs the establishment of its own motion, incidentally permitting no idea to come in that has not somehow business with it. Its energy, therefore, passes over of itself from the potential kinetic form. Its energy, also, is much the greater of the two. For to initiate action of itself shows more activity inherent in the idea than merely to respond to a shove from without. This explains the apathy of the general hypnotic state on the one hand, and the throe and subsequent quiver of the possessory trance on the other.

If the energy of the idea be not kept up by appropriate stimulation, it gradually falls, as is shown by the lapsing of the subject, when left alone, into a state of coma. But the aptitude of the idea to act remains relatively the same. For, on renewed incantation, the dominant idea again rises to a point of action before the rest of the brain.

Both entranced states thus differ from the normal condition, not in the mind's being curiously open, as at first one is tempted to think, but in its being curiously shut. For, in the normal state, unless some fixed idea chance for the time partially to have closed the avenues of approach, the mind lies open to all comers, incoming ideas as well as sensations, all of whom it eagerly welcomes, and then after admission quietly chokes such as on inspection it does not happen to fancy. In the entranced state, on the other hand, no idea is admitted at all unless personally related to the possessing idea, and when once introduced is permitted full play in the premises.

Whatever thus gains admittance through the dominant idea is, therefore, from meeting little or no opposition, all-powerful. In the perfectly hypnotized person, the slightest hint from the operator produces instantaneous and complete action. For, in that motionless mind, there are practically no counter-forces present to oppose it, nor are any such roused by its action to check it after it has started. There is nothing but it to act. Only when it clashes with another visitor does any hesitation or difficulty result. But the man's sense of his own identity does not change, because it is not a part of the dominant idea that it should. When by suggestion an idea of such change enters his mind, identity changes at once.

In perfect subjects there is no consciousness of constraint. It is only when the hypnosis is imperfect that side-ideas are roused enough to suggest the possibility of acting otherwise. The subject then becomes dimly aware of compulsion, without, however, having any definite conception of what that compulsion consists. He simply feels that he must do so and so ; and he does it.

In waking life, a fixed idea will often mask itself in the same manner. We feel that we must act in a certain way, often in a very trivial way, against our will, as we say, yet without questioning for an instant that it is we who act. As a matter of fact, it is the idea that for the moment is the I ; and the faint remonstrance of which we are conscious is due to such faint side-ideas as are roused by its action.

But in the possession trance the dominant idea consists consciously in a change of identity. The consciousness in the entranced state throbs with the sense of this new personality as waking life does with the sense of self. Consequently, all the possessed's thoughts, words, and actions conform to it; none that do not finding foothold in his mind. The man does not simulate the spirit or the god. Mentally, he is the spirit or the god, and his mechanism, in so far as in him lies, responds in its performance. His is anything but a case of acting; it is an absolute change of identity, the new ego being the man's conception of the god. Such may not be the god, but it also is not the man.

From all this, we perceive a certain parallelism between trances and dreams, with certain divergences. In both the mind is inactive, except along a particular line. In both the illumination is lightning-like, and in both no general illumination resulting in a general judgment of things as they really are takes place, because of the current's failure to rouse side-thoughts. But in the trance the dominant idea is much stronger than in the dream, and persists through the whole of it as a ground for all other ideas. Especially is this so in the possession trance. And the reason for this is more or less patent. The idea that causes the dream is much less consciously absorbing than the idea that possessed the possessed. The one is haphazardly entertained, the other is purposed. Secondly, it is probable that the brain, generally, is much deeper asleep in the trance than in the dream. The fact that of our own motion we are so close to waking when we begin to dream implies this, and the easy consequence of one idea upon another in the dream state goes to back it up. Lastly, the possessing idea in the trance is repeated and realized again and again in successive trances. This strengthens it immensely. How much so, is evident from the great development observable in trances. A trance that occurs for the first time is usually very embryonic; but by repetition the idea acquires momentum that rivals that of single-purposed waking action.

Habit is just as potent in the trance state as in the normal one. In both lives a self-educatory process goes on, any action gaining proficiency by practice. As we have seen, divine development is as duly marked in the Shintō trances as human development in every-day man.

Much of the supposed divinatory power of the possessed is attributable to the same cause that makes the hypnotic subject so supernaturally omniscient. The brain of any one is a register of sense impressions to a degree unsuspected by its owner. It is none too much to say that everything we have ever experienced is there, could we only get at it! The possessed does get at it, or at some of it, and surprises himself quite as much as others by having done so. Whence his honesty in denying that it is he that does it and the natural belief of others in its supernatural origin.

In conclusion it may be noted here how ill the self fares under these illusions and disillusions of the trance. That self can thus be snuffed out at a word from the operator, or by the mere idea of god in the possession trance, betrays it no transcendental thing. Self, indeed, would seem itself to be; and the bundle of ideas in that mass of machinery, the brain, alone to constitute the I.

XIII.

Certain differences between the Japanese possession trances and others of their kind are significant.   To begin with, one peculiarity of the Shintō trance is the *maeza's* connection with it.   This man is the official intermediary of the god, and he holds a curious intermediary position between the person spoken to in the mediumistic trance and the operator in the hypnotic one.   He is the *nakōdo*, or go-between, of the whole transaction.   He is the only part of humanity whom the god deigns spontaneously to recognize. He alone may speak to the god, and him alone the god condescends to answer.   Any one else, however pious, who desires to converse with the god, must first be brought in rapport with him by the *maeza*.   Until such rapport be established, the god pays the outsider's remarks no attention.   That he is not quite so deaf as he seems, however, is shown by his occasionally scolding the *maeza* for irreverential conduct on the part of such outsider.   I blush to say that I never knew this to happen except in my own case, when engaged in testing the reality of the god by making, too openly, a pin-cushion of him, or otherwise treating him with what he took for disrespect.

But the *maeza* does not affect the god's actions, and only incidentally suggests by his questions the current of the divine thought precisely as one person does that of another in every-day conversation. The *maeza* usually starts the topic, but the god is responsible for the replies. The *maeza* is thus, unlike the operator in the hypnotic trance, not the power behind the throne, but merely the master of ceremonies before it. In this he differs again from a person who has a sitting with a trance-medium, and who is not supposed to open his mouth except upon his own business. There is, however, a greater gulf between the god and the *maeza*, particularly pure as the latter is, than between the sitter and the informing spirit.

We now come to a very suggestive dissimilarity between the Shintō possessions and all others.

Of trances of the possessory sort there are manifold varieties to be found scattered over the surface of our globe. Believers grade them after the ethics of the possessing spirits, a pious if not over-profitable criterion. In Japan, for example, the rank of the god is gauged by the knowledge he displays of his own family mythology, while in America possessing spirits are valued for their proficiency in a certain milk-and-water philosophy, metaphysically tinctured of religion. The more milk-and-water their well of information proves, the purer proof-spirit is it esteemed to be.

To science the spirits' morals would be of more consequence did they not so singularly mirror the morals of the race which the spirits are kind enough to possess. As it is, so remarkable a resemblance in ethical standards between the immutable gods and ever-evolving man, observable at all times and among all peoples, proves too much for popular deity. Such concordance, further emphasized by the striking manner in which as a race advances in its conception of conduct the moral development of deity keeps pace with the moral development of the devotee, hints that between the orthodox and the true divine comedy, the parts of creature and creator have unfortunately got reversed.

The more abstract the conceptions of a

race grow to be, the more abstract become
its gods, and in consequence the less they
deign temporarily to inhabit mankind. A
growing incapacity to conceive how a more
and more abstracted god would act in the
concrete is indirectly responsible for this.
Among aboriginal peoples the gods themselves descend to embodiment in man;
among more evolved races the spirits of departed men take their place.

But it is not simply in their morals that
the gods show themselves in sympathy with
their people. In their characters generally
you shall see reflected the race characteristics. In Japan the gods are eminently
Japanese. They are dignified, artistic, simple
souls, of the most exceptional deportment.
Their life is made up of one long chain of
ornamental, if somewhat conventional, moments.

Especially is this agreement of gods and
men conspicuous in that most interesting of
Japanese traits — the race's unindividuality.
As we saw, one of the strangest features of
Japanese possession is the way in which
several gods deign to share one trance.
Now when this copartnership is closely scru-

tinized it will be found to afford proof of a curiously conceived impersonal kind of deity.

It is not that to one unacquainted with the gods there appears at first sight to be a very strong family likeness between them, so strong as to imply no very marked individuality in any, for such superficial resemblance is common to every race in the eyes of others. It is in the character of the divine consciousness that the peculiarity consists. For the consciousness of any one god is continuous in successive trances, and the consciousness of successive gods is continuous in any one trance. That is, in the person of the same man the god remembers what he did, said, and heard in different trances, and different gods remember what the others did, said, and heard in the same trance, while perfectly differentiating themselves from those others. But different gods do not remember about each other in different trances. The first of these capabilities is of course the usual trance - memory, as self-identifying a one as the man's normal memory. The second shows that an indefinite idea of god underlies the several special manifestations of it. The third indicates the extent of this common bond.

That each god thus knows his own acts and sensations from those of every other god, in the same trance, and remembers his previous acts and sensations in successive trances, fulfills all the phenomena that we recognize as constituting an individual self. It is therefore only natural for it instantly and irrevocably to have been taken for such. On the other hand, that one god should have any idea of the actions of his predecessor when embodied, hints at a ground-work of unindividual self.

The change of god evidently comes about by unconscious auto-suggestion. Certainly the subject himself has no inkling before-hand what gods will constitute his surprise party, if his seemingly honest profession to that effect is to be believed, and there is really no reason to doubt it. Nor is the change due to any suggestion on the part of the *maeza*, the official interviewer of the god. For the *maeza* asks no leading questions on the subject; he confines himself to asking after the fact who has come, and then to questionings about the cure of the disease, or other desired mundane or divine matter, quite apart from the personality of the god.

The auto-suggestion is of two parts, — the general idea of change, and its particular performance. The first is like the unintentionally induced hypnotic habits of the Salpétrière. The gods have learned that they are expected to come in Indian file, and kindly do so accordingly. That they did so initially is due undoubtedly to the underlying impersonality of the race.

That there is this general predisposition to rotation in office is proved by the earliness with which the change shows itself. It appears long before the possession is perfect enough for words. The boy whose divine development I instanced before was already several gods in turn, while as yet unable to talk as any. The particular change comes about from associations between the idea of one god and the idea of the other, contracted either in the normal or the entranced state, and then evoked in the course of the entranced's heavenly thinking. Sometimes the link becomes visible. A god will say that he is himself unable to answer a question put to him, and will report the matter to some higher god for solution, after which an attendant of the higher god descends.

that the thoughts it rouses there mingle unconsciously with a man's thinking most of the time. They constitute what we know as habitual ones in the normal state. When, therefore, the brain lies clogged in the general lethargy of the trance, these channels still remain relatively more permeable than the less pervious veins of more recently evolved sensations peculiar to the individual. Thus the activity that cannot wake the man wakes the race.

This brings us to confront the atavistic character of the general trance state. *A priori*, we have just seen that the state should hark back, and *a posteriori* that it does so in this particular case. But we have evidence that it is atavistic generally. The easy transition from one idea to another in the hypnotic state, the want of reasoning shown in it, the intentness and energy with which any given idea will be pursued one moment, only to be thrown over the next with a completeness which is caricatural, are states of mind that recall childhood for comparison. The man has become a sort of grotesque boy again. Could all *idées fixes* be eradicated, that is, could we have the perfectly normal man for subject, then if the operator could suggest some action colorless enough to let only native activity come into play, — a purity of experiment practically unattainable, — we should probably, as the trance state deepened and the man lost himself, see him lose first his individual characteristics, then his family traits, then the habits of his clan, and so down, till only the broadly human ones survived. The trance state would undo what evolution has done, and return to us a primeval savage in the body of an end-of-the-century man. But fortunately that most insipid individual, the normal man, whose mild portrait you shall see in any composite photograph, it is impossible to obtain. For the very essence of evolution consists in the survival of the slightly abnormal. The spirit of the cosmos is itself one great *idée fixe* working itself out. The normality of the whole depends upon the abnormality of each part. To be a trifle one-sided gives each of us our chance. Indeed, nothing is easier than to show that were everything, as the Roman expression had it, smooth and round, nothing could ever have developed, just as without irregularity no motion could have existed in the solar system except one vast self-crushing in the sun.

Thus idiosyncracies are a necessary part of us, but they are numerous and diverse in proportion to the height the individual development has attained. They are much less marked between man and man in Japan than among Aryan folk. The average Japanese more nearly approaches his own national norm.

This lands us in our investigation at an unexpected conclusion, to wit, that these gods really are what they claim to be. In Shintō god-possession we are viewing the actual incarnation of the ancestral spirit of the race. The man has temporarily become once more his own indefinitely great great-grandfather. It is a veridic incarnation, if ever there was one. If these his ancestors were gods in the past, gods they are that descend to embodiment to-day.